Clear Lake

Clear Lake

a novel

Nan Fink Gefen

SHE WRITES PRESS

Published 2013
Printed in the United States of America
ISBN: 978-1-938314-40-7
Library of Congress Control Number: 2013933381

For information, address:
She Writes Press
1563 Solano Ave #546
Berkeley, CA 94707

In memory of my sister,
Marion

*Truth is balance. But the opposite of truth, which is
unbalance, may not be a lie.*
     —Susan Sontag

Part One

2000–2005

1

On an August day in 2000, a truck swerved into the right lane of Oakland Interstate 880 and crashed into Rebecca Lev's rental car. The noise roared into her head, and she jammed on the brakes, careening to a stop on the berm. After a moment of shocked silence, Paul and Annie, who were in the backseat, began to scream. Rebecca reached frantically for them, reassuring them, checking them over. They seemed unharmed, but then she glanced down and saw that her own blue cotton shirt was stained with blood. A wave of nausea passed through her.

An ambulance and a fire truck appeared on the berm, sirens blaring, and a team of paramedics helped them out of the undamaged passenger side of the car. When Rebecca stood up, her legs gave way. "Put her on the gurney," someone nearby called. "She's injured. We'll take her to the hospital."

"Don't forget the kids," she managed to say. She closed her eyes, letting the paramedics strap her onto a narrow gurney and cover her with a blanket. For a moment she thought about Peter, her ex-husband, and wished he was there to take charge, but then she remembered how he had failed at that. When they were living in Chicago, before they split up, she had sliced her finger badly with a kitchen knife while chopping onions, and Peter couldn't handle the emergency because the sight of blood made him sick. She'd wrapped her finger in a clean dishtowel, and one of their housemates had rushed her to the doctor.

Rebecca gave way to the fogginess that was enveloping her. The gurney rolled along the berm and she felt herself being lifted into the ambulance. Somebody gave her a cold pack, telling her to hold it over her lip and chin. As though from a distance, she heard ten-year-old Paul ask the driver in his careful way about the shiny gauges on the front panel. Annie, her younger child, sat at her side, holding her hand and squeezing it anxiously. The ambulance sped along, the siren rising and falling, a comforting sound, and it seemed that they could go on like that for hours.

When they arrived at Oakland's Highland Hospital, the paramedics wheeled Rebecca through the crowded emergency lobby and into an examination room, the children following. She fingered her face under the cold pack, worrying about where all the blood had come from. One of the paramedics slipped her a piece of paper with information about the truck driver: his name, license number, and insurance. "Was he hurt?" she asked him. She hadn't even thought of that until now.

"Not a scratch. His vehicle was hardly dented."

"That's not fair," Rebecca said. The man shrugged.

The paramedics helped her transfer to the hospital bed, and after they left she put on the cloth gown a nurse had given her and looked around the room. With its drab beige walls and neon lights overhead, just large enough for a bed and a straight chair, it could have been any emergency examination room anywhere. "How dare that driver hit us," she said to the kids. "He should have watched where he was going. We've been looking forward to this vacation for so long, and now he's messed it up." She could have gone on about how frustrated she felt, but she saw Annie's bottom lip begin to quiver. "We'll still have a great time in San Francisco," she said as confidently as she could. "We'll make it to Fisherman's Wharf and all those other places. We won't let anything get in our way." She wanted more than anything for this vacation to be a success. It would help to make up for the troubles her children had gone through in the last two years. The worst had been the divorce and losing their father when he moved up to Wisconsin with his girlfriend, but she'd also hurt them by leaving them so often with sitters when she worked late at the psych clinic or stayed at the university into the night, writing her dissertation. The kids had been steadier than she expected through all this, but she feared it had had its effects.

The emergency doctor came into the room and introduced himself. Rebecca tried to remember his name, but it slipped away right after he said it. He examined her, rotating her arms and legs, palpating her abdomen, listening to her heart. She couldn't stop staring at his slender fingers, so beautifully brown. The children stood by quietly. "We're going to have to sew up your mother's lip," he told them. "Her teeth went right through the flesh just below the lip line."

"Yuck," Annie said with a worried look.

"It's just a few stitches, and then she'll be as good as new."

"Will there be a scar?" Rebecca asked. "That's the last thing I want." The doctor assured her that it would fade over time and be barely visible. "Let's hope," she said, thinking it was easy for him to say this.

When he was finished, a woman from the hospital admissions office appeared, asking for her medical insurance card. Rebecca rummaged through her jeans for her wallet and gave her the card, and then she raised herself in the bed, lightheaded, and started to answer the questions on the patient information form the woman left with her. "Closest person to notify?" she said to the kids. "I can't name the two of you."

"What about Grandpa Charlie?" Annie asked.

"He wouldn't want to be bothered."

"But he lives close by."

Rebecca looked at her daughter's earnest, upturned face. "Some things are not so simple," she said. She thought of the upsetting visit they'd just had with her father. They'd come to visit him at his new house after an absence of five years, and she had imagined, hoped, they'd have a warm reunion, a time of closeness. She should have known better.

Paul fiddled with the stethoscope the doctor had left behind on the bedside table. "Listen to my heart," Annie said, pulling up her T-shirt. "It's singing."

"Stop it, kids," Rebecca said. She continued to puzzle about who to name on the form. "I'll leave the space blank," she said. "Nobody will notice." She sank back on the bed, and for a moment the room swam around her and everything seemed unreal: the crash and ending up here in this hospital. If the accident had been much worse, they could have ended up in the morgue. She began to laugh, big gulps of sound that came out like sobs.

"What's wrong? Why are you doing that?" Annie asked.

"I was just picturing . . ." Tears flooded her eyes, her laughing and crying all mixed up. "What if I went like this to Grandpa Charlie's fancy house? What if I walked in the front door and said here I am, a big mess, and dripped blood all over their expensive rugs and antique furniture? Can you imagine how Vicky would freak out?"

Annie giggled, but Paul stared at her. "Don't say that."

Rebecca reached out to the children, drawing them close. "I'm so sorry about the accident," she said. "I never wanted that to happen." She felt like dissolving into them, letting go of the fear and anger that was choking her inside, but a nurse came into the room and gave her an inquiring look, and she straightened up. "By tomorrow, we'll hardly remember the accident happened," she said. "Right?"

The nurse announced that Rebecca's face would be stitched in a few minutes, and that the kids would have to leave the room. The thought of being separated from them felt like a rope breaking, but the nurse was right, they should be shielded from the sight. An aide came to escort them to the emergency waiting area, promising they'd be watched over there. Rebecca huddled on the bed and waited for the doctor to return. *Breathe*, she told herself.

Earlier that day, when Rebecca first saw her father's new house in Piedmont, she'd also had to remind herself to breathe. She had driven there with the children from their motel in San Francisco, expecting to find a small ranch home like the one she'd grown up in alone with him in Berkeley, a dozen miles away. But when they arrived at his new address, she was shocked to discover that he now lived in a dark, unwelcoming mansion with huge pillars in the front and shutters over the windows, sure to keep out the light.

"It's a haunted house," Annie had said slowly. "A scary one."

"Goblins and monsters," Paul said.

"Don't scare her, Paul," Rebecca said. But she had felt uneasy herself as she threw her camera bag over her shoulder and shepherded the kids to the front door, ringing the bell. The chimes inside played an arpeggio, and a Spanish-speaking maid let them into an entry that had a marble floor and a large bouquet of artificial flowers on a mahogany table.

The woman beckoned them to follow, and she silently led them down a long hall full of shadows. As they passed a gold-gilded mirror, Rebecca caught a glimpse of herself, her face strained and tired, and she scrunched up her mouth and tried to smile. She looked completely out of place in this house in her jeans, flip flops, and rumpled blue shirt, and she wished she had thought to put on a little makeup. She ran her fingers through her curly dark hair, trying to smooth it down.

"I don't like this," Annie whispered.

"Me either," Rebecca said, reaching for her hand. "We won't stay long."

The maid showed them into what must be the living room, a space crammed with objects made of jade, glass, and porcelain. It seemed that someone had gone on a wild shopping spree and dumped everything there without regard for taste or balance. A thin light shone from the crystal chandelier overhead. Rebecca and the kids sank onto one of the couches, a white velvet period piece, and she looked around to see if anything in the room was from Charlie's old house. "I don't understand what's going on here," she said to the kids. "All these things are new. I'm sure Grandpa Charlie didn't buy them. He always loved to fish and hunt, and he used to wear his grubby old clothes around the house when I was growing up. He was just a regular kind of guy."

"Then why does he have all this stuff?" Paul asked.

The door to the living room swung open, and Charlie walked in. "Dad?" Rebecca said, as unsteady as the children.

Charlie looked just as she remembered, a wiry man with receding, reddish hair, freckly skin, and thin lips. "Hi, sweetheart," he said in his soft voice, kissing her on the cheek and awkwardly hugging the children.

"Hi," Rebecca said, relieved to see him.

"When did you get in from Chicago?" he asked.

"Yesterday. The kids have grown a lot, haven't they? It's been five years since you saw them." Details like this always slipped his grasp. He'd probably forgotten she was married back then.

"Well, here I am in this new house," Charlie said, sounding excited. "How do you like it?"

"It's huge, that's for sure," Rebecca said.

He smiled at her. "It's Vicky's doing."

For years Rebecca had hoped her father would find a woman and settle down. He'd lived alone since her mother died when she was four, and it would be a relief if he had someone to watch over him now that he was almost seventy. She had always imagined him ending up with a sporty, congenial woman who'd go fishing with him and discuss his commercial real estate deals, drink cocktails, and crack jokes.

"Who's Vicky?" she asked. When she had called her father to tell him they were coming to the Bay Area, he had given her the address of his new home but he hadn't mentioned a woman.

"She lives here."

"You should have told us," Rebecca said. It was just like him to be so withholding with information. "Have you known Vicky very long?"

"A while."

"A short while or a long while?"

The doctor with the beautiful hands returned to Rebecca's hospital room, ready to begin the procedure. It wouldn't take long, he explained; they'd drape her face except for the wound, and they'd give her a shot of Novocain to numb the pain. He touched her cheeks, studying her face, and Rebecca was soothed by his light, gentle approach.

She had been attracted to Peter's hands, too, when she first met him in college. They were the hands of a poet, sensitive and yearning, but she had been deceived by them. The last time they made love, just before she left him two years ago, he'd reached out to her with those beautiful hands, and, despite her anger toward him, she had opened to his touch. But afterward, as they lay in bed, his eyes had taken on that hard, critical look he'd had for months, and he'd said, "I realize now that I no longer love you."

Rebecca was talking to her father in the living room in Piedmont when Paul nudged her and she looked up, seeing a woman posed in the doorway staring at them. If anyone ever looked like a 1940s movie star, she did, dressed in an off-the-shoulder black cocktail dress and gold spike sandals. Her platinum blond hair hung over one shoulder, and her ice blue eyes moved slowly from father to daughter. "Oh, there you are," Charlie smiled, noticing her. "Come in, Vicky, come in."

He seemed flustered by Vicky's presence, but she was as smooth as roller balls. "Hello, Rebecca," she said in a cool voice as she moved into the room.

Rebecca caught a whiff of what must be expensive perfume. Never in a thousand years could she pull herself together to look like this woman, even if she wanted to. "I'm glad to meet you," she said, rising from the white velvet couch, extending her hand.

Vicky ignored the gesture. "You arrived without mishap, I see," she said. "And these are the children."

"Right," Rebecca said, introducing them. There was an awkward pause, and she started to tell her about the two-hour delay they'd had yesterday at the Chicago airport and how frustrating it had been to wait in the plane while the mechanics fixed an electrical problem. "Anyhow, we made it here," she ended, when Vicky didn't seem interested.

"Children, would you like some cookies?" Vicky asked.

When they nodded politely, she pressed a button on the wall.

"That rings for Maria, the maid, in the kitchen," Charlie explained. "Pretty impressive, isn't it?"

Rebecca nodded, surprised he cared about such things. When she lived alone with him in Berkeley, he'd hired sitters and housecleaners, but never a live-in maid. It wasn't a matter of money—he'd been successful in the booming California real estate market—but he'd preferred to keep their home private and simple. She'd never known him to spend money on anything except necessities.

Vicky placed herself next to Charlie on a silk loveseat a few feet away, displaying her shapely, tanned legs. Close up, she was older than she first appeared, maybe fifty-five or even sixty. Her nails were carefully manicured, the pale skin on her face was stretched smooth, leaving it expressionless, and her lips were sealed together in a straight line. Vicky was a glamorous woman, Rebecca thought, one who would require a lot of upkeep and insist on expensive things. She never would have picked her for Charlie, but that was his business, not hers. "This is quite a house," she said. "When did you move in?"

"Mr. Stevens purchased it six months ago," Vicky answered.

"Mr. Stevens? You mean my dad."

"Vicky calls me that," Charlie laughed in a nervous way. "She likes me to feel important."

"You are important," Vicky said, placing her hand on his thigh.

Maria came into the living room carrying a tray of red fruit punch and sugar cookies. After she served the children, Vicky dismissed her with a curt nod. "Gracias, Maria," Charlie called after her as she slipped out of the room.

The children quietly munched their cookies. Rebecca felt Vicky's eyes on her, measuring her, and she sat up straighter. "Be careful with that punch," she said to the kids.

"Rebecca is a therapist," Charlie said to Vicky.

"So you told me."

"I just got my doctorate in psychology," Rebecca said. She looked at her father, hoping to see his approval, but he was examining his fingernails. "It was a long haul, but it's over now. I'm finishing up two years of internship at the psych clinic this fall, and when that's done, I'll take the state board exam and get my license. Then I can hang up my shingle."

"Mommy likes to help people," Annie said.

Rebecca looked gratefully at her. "It's been pretty exciting. I'm working with a lot of families at the clinic."

"Good for you," Vicky said in a sarcastic tone.

Rebecca stared at her, wondering why she was being so unfriendly. At the very least she could make an effort to welcome them since they were Charlie's only family. Perhaps she disapproved of Rebecca's appearance or something she'd said, or she saw her as a rival for Charlie's affection—but that would be ridiculous, because months went by between phone conversations with her father, and they hadn't been close for over twenty years. Paul slurped down his fruit punch next to her, making a sloppy sound, and she shot him a warning glance. "Do you have children?" she asked Vicky.

"She has one," Charlie answered. "Lana."

"Did you name her after Lana Turner?" Rebecca asked Vicky.

"Why would I do that?"

"Of course." Rebecca gave her a small smile. "Do you get to see Lana very often?"

"She lives in Los Angeles."

"We live in Chicago," Annie said in a bright voice. When nobody noticed, she sank farther back on the couch and folded her arms across her chest.

"Vicky's really interested in psychology. She reads a lot about it," Charlie said.

"Which authors do you like?" Rebecca asked, thinking they might find common ground here.

"Whoever's current," Vicky answered shortly.

"Vicky's the smartest, most cultured woman I've ever known," Charlie said. "She has her nose in a book all the time, except when she's working on decorating the house. Hasn't she done a great job?"

Rebecca felt like swooping up the kids and speeding away.

The doctor injected Novocain around Rebecca's wound and told her he'd be back when it took hold. She closed her eyes and braced herself for the procedure, worried it would hurt, hoping it would be over quickly. She took several deep breaths, trying to relax. The color of red filled her mind, brilliant red oozing downwards, staining everything it touched. The color had its own beauty, but it also was dangerous, too much to be let loose. She thought of the red blood of the crash and how frightening that had been, and then she remembered the red punch that Maria had served the children.

The punch had caused a dreadful scene, although it had started innocently enough. "Grandpa Charlie, do you have a dog?" Annie had asked during a pause in the conversation.

"Two, in fact. Grover and Daisy," he had answered.

"Oh, good. I love dogs." Squirming with excitement at this news, Annie tipped over her glass of red punch, spilling it onto the white velvet couch.

A horrendous roar erupted from Vicky. "Goddammit! Look what you've done!"

Rebecca rushed in. "Hand me the glass, Annie. Let's clean this up fast so it doesn't stain." She mopped the punch with paper napkins as best she could and dropped the soggy mess on the tray.

Vicky's face was filled with rage. She leaned toward Annie, speaking in a loud, shrill voice. "You're a bad, bad child. You ruined my couch. We had to wait months to get it."

"It was an accident," Rebecca said, trying to keep her voice calm.

Vicky shifted her glare to her. "There are no accidents."

Annie's round blue eyes filled with tears. "I'm sorry," she whispered.

10

"Sorry is not good enough."

"It's okay, honey," Rebecca said, furious at what was happening.

"You should be more vigilant with your child," Vicky said sharply to her. "You're her mother, aren't you? She should be taught to respect other people's property."

"Annie and I are both sorry, then," Rebecca said, glaring back at her. "But you shouldn't scream at my daughter like that. It's not her fault that you served her red punch." She thought of other things to say, but she was too shaken by what was happening to fight any more. She glanced over angrily at her father—why wasn't he doing something to stop this?—but he had a resigned expression on his face.

"Call Maria," Vicky said to Charlie. "Get her in here right away with the fabric cleaner."

"If the couch is ruined, I'll buy a new one," he said in a discouraged tone.

"You're damned right you will."

The doctor described what he was doing to Rebecca as he sewed up her injury, and she focused on his comforting voice, trying to ignore the strange sensation of the needle entering her numbed flesh. When he finished, he told her how to care for the wound so that it wouldn't become infected, and he wished her well and left. She sat on the hospital bed, relieved the procedure was over, but then she began to worry about the wrecked car. She'd have to call the rental car company right away, but she couldn't remember if she had checked the box for insurance coverage or decided to forego it because of the extra cost. Money was so tight these days, and she wouldn't be able to cover the damages of the accident, but then again, she wasn't responsible for it and the truck driver's insurance company should pay. All these details seemed so confusing.

The kids would be wondering about her in the waiting room, and she pictured Annie asking Paul over and over again in a worried tone what was happening. He'd finally tell her to shut up and stop bugging him. Rebecca rose from the hospital bed and washed her hands slowly in the little sink, taking as much time as she could. Without a mirror, she couldn't see what her face looked like with the bandage stretched over the stitches, but it wouldn't be pretty. She sighed deeply. If only there was someone she could call to rescue her and the kids, someone to sort out the mess about the damaged car, someone to get them back to the motel in San Francisco. If only she had a mother—it came back to that, as it always had. But no mother existed, and though her father was alive, he was no help, or at least he had not been since she was young. And now there was Vicky, who'd only make matters worse. Rebecca felt so alone, so bitter, so adrift; her eyes welled with tears. But her children were waiting for her. She yanked a wad of rough paper towels out of the container and blotted her eyes.

After Annie spilled her red punch, Vicky stomped out of the living room and Charlie stared after her, blinking hard. Maria appeared with the fabric cleaner and silently sprayed it on the couch, but a faint stain remained despite all her efforts. "Let's go see the dogs," Rebecca said, disgusted by how the visit was going.

"Sure," Charlie replied without enthusiasm.

Rebecca threw her camera bag over her shoulder, and they trooped out to the kennel at the rear of the yard, fenced off behind a wall of tall silver bamboo. "Daisy, come here," she called to a familiar collie whose tail wagged her whole body. A few years after she left Berkeley for college in Ann Arbor, Michigan, her father had bought Daisy, who had slept next to his bed and eaten scraps of food off his fork in their old house. "What are you doing out here, old girl?" Rebecca crooned. "They won't let you in their fancy mansion?"

Charlie overheard her. "Dogs mess things up," he said.

"That sounds like something Vicky says, not you."

He glanced over at her. "The air is good for them."

"Come on, Dad," Rebecca said. "You used to love Daisy."

Grover jumped up, licking Annie's face, and she laughed, then Paul threw a ball high into the air and the dog rushed to catch it, kicking up dust. "Do it again," Charlie called, and Annie shouted happily, her blond curls looking like gold rings in the sunlight.

It pleased Rebecca to be together like this, light and easy, and she relented a little toward her father, remembering how good he had been to her after her mother died. He had made her feel loved: When he'd come home from his office, he'd lifted her up and kissed her and called her his little sweetheart, and she'd followed him around the house, chatting with him. He'd been her playmate, her beloved father, and sometimes he'd chased her around their small, woodsy backyard, whooping with excitement, and Sparky, their dog, had rushed after them, barking, until they fell into a laughing heap.

Glancing over at the huge house, through the bamboo, she noticed Vicky staring at them from the second-floor window, her face set in harsh lines. She stared back at her, determined not to be intimidated. "Vicky has a nasty temper," she said to Charlie.

"She doesn't like anything to happen to her things, that's all."

"That woman's going to give you a lot of grief," Rebecca said. "You know that, right?"

Charlie turned away from her and looked up at the second-floor window, where Vicky still was observing them. "We'd better get inside," he said. He started across the lawn, his step urgent.

"Watch out for her," Rebecca called after him. The kids stopped playing, hearing her tone. "Come on," she said to them. "Say good-bye to Grover and Daisy."

"Aren't you going to take any pictures?" Paul asked her.

He and Annie were used to her bringing her camera along wherever they went. Rebecca had discovered photography at a summer camp in the Sierra Mountains when she was ten, and she had been hooked ever since. Through the lens of the camera she was able to see the beauty and balance in everything around her, and it seemed that a deeper truth was being revealed. She went into a kind of altered state: time slowed way down and the jaggedness within her disappeared. But she was too busy for photography these days and took pictures only on the run, which left her frustrated. Someday, somehow, she'd find a way to enter more fully into the world the camera offered her.

"Sorry, no pictures today," she answered Paul. "I'm not in the mood."

The surgical procedure was finished, and it was time to leave the hospital. "We need to catch a bus back to the city," Rebecca said to the kids. "It'll be chilly outside with the summer fog beginning to roll in at this time of day. Better put on your sweatshirts."

"But where are they?" Paul asked.

"You don't have them?" Rebecca started to scramble through the hospital sheets, looking around the room. "Oh god, I can't believe our things aren't here. The paramedics should have brought everything with us in the ambulance. My camera was in the car, and I can't lose it."

She stuck her head out the door of the room and flagged down a nurse she hadn't seen before. "Our things, do you know where they are?" she asked.

The nurse promised she'd investigate, and Rebecca paced around the room until the woman finally returned with a plastic sack holding the camera bag, the kids' sweatshirts, and an assortment of maps, kid's books, and snack food. "Oh, thank you," Rebecca said in a loud voice.

The nurse looked closely at her: "Are you sure you're well enough to leave the hospital?"

"Just a little shook up," Rebecca answered. "I was really worried about my camera. It would be a disaster if I lost it, but now I'm okay. We'll be on our way once we figure out where the bus stop is."

"You shouldn't be taking a bus," the nurse said. "You've been through quite an ordeal."

"But we have to get back to San Francisco. We have nobody to pick us up, and a taxi is too expensive."

The children whispered to each other for a moment. "Annie and

I can pay for a taxi," Paul said to Rebecca. "Grandpa Charlie gave us some money, remember?"

"What a lovely thought." Her eyes filled with tears. "But keep it for yourselves. I'm sure your grandfather would want that." At the end of their visit with Charlie—now only a few hours past, but already it seemed so long ago—she had drawn him aside and asked him to give the kids a little cash for souvenirs. It was the least he could do, and it would mean a lot to them. And then she'd hugged him good-bye and held on to him, her yearning for him strong despite her disappointment about the visit. For a moment he'd seemed to return her feeling and he'd lingered, but then he'd broken away, saying he had to get back to Vicky.

"Please, Mommy," Annie said, pulling ten dollars out of her pocket. "Take it. We don't need it."

"You kids are unbelievably great, the best in the world," Rebecca said, brushing away her tears. "I really appreciate your offer. But the money is yours, and you deserve it." She sucked in a deep breath. "Okay, we'll take a taxi. I'll find some way to make the money work." The children looked anxiously at her, and she did her best to smile. "Everything will be fine. You'll see."

2

One evening after returning to Chicago, Rebecca prepared to go to a party at her close friend Ella Jacob's apartment. She pulled on her newest jeans, tight and sexy the way she liked, and a silky crimson blouse. But as she examined her face in the bathroom mirror, she grimaced. "What's wrong?" asked Annie, who had been following her around all evening.

"That scar from the accident—it's better, but it still shows." Rebecca searched in the bathroom drawer for a tube of cover-up cream and patted some on. Her most expressive feature, her warm brown eyes, looked tired tonight, and she found some mascara and eyeliner to brighten them up.

"Let me do your hair," Annie said. Rebecca nodded, although the sitter was arriving any minute. This was a ritual they had, a special mother-daughter thing, and she'd never say no.

Annie stood on the toilet and ran the brush through Rebecca's thick dark hair, untangling the knots, and she finished by twirling around a strand and tucking it back with a silver comb. Rebecca surveyed herself in the mirror. Not bad.

The sitter was already a little late, and she busied herself by straightening a pile of client notes on her desk in the living room. She really needed a night out after the upsetting afternoon she'd had at the psych clinic. The memory of what had happened still burned in her mind: She had been talking to a client, an unemployed, depressed man, who was telling her about his frustrating search for a job. She had suggested a few resources that might help him, and he'd brightened. Suddenly the harsh sound of the buzzer on her desk had jolted them. It was her training supervisor, Winston, who was watching the session through a one-way window. When she joined him behind the observation glass, he told her she was making a mistake. "This client needs to be dealing with his depression, not his employment situation," he'd said in a crisp tone. "Remember, you're a therapist, not a social worker or an employment coach." Rebecca had been stung by his criticism, and when she couldn't come up with a quick defense, she had felt even worse.

That humiliating moment had stayed with Rebecca for the rest of the afternoon, and it was in her mind as she drove across town to the party at Ella's place. *Let it go*, she told herself. Every intern had to endure this kind of criticism; it was part of becoming a therapist. She pictured herself in the future, a full-fledged professional making good money and having a certain status. The fact that she would be helping people made the vision all the sweeter. She had dreamed of being a psychologist since she was thirteen and saw a TV program about one who was working with troubled kids from divorced families. The therapist had seemed so self-assured and so wise, a kind of hallowed being, and she'd wanted to be like that.

By the time Rebecca walked through the door of Ella's apartment, she felt much lighter. A dozen or so therapists and people she recognized from the university had already congregated, and she heard the sound of laughter, gossip, and end-of-the-week letting-down. She rushed over to Ella and they hugged; they had become close friends toward the end of graduate school, but now their schedules didn't allow them much time to get together.

They chatted for a few minutes, then Ella went to greet someone who had just arrived and Rebecca joined two people she knew, Carl and Miranda, both of whom had private therapy practices. The subject of her internship came up, and she described what had happened at the clinic that morning. "Winston came down hard on me," she said. "I was so flustered I couldn't even explain myself."

"What would you have liked to tell him?" Carl asked.

"My client's depression is situational," she answered. "He wasn't depressed before he became unemployed. His depression will ease if I help him figure out how to get a job."

"Sorry, but I agree with your supervisor," Miranda said, adjusting the beret she always wore. "It's a mistake for a therapist to get caught up in trying to solve a client's life problems."

"You have to work with the underlying depression," Carl echoed.

"But realistically, unemployment causes depression," Rebecca said.

"Over time you'll learn what you can do as a therapist and what you can't," Miranda said.

Rebecca eyed the two of them. They were like Winston, who worked by the book. She felt unsure of herself, wondering if she was right in her approach and embarrassed that she had revealed so much to them. "Thanks," she said, turning away. "Time to party."

Across the room she noticed someone she hadn't met before, a large man with nappy black hair and thick eyebrows that joined just above his nose, telling stories and laughing louder than anyone else there. Ella walked by, carrying a bowl of potato chips. "Who's that?" Rebecca whispered.

Ella glanced over. "Stan Felder, a friend of my brother's."

Rebecca watched Stan gesturing and guffawing. "Is he always so talkative?"

"He's a nice guy." Ella offered her the potato chips. "Here, eat. You can afford to put on a few pounds. Not like me."

"What do you mean by nice?" Rebecca asked, taking a handful.

"Don't be so suspicious. Not all men are like Peter. Stan's a good, dependable guy who works in his uncle's sporting goods business."

"Not a therapist? That's refreshing."

"Carl and Miranda got to you, I can tell," Ella laughed. "They can be condescending."

"I had a hard day at the clinic, and they didn't make it any better."

When Stan's conversation on the couch had finished, Rebecca went over and introduced herself and they began to talk. She noticed that his hands were stubby—the kind of hands that pound and hammer, practical hands that get things done. Soon they drifted toward the kitchen where it would be quieter, she leading the way and Stan lumbering behind, almost twice her size. "We're off to the inner sanctum," he joked, and she turned to smile at him.

In the kitchen they made themselves tall drinks of rum and coke. He asked her what she had done that summer, and she told him about the trip to California and the accident. "The wrecked car didn't cost me anything in the end, and the kids had a good time," she said. "I pulled it off, I'm proud to say."

"Kids always know how to have fun," Stan said. "Sometimes I wish I was young again."

"I can just see you running out of the house with your baseball glove, looking for your gang," she laughed.

"Every day," he said. "We used to play ball on the empty lot near my house. How did you know?"

"I'm a therapist, didn't I tell you?" She was enjoying this conversation; Stan was transparent, and it didn't take much to see that he was in some ways like an overgrown kid. "Is your whole family into sports?" she asked.

"My dad was."

She saw a flicker of sadness in his face. "Was? Meaning that he's lost interest? Or is he no longer around?"

"He died ten years ago, when I was thirty."

"I'm sorry," she said. "My mom's dead, so I know what that's like."

"But you still have your dad?"

"We drifted apart a long time ago and hardly ever see each other," Rebecca answered. "This summer I discovered he's living with a woman, Vicky. I really wanted to like her, but it turned out that she's one scary lady. When my daughter accidently spilled some punch on her precious couch, I thought she was going to attack her."

"What did your dad do?"

"He just stood by and watched. He has no control over the situation," she said. "I think he's in for big trouble. I tried to tell him, but he didn't listen. There's nothing I can do about it, I'm afraid."

"So Vicky is a dragon lady," Stan said, putting on a heavy Yiddish accent, making claws and lunging at Rebecca. A little drunk by then, she convulsed with laughter at his description, thinking that he'd gotten it just right.

"Any dragons in your family?" she asked when she recovered.

"My ex-wife, Amy. And then there's my mother, but that's another story. Really, I'm lucky. My family has its share of craziness, but there's a lot of love."

"That sounds like a cliché."

"It's for real."

Rebecca smiled at Stan. A family with a lot of love sounded good to her. Peter had been down on families from the beginning; he claimed that his creativity as a poet depended on him living in an unencumbered way. He hadn't wanted to marry, but when she'd become pregnant with Paul, he had reluctantly agreed. Rebecca had always felt the burden of being the one who had pressured him into it.

She moved closer to Stan. She felt beautiful, a woman in her prime wearing her favorite crimson blouse and having a better time than she'd had in months.

A week later Rebecca and Stan met for drinks. She couldn't stay long—the kids were with a teenager who had to leave by seven o'clock—but she liked being with him and hearing his funny stories. He was a jolly clown, she thought. "Call me tomorrow night," she said to him when it was time to leave. "It's hard for me to get away in the evenings, but I can always talk."

In the following weeks Rebecca and Stan spoke often late at night. She curled up in the green armchair, propping the phone under her chin, listening to his cheerful voice. On the wall of the living room was a photograph she'd taken at the Lincoln Park Conservatory after her divorce, and she gazed at it as they talked. It was of a tropical plant—she didn't know its name—and she'd been intrigued by the way its florid leaves opened to the light and the single, yellow, horn-shaped bud burst forth.

She liked getting to know Stan in this slow, easy way. They often spoke about the breakup of their marriages. "When my ex walked out, I was really pissed," Stan said.

"Why did she leave?" Rebecca asked.

"I couldn't do anything right. She was the most critical person I've ever known. I guess she got fed up with me."

"Peter was critical, too. Except I was the one who left."

"I don't miss her," Stan said. "But I liked having someone next to me, a partner."

"I feel free for the first time, now that I'm on my own," she told him. "Although I don't see spending my entire life like this."

They were circling each other, and Rebecca was not sure if she wanted Stan as a friend or a lover. When he talked about sports, which he did a lot, she lost interest, but she had a feeling of comfort and safety with him, and she was drawn to his enthusiastic manner. His habit of saying "That's great!" about most things made her laugh.

She began to tell him more about Paul and Annie, describing the little events of the day and the household crises. "My sitter quit," she said one time. "I don't know what I'll do." She had been trying to find someone else, rearranging her work schedule in the meantime.

"Don't worry, something will work out," he replied in a light tone.

"That's easy for you to say," she said, but his optimism helped her remember that the crisis would pass, and her spirits lifted.

Two months after Rebecca began having her phone conversations with Stan, he asked if he could meet her kids. She hesitated, thinking it might confuse them since she hadn't brought any men home since they'd moved into the apartment, but then she pictured Stan's well-meaning, open face and thought that they could use some of his warmth in their lives. "Sure," she answered. "Why not?"

A week later, Stan arrived at the door of Rebecca's third-floor apartment with yo-yos for the kids. It was a few days before Christmas, and he was wearing a Santa Claus hat. "Merry Christmas," he said in a hearty way, and she drew him in, pleased he was there.

"Santa has arrived," Rebecca called to the kids, and they emerged from their shared bedroom, eying him curiously. "Ho, ho, ho," Stan grinned at them.

Paul stared back at him, but Annie laughed, and it didn't take long for her to move closer to him. "Do you like jokes?" she asked. Before he could answer, she started in: "Why are fish so smart?"

"Because . . . they're born that way?"

"No, no." Her face filled with delight. "Because they live in a school."

"Hey, that's great," Stan clapped, and he threw a joke back at her. Paul stood by, listening with a guarded look on his face.

"I see you're ready for Christmas," Stan said, looking at the tree Rebecca and the kids had decorated with ornaments and strands of popcorn and cranberries. "Here's an early present." He brought out the yo-yos, and the kids began to play with them, excited that they lit up in bright colors when they spun them around.

"Show me the rest of your place," he said after a while. Annie led him into the kids' bedroom, Paul following, and she introduced him to her favorite stuffed animals, Muffy and Duffy and Polly. Paul's miniature cars were lined up tidily on a high shelf. "I like model cars, too," Stan said to him. "I collected them when I was a kid."

"Nobody touches them," Paul said.

"But I can look, right?"

"Just don't pick them up."

"Okay," he laughed.

Rebecca listened happily to Annie's continuing chatter and Stan's booming voice from the kitchen, where she was finishing up dinner. Even Paul was talking to him. "Time to eat," she called. Usually she threw something together quickly for the kids, hot dogs or chicken fingers, but tonight she'd gone to more trouble, making pasta and meatballs and a salad and buying a bottle of Chianti, a treat.

"Great place you have," Stan said to Rebecca as they settled around the table.

"It's home," she smiled. The windowsill above the sink needed repainting and the yellow linoleum floor was patched and faded, but she'd put her cooking utensils in a bright pottery crock and a vase of daisies sat on the table. For nine years she'd lived with Peter in communal houses, first in Ann Arbor when they were at the university and then in Chicago. It had been a way of saving money since Peter didn't make much teaching poetry and Rebecca made even less at the part-time jobs she cobbled together. But even if they could have afforded their own place, Peter would have insisted that they live communally; he'd said he needed the stimulation and company of housemates to survive. Rebecca thought this was because he was trying to make up for the loss of his parents when he was a teenager—they'd been killed in a freak car accident—but he'd disagreed, saying it was just the way he was, coming from a big Russian family that sat around the kitchen table and talked a lot. At first she had loved having so many people around, but later she'd tired of all the drama, the ideas, the interacting, and she'd begun to yearn for a quieter home. When she left Peter two years ago and rented this apartment, she had felt relieved to have a place of her own. She was now more settled than she'd ever been.

"Mommy sleeps in the back room," Annie said. "We jump on her bed and wake her up in the morning."

"That sounds like fun," Stan laughed.

One late night in March, Rebecca led Stan to her bedroom. It was decorated with softly-patterned Indian cloths she'd bought at an import shop and tacked to the walls and ceiling. The room had a gauzy, floating feel, different from the rest of the apartment.

She lit the candle beside her bed and invited him in. For a moment he held back, shyer than she'd expected, and then he became all hands, all mouth. He was quick in his passion—so different from Peter, who could go on making love for hours—and for a moment Rebecca missed her ex-husband greatly. But then she guided Stan in what she liked, and even though he was clumsy and unsure, she found a measure of satisfaction from his touch. Not too bad a start, she thought, resting beside his big, snoring body.

When Stan awakened, he gazed at Rebecca. "You're really something," he said, his voice gentler than she'd heard before.

"Yes?" She fluttered her eyelids, amused by his seriousness. Her hair was wispy around her face, and her breath tasted of the pizza she'd eaten for dinner. "I must stink of garlic."

"You're beautiful however you are," he said. "And you even have your doctorate. I couldn't do that."

"That's because you never studied in college," she smiled. "You probably hung out in the gym the whole time. It's amazing you made it through two years."

"I know how to enjoy myself." He stroked her hair. "Compared to you, with all your books."

"Salt and pepper, that's you and me."

"I'll teach you how to play basketball," he said. "Forget it. I'm too short," she laughed.

"You're just right," he said, drawing her closer.

Rebecca, who had learned a lot about families at the psych clinic, awakened the next morning worrying how the children would feel about Stan being there. "They've had me all to themselves for two years," she said to him. "They might not like sharing me." She quickly slipped into her old flowered kimono and Stan pulled on his pants and fastened them.

But when Annie bounced into the bedroom just as he finished, she seemed pleased to see him. Paul trailed in after her, his brown hair sticking up in spikes. "What are you doing here?" he asked.

"He's Mommy's friend," Annie said.

"I was too tired to go home, so I stayed," Stan said. "That's okay, isn't it?"

Paul's eyes narrowed for a moment, and Rebecca reached out to give his hand a squeeze, hoping he'd soften. "I guess so," he said.

Rebecca began to make breakfast. The smell of coffee filled the kitchen, and the sun shone brightly through the window. Spring had come to Chicago early this year with its budding chestnut trees and flowering shrubs; this would be one of the first warm days of the season. The children and Stan drifted into the room, drawn by the promise of pancakes and bacon, and they sat around the kitchen table, a little family.

"Let's toss a baseball today," Stan said to Paul after breakfast.

Paul paused before nodding. He loved playing ball, and since he didn't know any kids in the neighborhood, Stan would have to do.

"Good idea," Rebecca said, impressed that Stan had thought of this. "We just happen to have a baseball." She jumped up from the table and rummaged around in the hall closet until she found it. "Go enjoy yourselves."

The children settled in with Stan, Annie the easiest, always happy to hear a new joke, and Paul playing ball with him but holding himself apart. Rebecca's greatest feeling for this new lover was gratitude. Many nights he came to her apartment to stay with Paul and Annie while she worked late at the clinic, and he dropped them off at school in the morning. Rebecca sometimes worried that she was taking advantage of him and he'd grow resentful, but when she asked him about this, he said, "Who me? I'm having a good time."

As long as the children were thriving, Rebecca cared most of all about her career. She didn't say this aloud because it sounded so coldhearted. She appreciated Stan's easy manner, but she wasn't sure if he'd ever get the love from her that he deserved. One night she sat him down and told him clearly about her priorities for the future. He looked at her blankly and said, "What's the problem? Of course your kids and your work are important. I just like being with you." She also told him that she didn't want to have any more children in the future because they would tie her down. "That's okay," he answered. "Paul and Annie are enough for me."

Stan seemed to accept her as she was, with her ambition and commitments, and that was reassuring—but sex was a problem. When he became aroused, he became slick with sweat, and the pungent smell and salty taste were hard to ignore. Even worse, she had to guide him anew each time they were together; he was like a dance partner who cannot seem to learn the steps. She'd never have the same shaking vulnerability, the same feeling of union, the same unselfconscious giving over of herself with him that she'd had with Peter.

But sex wasn't everything, she reminded herself, and Stan was a decent, safe person. With Peter, she'd had to fight against his attraction to other women the whole time they were together. She had often discovered sexy notes from women in his pockets, or the phone would ring and the caller would hang up upon hearing her voice. Each round of this meant fights and recriminations, then promises of monogamy on his part and forgiveness on hers. The end had come when she'd discovered he was sleeping with one of their housemates, a friend of both of theirs. Exhausted and raw, she'd packed up the kids and moved out, vowing she'd never let herself be hurt like that again.

On a warm Sunday afternoon late in spring, Stan took Rebecca and the children to meet Miriam, his mother, who lived in a rambling old house in nearby Evanston. "My mother's an artist. She's a large-scale woman," Stan had said before they arrived. Rebecca didn't know whether that was a compliment or a complaint.

As they entered the house, Miriam kissed Rebecca and the children as though she'd known them for years. Her old beagle rose on unsteady legs from a cushion, barking half-heartedly. "Hush, Ruby," she yelled. "These are our friends."

"I don't get a kiss?" Stan laughed.

"You're not a special visitor," Miriam said, her voice loud and gravelly.

She had close-set eyes in a long, horsey face, and her cropped gray hair stuck up at odd angles. She turned her attention to Rebecca: "You're a good-looking woman. I see why Stan has been making himself scarce."

"You're embarrassing us," Stan said.

"No, you're not," Rebecca laughed.

"Yes, you are."

Miriam led them toward the living room, and Rebecca noticed a painting on the wall, a big canvas with bold swathes of red and orange. "Is that your work?" she asked.

"Yes. What do you think?" Miriam asked.

"I really like it. It's so vibrant and alive."

"Stan says you're an artist too."

"A photographer, but only an amateur."

"We have that in common, then," Miriam smiled.

Taking Annie and Paul by the hand, she led them to see her fish tank in the living room. They spied three stray cats draped on the couch and could hardly contain their glee. She chatted easily with them, and when she asked them to help her cook dinner, they disappeared into the kitchen. Stan and Rebecca settled on a couch nearby.

"Your mother has a way with kids," Rebecca said to Stan.

"She has a way with everyone," he said. "Nobody can resist her."

"Including you?"

"I suppose so."

"Meaning what?" Rebecca asked.

"She's always liked David, my younger brother, better than me," Stan shrugged. "He's the funny one who makes her laugh. He even turned out to be an artist like her."

"That sounds painful." Rebecca filed away this subject for further conversation.

"But since he lives in England, she doesn't see him much. I'm the one who figures out her bills and fights with the garbage service if they don't show up."

"Too bad for you."

"I don't really mind."

Through the kitchen door Rebecca could hear Miriam giving the kids instructions for making the salad and chatting with them. "Do you have grandparents?" she asked.

"No," Paul answered quickly.

"But there's Grandpa Charlie," Annie said.

"He doesn't count."

"Well, I don't have any grandchildren," Miriam said. "It sounds like we have a match."

Annie giggled.

"Where's your dad?" Miriam asked a few minutes later.

"He's gone," Annie said, in a matter-of-fact voice.

"We don't ever see him," Paul added.

"That's too bad," Miriam answered. "But families change sometimes."

"They've written off their father," Rebecca whispered to Stan. "I don't blame them. That bastard was the one who abandoned them, after all."

Dinner was ready, and Annie came out of the kitchen to find Rebecca and Stan. "Come and get it," she called happily, draped in Miriam's soiled striped apron.

The kitchen table was a colorful sight with its red-checkered tablecloth and platters of hamburgers, mashed potatoes, and salad. In the center was a bowl of pitless black olives; the children dove into it, putting them on their fingers and wiggling them. "Mom never lets us have these," Paul told Miriam.

"What are you talking about?" Rebecca said. "I do on special occasions."

"Like this," Annie said.

"Stan tells me you're from California," Miriam said as they settled into eating.

"I was born there," she replied, "but I left for Ann Arbor to go to college and then I moved here."

Miriam chomped on a bite of salad. "Are your folks still out west?"

"Just my dad. My mom died when I was four."

"That must have been hard, growing up without a mother," Miriam noted.

Rebecca paused. "It was, but here I am." She felt a familiar sadness, but when she saw the look of sympathy on Miriam's face her sadness eased.

"Your father took care of you?"

"At first he did, but then he got involved with work and was away a lot."

"So he's the grandpa who doesn't count," Miriam mused. The children were busy with their hamburgers, piling them with catsup and pickles, and she helped herself to more salad.

"Are you close to your father?" she asked Rebecca.

"Stop with the interrogation, Mom," Stan said sharply.

"It's okay," Rebecca said, appreciating her interest.

"I'm asking a perfectly reasonable question," Miriam smiled.

"My dad and I have gone our separate ways," Rebecca said. "We did a lot of things together when I was a little kid, but that ended when I was about eleven. That's when he seemed to lose interest."

"He probably didn't know what to do with a growing-up girl. Lots of men are like that," Miriam said.

"Right," Rebecca said. "It took me two years of therapy to realize that."

"And probably a lifetime to get over being hurt," Miriam added.

"Enough," Stan said. "You're being too personal."

"Don't be so uptight," Miriam laughed. "Rebecca and I are just getting to know each other."

"Are you Jewish?" Annie asked Miriam.

"Where did that question come from?" Rebecca asked.

"Kimberly in my class is Jewish. She has a lot of pets, just like Miriam."

Miriam smiled at Annie: "Yes, of course I'm Jewish. Are you?"

"Mommy, am I?"

"Not really," Rebecca answered. "Your dad's parents were Christian and Grandpa Charlie isn't anything. But my mother—who you're named after—was Jewish."

"Well, then, that makes you a Jew, too," Miriam said, patting Annie on the arm. "We'll be Jews together. How is that?" Annie smiled up at her with gratitude.

The dinner continued a while longer, but Stan began to look at his watch. "Let's get out of here," he said. "I'm already late for my racquet-ball game."

"Can't we stay longer?" Paul asked.

"I'd also like that," Rebecca said, pleased by her son's show of enthu-siasm, "but we need to ride back with Stan to Chicago."

"You're welcome here anytime," Miriam said, her face alight with satisfaction. "Every day, if you wish."

"You won't forget us?" Annie asked.

"How could I do that? Now that I've found you, I'll never let you go."

In the weeks that followed, they visited Miriam's house several more times, and Stan continued coming and going from Rebecca's apart-ment in his usual way. She was satisfied with this arrangement—and Miriam was a great addition to their lives—but she began to notice a change in Stan, a growing restiveness. At first it wasn't obvious, but on a humid, hot evening in June, as they sat in her kitchen with the fan blowing, he began to drum his fingers on the table impatiently. He'd been irritable since he walked through the door, and at dinner he had snapped at Paul when he didn't pass the salt quickly enough. "What's going on?" Rebecca asked him. "Too much heat?"

"I'm fed up with ping-ponging back and forth between my apart-ment and yours," he said. "I was supposed to play tennis tonight. I thought my tennis racquet was here but it's at my place, and now it's too late to go get it and make it back to the court in time."

"That's a bummer," she said tiredly.

"It happens a lot. I don't like it. I don't want to do it anymore."

Rebecca was silent for a moment. "What do you suggest?"

"I don't know." He slumped in his chair.

She took a deep breath. "I suppose you could move in here with us. That way, your things would be in one place. That would be the simplest solution."

"You'd need a shoehorn," he said. "I can barely fit in your bed, and where would I put all my sports gear? We need more room."

Rebecca sighed, knowing he was right. "But I love it here. The neighborhood with all the little shops and greengrocers and everyone out on the streets. I really don't want to move."

"Then what?"

That was the question, and it took several weeks for it to be resolved. Rebecca continued to resist the idea of moving. She'd worked so hard to make a home for herself and the kids, and she liked the freedom of having her own place—but she also knew that if she and Stan were going to continue together, there was no other alternative.

During this period of uncertainty, she called her friend Ella late one night and spoke to her about her confusion. "I'm afraid I'll lose, whatever I do," she said.

"The core of your dilemma is Stan, right? Do you love him?" Ella asked.

This question, which was so simple, threw Rebecca, and she felt her face redden. "I don't really think of him in those terms," she answered. "But I think we'd create a solid, strong family."

Ella paused. "Are you sure? You told me he's been sharp with the kids a few times recently."

"That's true," Rebecca replied. "But he has a lot of good things about him. And I really like Miriam so much."

"You're not moving in with his mother, you know," Ella said, but then she backpedaled. "Whatever you decide, I'm sure you'll make it work."

"You're a really good friend," Rebecca said.

Ella laughed. "You owe me. Next time I'm upset about something, I'll call you late at night."

Rebecca hung up the phone feeling even less sure about what she was doing.

In the end Rebecca told Stan she was willing to consider moving. "I'm not promising anything, but how about we look for a place near Miriam's in Evanston? The kids would love living close to her, and so would I. I could open my practice in that town as easily as Chicago."

"Forget it."

Rebecca was surprised by his vehemence. "Too much togetherness?"

"I was thinking of Skokie instead. It's a nice little suburb," he said. "It's closer to Chicago. Real estate there is pretty cheap, and the gym is nearby."

"I see you've already been investigating this," Rebecca said coolly. "But hey, didn't the Nazis march in that town in the late seventies? I remember reading about it."

"Don't worry, it's safe. People organized against them, and they kicked their asses out."

"No Nazis and there's cheap real estate?" she sighed, shaking her head. "It sounds like a real family wonderland."

Rebecca gave in to Stan's desires, and they soon found a two-story house with sprawling maple trees and a yard on Creston Street in Skokie, just north of Chicago. She realized she could open a therapy office nearby, and the house wasn't far from Stan's store, where he now was assistant manager. If they moved there, they'd be able to adopt a dog from the Animal Shelter, something the kids had been clamoring for and that she'd like too. A picture of the life ahead of them was emerging.

Miriam came by as Rebecca, Stan, and the children were checking out the house, peering into closets and throwing open windows. "There's even a room for you, Grandma Miriam," Annie yelled.

"She's calling her 'Grandma' now," Rebecca whispered to Stan. "I like that."

"I snore. I'm better in my own bed," Miriam said back to Annie. "But I'll come sometimes."

The neighborhood appealed to Rebecca, although she'd miss the excitement of city life. Next door lived Richard and Gus, a likeable couple who dropped by and introduced themselves, saying they were opera fans and passionate about listening to their recordings but that they'd be careful not to play them loud late at night. If Rebecca had to move—and she had now convinced herself that it was the most sensible choice—it seemed that this neighborhood and this town would work.

Stan and Rebecca made a down payment on the house. It was mostly his money, but she sold some shares of the stock Charlie had given her when she reached twenty-one—her early inheritance, he had told her—to pay for part of it. "If I'm a co-owner, you can't throw me out," she said to Stan half-jokingly. "And you can't make all the decisions." They talked about getting married later, after they settled into the new house and saw how things were going. Stan rushed around in a fever of excitement, taking charge of the move, packing up Rebecca's and his apartments, planning on where everything would go. His enthusiasm was running wild, and he was bossy in a way she hadn't seen before.

"Slow down," Rebecca said to him one evening as he was transferring the contents of her kitchen drawers into a moving box. It was a relief that he was doing all the work since she didn't have the time, but his frantic activity was starting to get on her nerves. "You need to check everything out with me. There are two of us, remember."

"I'm having fun," he laughed.

"The kids don't like you telling them what to bring to the new house," she said. "Everything of theirs should come along."

"Why should I pack up stuff they're just going to throw out later?"

"I'm telling you, take it easy with them." Her voice was angry. "Last night Paul was really upset. He said you threw his model car collection into a box with a bunch of other stuff without asking his permission. You know he doesn't like anyone touching those cars. And in case you haven't noticed, if Paul is upset, Annie isn't far behind. I don't want the kids to start resenting you."

"Okay, okay. I'll be good."

"I'm counting on you," Rebecca said as positively as she could.

Later that night Stan went back to his own apartment to do some final packing, and the kids were in bed. Rebecca sank into the green armchair, thinking of the two years she'd lived in this small space and how good it had been for all of them. She glanced up at the bookcase and noticed that the CD player hadn't been boxed up yet, and she rose and rummaged in one of the moving boxes to find a favorite Miles Davis CD. It was just the right music for her tonight; his mournful tone would mirror the sadness she felt about leaving the apartment.

When the music began, she let it wrap around her, lower registers first, slow and easy. Her body was stiff from sitting all day at the clinic, and she began to sway. Legs, hips, the movement climbed up her spine to her shoulders, her arms. The trumpet grew in strength, the sound becoming more complex, more piercing. She turned up the volume as loud as she dared with the neighbors in the apartment downstairs and the children sleeping. The room howled with the rhythm and beauty of the music.

Her sweatpants and shirt were too hot, and she ripped them and her bra and panties off. She was swept into the sound—Miles's trumpet wailing and weeping, the intensity growing—and she danced wildly with all the feelings she had within her, tears running down her cheeks. A huge sound grew inside her and she opened her mouth to let it out, but she stopped herself. The children would be frightened.

Miles now began to wind down, and Rebecca's movements became smaller, slower. Her breath, less rapid now, filled her chest and streamed through her body. She felt as though she had entered into a truer state of being. But the music stopped, and it was time to get back to work, back to the move, back to the life she was so carefully constructing.

3

In the autumn of 2002, the phone rang in the kitchen of the Skokie house as Rebecca lugged in the last of the bags of groceries she had bought on her way home from the office. She rushed to pick up the call. Charlie's soft voice came over the line: "Hello, sweetheart."

"What a surprise," she said. It had been over three months since they last spoke, and it was always she who called him. "How are you doing, Dad?"

"Not bad, not bad."

As usual, she couldn't tell a thing by his response. "Anything new?" she asked, glancing over at the dirty dishes in the sink. She didn't have much time to talk. She had to pick up Annie at middle school in a few minutes then stop by the bike shop with Paul's flat tire, throw together something for the kids to eat, and get back to her office to see a family with a petulant teenager who had been picked up for shoplifting.

"I closed a mall deal in Modesto," Charlie said.

"That's good," Rebecca said in a tone that didn't encourage further details. Once he got going on this subject, he could go on for a long time.

"At first it looked like the deal wouldn't go through," he said. The line was silent for a moment while he cleared his throat. "Did I tell you Vicky and I tied the knot?"

Rebecca dropped a bag of apples, and they rolled in all directions. "Damn. Wait a minute." She rushed to collect them, but as she jammed them back into the bag, it tore apart. "When did this happen?" she asked.

"A while back. A few months ago."

Rebecca had hoped that Vicky would disappear. "If you'd told me, I would have come to California for the wedding," she said.

"We didn't want to make anything out of it."

Stan and Rebecca were getting ready for their own wedding, a simple ceremony in their living room with a dinner afterward for their closest friends and family. They'd argued about what kind of wedding to have before settling on this plan. Stan had wanted a big celebration with a few hundred guests, but she thought a small one was more suitable. And less work. Fortunately, she had prevailed. "You remember I'm getting married, too?" she asked. "In November. I sent you an invitation. Stan and I decided it was time since we've been living together for almost two years."

There was a pause. "That's right."

"Can you come?" Rebecca asked.

"Not to the wedding."

"That's too bad," she said, disappointed even though she'd never expected he'd make the effort.

"But we'll be seeing you soon," he said. "Vicky and I are driving to Chicago in our new RV."

"You're coming here? I can't believe it. That's really wonderful, Dad." A warm smile spread through her.

"It's Vicky's idea," he said. "We bought this new luxury RV, and she said she's never seen Chicago."

"I got the impression she didn't want to have anything to do with us."

"Well, she's coming." Charlie paused. "Can we park in your driveway?"

Rebecca imagined a huge silver blimp taking up all the room in their short driveway. "Sure, Dad," she laughed. "We'll figure it out when you get here."

"We're leaving California right now."

"Today?"

"Vicky's just putting the final things in the RV," he said in a cheerful tone. "See you later." He hung up before she could ask him what day they were planning to arrive. She dialed his number again, but there was no answer.

When Rebecca saw Stan that night and told him that her father and Vicky were coming, he immediately began to make a list of things they could do. "Better wait to see what they're like," she said. "They're not what you'd call normal people."

"Nobody's normal," he replied.

"Remember the night we met and I told you about Vicky? You called her a dragon lady."

He laughed. "Maybe she's changed."

"I doubt it."

Stan rubbed his hands together gleefully. "I can't wait to meet Charlie. My new father-in-law."

Rebecca was not surprised by Stan's enthusiasm; he still missed his own father, Mort. "Don't count on him to be like your dad," she said.

"We'll take everyone to a football game, and Miriam can come, too," Stan said. "It will be a real family outing. We'll all get to know each other."

"I wouldn't buy the tickets yet."

"Call your father right now and see if they want to go."

"Slow down," Rebecca said. "Just because you like football doesn't mean everyone else does. Besides, I have no idea where he is. They're already on the road in the RV, impossible to reach."

"Doesn't your dad have a cell phone?"

Rebecca sighed. "I don't know, Stan. If he does, I don't have the number."

Since the move to Skokie, Rebecca had made her peace with the new house. She loved the light that filtered through the big windows in the kitchen and the extra bedroom space upstairs, and the backyard was a bonus now that they had Ruckus, a flouncy black mutt that followed Rebecca everywhere. But when she thought of the upcoming visit with Charlie and Vicky, she saw the house through more critical eyes. The yard was a mess, and something had to be done about the frayed green armchair in the living room and the tacky shower curtain upstairs. Stan always left his sports gear in a pile in the hall—she made him put it away in preparation for the visit, and she got the kids to pick up their belongings, which were scattered all about. In the living room she hung up six favorite photographs she'd taken of the mountains in Mexico, where she and Peter had traveled the summer before Paul was born.

If Charlie and Vicky had left California when he said, they might appear by the end of the week—but then again, they might stop along the way and not even bother to call. As the days progressed, Rebecca became increasingly frustrated by not knowing when they'd arrive. She couldn't just wait around the house, and yet she wanted to witness that grand moment of the RV pulling up and her father and Vicky alighting.

There also was the matter of figuring out what to do with the RV. Stan and Rebecca usually parked in the driveway, but that's where the RV would have to go. In anticipation of this, they left their cars on the street, but space was limited and the cars had to be juggled. Richard and Gus didn't mind, but a neighbor down the street, someone she hadn't even met and who sounded unfriendly on the phone, called to say that he had heard a RV was arriving soon and that he was concerned. Rebecca explained that it would be there only temporarily, but she worried that other neighbors might be bothered. The longer the wait until they arrived, the more irritating it was.

During those days, she continued to see clients in her therapy office. She now had her own private practice in a professional building where Ella also leased space. Sometimes they passed in the hall between clients and had a few minutes to chat. "Are Charlie and Vicky here yet?" became a joke between them, although it was becoming less funny to Rebecca. Stan called often during work hours, asking if they'd arrived, and the kids came home from school with the same question.

Two weeks after Charlie's phone call, Rebecca drove down Creston Street late in the afternoon, having finished a session in her office with a woman who couldn't decide whether to leave her verbally nasty husband or stay for the kids' sake. In the driveway sat a huge silver RV. She rushed into the house. "Dad, are you here? I'm home," she called.

"He's sleeping," Paul said from the kitchen.

"Upstairs?"

"In the RV." Paul's manner was even flatter than it usually was these days.

"Did you talk to him?"

"When I went outside to say hello, he barely even said hi. He told me he and Vicky were going to take a nap in the RV and they'd see me later. That was hours ago." Paul's voice cracked, as it often did these days. He was on the verge of adolescence, growing tall and skinny.

"That's a disappointment," Rebecca said, wishing the visit had gotten off to a better start for him. He could use a little grandfatherly love since his father had disappeared and he had never warmed up to Stan. "But don't take it personally. At their age, it's quite a strain to drive so far. Of course they're tired."

"Guess again, Mom. Last night they stayed only thirty miles away."

"Oh, dear," she grimaced.

Annie buzzed through the door in her soccer clothes, excited. "Where are they? I can't wait to see them." She had become quite an athlete since they moved to Skokie, joining whatever sport happened to be in season.

Paul gestured toward the RV. "In there."

"Well, they'll be hungry. I'd better do something about dinner," Rebecca said. "You kids start in on your homework." Paul shot her a disgusted look, but he didn't argue.

She rushed to the supermarket and bought steaks to grill, the makings of a salad, a fresh baguette, and a good bottle of Merlot. By the time she returned, Paul had disappeared to his room and Annie, the diligent student, was finishing up her homework. "Can I help?" she asked. Together they put a white tablecloth on the dining room table and set it with their best stainless silver and white dishes from Pottery Barn. Rebecca sent Annie outside to pick a bouquet of the golden chrysanthemums that grew by the side of the house; they'd go on the table, along with two tall candles. Still no sign of Charlie and Vicky, but when Stan got home, they'd have a big celebration. Rebecca imagined it would be awkward at first, but she hoped they'd settle into a long, pleasing evening together.

Stan burst into the kitchen an hour later. "I met your father and Vicky outside," he said.

"Oh, good. Did you invite them to come in?"

"That's not going to happen," he replied. "They're all dressed up and waiting for a taxi. They said they're going to one of those expensive downtown restaurants."

Rebecca stared at him. "Shit."

Stan gave her an amused look. "You warned me."

"It's not funny."

Rebecca tromped outside, Stan and the kids following. If Charlie and Vicky were going to be so rude, she, at least, would put on a good face. She greeted Vicky and hugged her father. "I'm so glad you're here," she whispered to him. "Welcome to Chicago, at last."

"Thanks, sweetheart."

"How was the drive?" Stan asked Vicky.

"Long," she answered, giving him a little smile. "But we made it." She was stunning in her sleek black dress, her platinum hair piled high, a glittery necklace around her neck—and Charlie, too, was spiffed up in a dark suit, his thinning hair slicked back. "You met Paul and Annie two years ago, remember?" Rebecca said, thrusting the kids toward Vicky.

"Of course I remember," she said, nodding at them.

"Hi," they said to her in unison.

"Can I see the inside of your RV?" Paul asked Charlie.

Charlie started to answer, but Vicky interrupted him. "No, you can't. It's our private place. Nobody goes in there but us."

Paul's face fell in disappointment. "I wouldn't touch anything."

Stan put a heavy hand on his shoulder. "They're entitled to their privacy, Paul. Their RV is like your bedroom—you don't want anyone to come in there, right?" Paul glanced up at him in a resentful way.

"So you're going out to dinner?" Rebecca said. "This is the first night of your visit, and I thought we'd eat together."

A look flashed between Vicky and Charlie, and he quickly spoke. "Some other night, sweetheart. I have a date with this gorgeous woman. We called from the road to make a reservation at La Spezia on the Magnificent Mile. I understand it's one of the best restaurants in town."

"As you wish," Rebecca said, her eyes narrowing. "Although the reviewers say the quality has dropped."

"You could get a really good dinner at our house," Annie said. "Mom's the best cook."

Rebecca gave Charlie and Vicky a moment to respond, but they just stood there. "You've made up your minds, I see," she said, "but at least we can have an after-dinner drink together when you get back."

"If it's not too late," Charlie said.

"I'll give you a key to the house," Rebecca said. "That way, you can let yourselves in. The guest bedroom is upstairs, on your left, and there's a bathroom across the hall."

"We'll sleep in the van," Vicky said quickly.

"I've made the bed up. You'll be much more comfortable inside the house."

"That won't be necessary."

Stan jumped in. "It looks like they're set in the RV, hon. Let it be."

"It's a little palace in there," Charlie said. "As long as we're hooked up to electricity, we have everything we need."

"Well, at least knock on the door when you get back and see if we're awake," Rebecca said.

The taxi drew up to the curb for Charlie and Vicky. He opened the door for her and took her arm in a courtly way, helping her into it. "Enjoy your dinner, you two," Stan said in his hearty voice. Rebecca turned away.

"That's weird," Annie said, waving good-bye to them. "Why don't they want to eat with us?"

"They will another time," Stan said. "They're probably tired of cheap meals, and they're hungry for something special tonight."

"Like we don't have special food at our house?" Paul said. "Who do they think they are, the king and queen?"

Ruckus came bounding over to them, frisky as always. Ordinarily Rebecca warmed at the sight of him, but tonight she pushed him away. "I hate what they're doing," she said. "I bet Vicky insisted on going to the restaurant."

"She isn't so bad," Stan said. "She was friendlier than I expected."

Rebecca gave him an irritated look. "Just wait."

Later that night Rebecca sat at the kitchen table, organizing the client notes she'd made during the past week, listening carefully for sounds in the driveway. Stan had fallen asleep on the couch in the living room, and Ruckus snored loudly on his round cushion in the corner. At eleven thirty, she heard a faint knock on the kitchen door. It was Charlie. "Oh, good," she said, letting him in. "I thought you weren't coming."

"Vicky's sick," he told her. "Something in the restaurant upset her stomach."

"Sorry," Rebecca said, thinking that the woman deserved whatever ailment she had. "I guess those reviewers were right about that restaurant. But have a seat anyhow."

"Just for a moment. I can't leave Vicky alone."

Stan roused himself and came into the kitchen. "A glass of wine, Charlie? Red? White?"

"No, thanks." Charlie seemed unsteady and unsure of himself as he lowered himself onto the kitchen chair.

"Are you having a good trip?" Stan asked.

"Pretty good." Charlie even looked a little pale.

"The RV is working out?"

"No complaints."

"It must eat up a lot of gas."

"Leave the questions for tomorrow, Stan," Rebecca said. "Dad's exhausted, you can see."

Charlie drew himself up with a determined sigh. "Well, I'd better get back to the RV. Vicky might need me."

"We'll talk in the morning, then," Rebecca said. She paused for a moment, remembering the silly thing they said to each other before she went to sleep as a child. "Sleep well, Dad. Don't let the bedbugs bite," she repeated the words to him.

He looked startled. "You, too," he smiled faintly. "Don't let the bedbugs bite, sweetheart."

After breakfast the next day, Rebecca left at the last possible moment for her office, hoping that Charlie would appear, but the RV remained closed and quiet. She slipped a note behind the screen door: "Let's have dinner together tonight. There's a good Thai place nearby."

When she returned home after work, the RV sat empty outside. "I saw Grandpa Charlie and Vicky leave," Annie announced, circling around her on her red bike, streamers flying.

"Another taxi?" Rebecca asked, crestfallen.

"They said they're going to a play. They've been sightseeing all day, and they came back to change. They're all dressed up again."

"I can't stand it," Rebecca shouted. "What kind of people are they? They're just using our house as a parking lot."

Annie threw her arms around her, and Rebecca ran her fingers through her daughter's tangled blond curls and held on to her until she calmed down. "I guess we can't count on them for anything," she sighed. "Some people are that way."

"But not everybody," Annie replied.

Rebecca awakened early the next morning with an overwhelming feeling of sadness. Perhaps it had come from a dream or one of those half-awake thoughts, but she felt she'd gone back in time to when she was eleven. Her body was stick-straight except for tiny, budding breasts, and dark hair had sprouted up unexpectedly in her private parts. She didn't know how to stop the noxious odor that appeared under her arms—she had no one to teach her, no mother to tell her what to do, and she surely wouldn't ask her father. In desperation she took a bar of soap, wetted it, and rubbed it there, letting it dry. It was only later, when a rash developed, that her girlfriend saw it and told her about deodorants.

She remembered one Sunday in particular. She had padded barefoot into the Berkeley kitchen in her nightgown and found her father reading the newspaper in his terrycloth bathrobe and beat-up leather slippers, his usual weekend morning attire. "Daddy, can we do something together today?" she'd asked hesitantly. Recently she hadn't felt sure of herself around him; he'd seemed to have lost interest in spending time with her, and his mind was always somewhere else.

He'd looked up, his eyes unfocused. "Aren't you supposed to go to the zoo today? I thought your friend's mother was going to pick you up."

"I'd rather be with you." She had felt brave saying this, but then she saw his face tighten.

"I'm sorry, but no."

Despite her pride, she began to weep. But instead of comforting her, he turned away and began to read the newspaper again. "You never want to do anything with me anymore," she flung angrily at him. "It seems like you don't want to be my father." She waited a moment for his reassurance, but it didn't come. Instead he put more sugar in his coffee.

This incident—which she had always thought of as a turning point in her childhood—stayed in her mind as she felt the sweaty warmth of Stan's body next to her in the bed. She'd given up on her father after that, but here Charlie was, in the RV in her driveway, rejecting her in the same way. It made her angry. He'd come all this way to her house, supposedly to see them, but he acted like he didn't care.

This was unacceptable. Rebecca climbed out of bed and stomped down the stairs. The sun had risen and the day was crisp and clear. It was Saturday, a good day for the children to rake up the maple leaves that had fallen from the trees, their job in exchange for their allowance. She'd get them going early on this project, and the crackling of the leaves, the sound of the rakes, and their shouts to each other should rout Charlie out of the RV.

She made a pot of coffee and sat in the kitchen, warmed by the sun streaming through the big windows. In the driveway the RV looked like a ridiculous silver blob. She began to smile at the bizarre happenings of the last few days. How strange it all was. If somebody came into her office describing a similar experience, she would help that client realize that these rude, rejecting relatives weren't worth sleepless nights and all that anger. She'd say that boundaries are important, that you could tell this father and his no-good wife to leave if things get too bad.

Breathing deeply, she vowed to handle the next few days, or however long Charlie and Vicky were around, in a different way. She wouldn't let them get under her skin like they had: being upset only hurt her, not them. The smell of coffee soothed her, and she settled into the promise of a beautiful autumn day.

The kids trundled into the kitchen, and she greeted them with morning hugs. After making French toast for them, she sent them outside to rake. Stan came down a little later, ravenous and ready for his morning coffee. Sitting around the kitchen table, they began to fantasize about what went on in the RV. "I bet they have sex toys in there, a whole scene," Rebecca said.

"Disgusting," Stan whooped.

When they heard a knock at the kitchen door, they looked at each other, hardly able to contain their amusement.

"Come on in," Stan said, opening the door for Charlie. He pulled a chair up to the table for him and poured him a cup of coffee. "Cream? Sugar?"

"He takes it black," Rebecca said.

Her father settled into the kitchen chair, holding his cup with both his freckled hands. "I'm glad to see that you still slurp the top off of your coffee," she said, smiling. "How's Vicky feeling this morning?"

"It took a day for her to get over that stomach bug, but she's fine now."

Rebecca noticed that his face was drawn and he had a whole set of wrinkles around his eyes and mouth she hadn't noticed before. "You look like you didn't get much sleep. Your eyes are all puffy," she said.

"Have you and Vicky been enjoying your sightseeing?" Stan asked.

"We went to the top of the John Hancock building yesterday."

"I love that view," Rebecca said.

"Where else do you want to go?" Stan asked.

Charlie looked away. "Unfortunately, we have to leave."

"Leave?" Rebecca's voice rose. "You mean you're going back to California? But you just got here. And you look really tired. You're not in any shape to make a long drive."

"We'll be fine. Tonight we can stop in Cedar Rapids, and that's only four hours away."

Eyeing her father coldly, Rebecca spoke in her most rational voice, as she would to a misbehaving child. "I want you to know, Dad, that I'm really, really disappointed. We looked forward so much to your visit, and we haven't even seen you."

Charlie squirmed in his chair. "Vicky needs to get back."

"What possible reason could there be?"

"She wants to start the kitchen remodel right away. She's on a mission, and when she's like that, there's no stopping her."

"Surely the kitchen can wait a little longer. And what about you? Don't you have a say?" Rebecca's voice became even sharper. "You're letting her decide everything. I bet she gave you an ultimatum to leave right now or some terrible thing would happen, but you shouldn't cave in. We're your family, after all."

Charlie sat there without answering, looking miserable. Stan jumped in. "Are you a baseball fan, Charlie?"

"Sure."

"Those Yankees, weren't they something, winning the World Series four to one this year? The Mets didn't have a chance with that lineup of pitchers."

"You're changing the subject, Stan," Rebecca said.

He gave her a "Cool it, hon," look, and the two men took off talking about the players they liked and their batting records. She considered interrupting again but decided it wasn't worth it. Disgusted, she sat back watching them. Stan seemed so eager to please, throwing out facts and figures, and Charlie seemed to warm to him. Stan shouldn't have shut her up like he did, but her father was the worst, disappointing her and failing to come through once again.

I'll never put myself out to see him again, she decided.

But then Charlie reached over and took her hand in his, holding it with tenderness. She felt his warmth; it was as though a current surged between them. "I'm really sorry, sweetheart," he said simply, looking into her eyes. For several moments the room became still, and Rebecca saw the deep sadness there.

"I am, too," she said.

Annie and Paul burst into the kitchen, carrying their rakes. "Water, water," Annie said. "We're working too hard."

"Take a break," Rebecca said. "Your grandfather is here."

The atmosphere in the room changed as the kids asked Charlie about Grover and Daisy and the tricks they could do. "Ruckus can roll over," Annie said to him. "Paul, make him do it." Paul waved his hand, and the dog rolled over and over across the kitchen floor like a circus animal.

"That's something," Charlie smiled. "Come here, Ruckus." He leaned down and scratched behind his ears. "You're a good old boy."

"Remember Sparky?" Rebecca said to Charlie.

"Sure, we had him for fifteen years."

"Remember that time we took him to Clear Lake?"

"Clear Lake?" Charlie's eyes hazed over.

"I was eight. You and I went on a trip together, and we brought Sparky along. One day we went fishing in a little speedboat, and everything was fine until it broke down in the middle of the lake," Rebecca began to chuckle. "Sparky was in the boat with us, and we tried to get him to swim for help."

"What happened?" the kids clamored.

"I remember now," Charlie said. "Sparky wasn't good at swimming, and he just paddled in the water around the boat like this." He made funny dog-paddling movements. "We yelled, 'Go on, go on,' but he didn't know what to do."

Everybody was laughing hard. "And then another boat came by," Rebecca said.

"A model class speed boat, with all the extras," Charlie added.

"And after we got Sparky into our boat again, we were pulled to shore."

The kids sighed with satisfaction at this story. Rebecca wanted them to stay like this for hours, for days, but soon they heard a sharp rap on the door. Vicky stood outside, a determined look on her face. "Where's Mr. Stevens?"

"He's here with us," Rebecca answered. "Come on in and join the party. I just made a fresh pot of coffee."

"We need to get on the road right away."

Rebecca eyed her. "What possibly can be so important?"

"If you must know, I have an important meeting with the contractor set up."

"Surely that can be postponed."

"If you knew anything about remodeling, Rebecca, you would realize that's impossible."

Rebecca folded her arms angrily. "It seems like you came here just to see Chicago."

"And we've seen it."

"I can't believe how rude you are," Rebecca sputtered.

Vicky looked into the kitchen and caught Charlie's eye. "What's the matter with you?" she said. "You know we have to leave."

Rebecca saw an expression of fear and trepidation pass over his face. "I'm coming, Vicky. I'm coming," he said, jumping up from the table.

"Don't do it, Dad," Rebecca said. "You can stay with us longer. You haven't even seen the rest of the house."

But he just shook his head and headed out the door, mumbling good-bye on the run. In a few minutes they heard the engine of the silver RV turn over, and through the window they watched it slide down the driveway, into the street. "There goes Grandpa," Annie said sadly.

"I bet he'd show us the inside of the RV if Vicky wasn't here," Paul said.

Stan gathered up the rakes and handed them to the kids. "Get going, you guys," he said. "There's still a lot of leaves out there waiting for you."

After Stan and the children left, Rebecca sank onto the kitchen stool. Something disastrous was going to happen to her father, she was sure. She didn't know what it would be, but darkness lay ahead, a darkness as tangible to her as the kitchen table she was leaning upon.

She held up her hand, the hand her father had touched, and turned it around and around, seeing it from all sides. It looked like a separate being, pale and luminous. She brought it to her lips and slowly kissed it.

4

In the months after Charlie and Vicky left, Rebecca worked hard to build up her therapy practice, and her number of clients steadily increased. Her nameplate, Dr. Rebecca Lev, was on the door to her office, a room twelve by fourteen feet, and when she walked into the space, she felt proud that she was now the professional woman she had so determinedly set out to become. Potted plants sat by a large window, and a leather couch with bright cushions and two armchairs were arranged in an inviting way. Several photographs she'd taken of a misty Michigan lake hung on the wall, and her psychology books were neatly stacked in the bookcase. On her tidy oak desk was a box of Kleenex.

But underneath Rebecca's calm professional exterior, she was not doing well. It was nothing she could put her finger on, nothing she even named to herself, but as she rushed from home to work and back again, she felt a frightful shaking within. She tried to push the feeling away, and she never confided in anyone about it. After working so hard to become Dr. Rebecca Lev, she couldn't fall apart—she had to hold herself together for her clients and the children.

Certainly every therapist she knew had issues. This fact reassured her. Ella struggled with depression, especially during the dark winter months, and she often talked about her unhappiness, wondering if she should go on medication or do more yoga. Kyle, who had an office upstairs, had nasty, unproductive fights with his wife, and sometimes he came into work in the morning distraught and exhausted. The other psychologist in the building, Karen, was attracted to men who wouldn't make a commitment, and she always ended up rejected and hurt. Everyone had a problem, but theirs were common. Rebecca wasn't so sure about hers.

On a freezing Saturday in February 2004, when winter seemed like it would go on forever, Rebecca left her house and headed north on Interstate 94 in the black Audi she'd bought recently, after her old Volvo died. She and her officemates had signed up to go to an all-day workshop for therapists on multicultural differences an hour's drive away. Rebecca had intended to ride there with the other three, but at the last minute Annie needed to be taken to a friend's house, so she told her friends to go ahead.

An ordinary day with an ordinary plan. But as Rebecca was driving along the crowded freeway, she began to feel breathless—not the usual kind of breathlessness where a change in position or a few deep inhalations made it go away—and her heart raced and her skin felt clammy. Her panic grew and she was sure that the Audi was going to veer out of control and crash. Clutching the steering wheel, hardly able to breathe, she pulled off at the first exit and drove to the back of a Shell station where no one would see her.

Now that she was in a safer place, she felt a little better, but she was shaking all over. It was as though she had been seized by a mighty force and bent into a ragged shape. She had had a panic attack, she realized, something she heard about occasionally from clients but had never experienced herself. The idea of getting back on the freeway and driving the remaining fourteen miles seemed impossible, and she was sure she'd have a monstrous accident. *But you have no choice, you have to drive on*, she told herself.

After recovering for a few more minutes, Rebecca willed herself to return to Interstate 94. She drove in the slow lane so that she could pull to the side if she had to. The whole time she was trembling and nauseous, afraid she'd miss the exit, afraid she'd crash. The traffic zoomed around her in a threatening way, but she managed to make it to the auditorium where the workshop was being held.

When Rebecca slipped into a folding chair next to Ella, the facilitator was talking about the unconscious assumptions therapists make about race; it was a topic she ordinarily would have found fascinating, but his words floated right over her and he might as well have been talking gibberish. Rebecca's most immediate worry was how to get home after the workshop. She never wanted to drive on a freeway again, but if she gave in to that impulse, she feared she'd end up with a full-blown phobia. Her only choice was to force herself back onto the interstate despite her panic. She decided she would ask one of her officemates to ride in the car with her, and hopefully their conversation would keep the demons at bay.

As Rebecca sat in the workshop, she struggled to understand why she'd had a panic attack. That terrible shakiness she'd been carrying for months was bad enough, but what had happened today was even worse. True, she was under a lot of stress. There was the constant pressure of trying to help her clients, some of whom were very difficult, and she fretted about meeting her share of expenses for the household and the office. Plus there was Charlie. She called him every month or so and asked him how things were going, but all he said was "fine" or "okay." She couldn't force him to talk, and she had no way of knowing what was going on, but he weighed on her mind.

But for now, the worst tension was what was happening at home. The friendliness between Stan and the kids had steadily evaporated in the eighteen months since Charlie and Vicky came to visit. At first the rift wasn't noticeable—the family had made it through Rebecca and Stan's small wedding without incident—but then it grew out of bounds. No longer would the kids tolerate Stan's silly jokes and teasing manner, and Paul, now fourteen, backed off whenever Stan came near. He told Rebecca he'd never been able to stand his stepfather, and this was no surprise—but when Annie, who was now twelve, said the same thing, Rebecca didn't believe her. "Come on, honey, you used to tell him jokes and laugh with him," she said. Annie yawned in an infuriating way: "I don't remember that."

A few weeks ago, during the winter holiday break, Stan had ordered the kids to clean out the basement, which had become the dumping ground for the family's unwanted stuff. "I can't, I have to play basketball," Annie had said, breezing off, and Paul hadn't even bothered to answer. Stan had lost his temper and screamed at them: "You fucking kids, you're selfish and spoiled. You never do anything to help." But they still didn't obey, and Rebecca, who witnessed this, had had to grab hold of them and insist on them helping: "We're a family, and even if you don't like it, you have responsibilities."

When the kids stomped down to the basement to clean it out, she had glared at Stan. "It's not okay for you to swear at them," she said. "No matter how mad you are. I won't have it."

"But they don't do what I tell them to," he'd fumed. "What's wrong with them?"

"They're just kids. And they don't like being yelled at. Nobody does."

"They should give me more respect." Stan had looked like a child himself, petulant and pouting, his arms hanging uselessly by his side.

"Don't take it personally," Rebecca had said crisply.

"How can I not?"

Stan began to stay away from the family more often in the evenings and on the weekends, taking responsibility only for the occasional stopped-up toilet or malfunctioning electrical outlet. The running of the household and the supervision of the kids rested entirely on Rebecca's shoulders. She felt that weight as she hurried back each day from the office, tired and pressured. Annie, it turned out, had problems with math and needed daily tutoring—her math teacher had called, suggesting this to Rebecca—and Paul was moody and inward, spending too many hours alone in his room, sprawled on his bed with his earphones on, listening to punk rock, avoiding his homework.

The children had been damaged by the trouble with Peter, Rebecca was sure. She could blame their father for that much, though she knew she was the cause of a fair share of their problems. Once she overheard an argument between them in the kitchen that began when Annie asked Paul the name of the drummer for Good Riddance, one of his favorite rock groups.

"You're so stupid. You don't know anything," he started in a scornful voice, as cutting and disparaging as his father had been when Rebecca and he were together.

"No I'm not," Annie screamed back, trying to defend herself just as Rebecca had always done.

"Stop that!" Rebecca said. "Don't you see what's happening?" They looked blankly at her, and she walked out, unable to explain.

In the midst of this, Stan and Rebecca had grown further apart. Rebecca ate dinner with the kids before Stan came home, a separate little family—it was easier that way—and in the evenings she often rushed back to the office to see clients or she counseled them on the phone. It always seemed that one or another of them needed extra support, and she couldn't just turn away. Stan filled his evenings and weekends playing tennis or basketball or racquetball or poker with friends, or he stayed late at the store. He ate dinner on the run, heating up food in the microwave or ladling soup from a pot that Rebecca had made. When the two of them went out to a restaurant or a movie alone, which happened seldom, it seemed that they had hardly anything to say to each other, although they both chatted away easily enough with friends at parties or other gatherings. Sometimes Richard and Gus from next door dropped by for a drink, and they gossiped about the neighborhood and the latest operas, but after the men left, the same sad silence settled between them.

Rebecca felt achingly lonely, even though she seemed to be always talking to a client or a friend or a child. Sometimes she thought about escaping from her marriage into an affair. At conferences and professional meetings, which she attended as often as she could, she met men who asked her out for drinks or coffee, but nothing came of it. Her officemate Kyle, with his lanky good looks and wry humor, attracted her. When he came downstairs to see her between clients, she found herself laughing more than she usually did these days, and she fantasized about going off with him to a nearby motel, a getaway from both their unhappy marriages. But then she'd have to see him in the office the next day, and that would be awkward.

In the end she decided she didn't have the time or the energy for an affair with any man. She would endure this second marriage—she couldn't bear the thought of another divorce—and she'd do the best she could.

After the therapists' workshop was over, Rebecca asked Ella to ride home with her. She thought about telling her about the panic attack, but it would make it more real if she discussed it and she wanted more than anything to forget that it had happened. Ella filled up the space anyhow, worried about her nephew Ben's upcoming bar mitzvah and all the family squabbles that had surfaced. "This should be a happy time but it isn't, with so much fighting," she said as they headed out of the parking lot.

"It must be hard on Ben," Rebecca said in as concerned a tone as she could manage with her fear of driving distracting her.

"He's a sensitive kid. I'm sure he senses the tension." Ella's voice was filled with concern. "My brother is hardly speaking to my parents, and their feelings are hurt. My sister keeps calling me, telling me I should get them to patch it up. When I say I can't do anything about it, it's up to them, she gets mad. I need you to come to the bar mitzvah to support Ben and protect me from my family. Will you?"

"Sure, I wouldn't miss it," Rebecca said. She had pulled onto the freeway now, and her hands were trembling and her heart was racing. But yes, she could do it, she could make it back to Skokie.

Ella had been talking about the synagogue where the bar mitzvah would take place since she'd started going there for services regularly a year ago, after her longtime boyfriend, Gary, broke up with her. She'd been devastated; her dream had been to marry him and have kids. "That synagogue helps me when I'm depressed about my life," she said to Rebecca. "I can sink into my seat there and just be quiet. Nobody wants anything from me, but I'm surrounded by people. It makes me feel peaceful."

Today, after the frightening panic attack, Rebecca warmed to the idea of being in a place where she'd find peace. "Who knows, I might really like it there," she said.

Three nights later, Stan went off to play handball and the kids were in their rooms, Paul listening to music, Annie doing homework. Miriam stopped by with a painting she'd promised months ago. It had been part of a retrospective of her work at an Evanston art gallery—the reviews had been laudatory—and Rebecca had chosen this one for the house.

She asked Miriam to stay for coffee. Stan often claimed that his mother loved his wife more than she did him, and although Rebecca brushed this off, saying she wasn't in the business of rivalry, a deep bond existed between the two women. The two women settled around the kitchen table. "How's Stan doing?" Miriam asked, stirring three teaspoons of sugar into her coffee. The kitchen was toasty warm, the warmest place in the house on this cold night.

"I don't see him much." Rebecca sipped her chamomile tea. Unlike Miriam, she'd stay up all night if she drank coffee at this hour.

"Neither do I," Miriam said, "but I'm not his wife."

"He keeps busy."

"Don't let him drift away." Miriam's voice was sober.

Rebecca shifted in her chair. She could try harder to please Stan, but she didn't have the interest or patience these days. "We're just in a down period," she said. "There's a lot of good in our marriage."

"Spoken like a true therapist."

"It's my day job," Rebecca said. "But Stan and I are committed. We both mean well."

"Meaning well is one thing, and delivering is another."

Rebecca gave Miriam a long look. "The truth is that our marriage is in trouble. But he's your son, and you don't need to hear about that."

Miriam took a sip of coffee. "Okay, we'll leave it there."

The women sat in silence for a few moments, then Rebecca glanced over at the painting Miriam had brought, a canvas with abstract swirls of color. "Those reds and golds, they're so beautiful. And the purple lines," she said. "The painting makes me think of a circus with all its hullabaloo. I'll hang it here in the kitchen."

Miriam scanned the room: "On that wall by the kitchen door. That would work."

Rebecca took her hand and squeezed it—how much she loved and depended upon this woman. "You're such a good artist," she said.

"But so are you."

"Not anymore."

Miriam gave her a stern look. "You should be out there with your camera every day. You have a fine eye and lots of talent."

"Latent talent, you mean. There's no time for anything except work and family." As Rebecca said this, she felt a heavy weight.

"So where's the satisfaction in your life?" Miriam asked.

"The clients," Rebecca said, "at least sometimes. Although today one man stormed out of my office because he didn't like me challenging him about his flirtation with the teenaged girl next door."

"And the kids?"

"There's satisfaction when they're in good moods—although that's happening less and less. They're fighting a lot with Stan."

Miriam lounged back in the kitchen chair, her rangy body extending over the sides. "Well, shame on all of them." She said this lightly, but Rebecca heard an undertone of concern.

"We'll work the family stuff out," Rebecca said, wanting to reassure her. She recently had been thinking they should go for family therapy, but when she'd raised the subject with Stan he'd been adamantly against it, and she hadn't even asked Paul and Annie. Surely therapy could help her family, but it would take a lot to get them there. Besides, it would be tricky to find the right therapist for them; she had professional associations with the good ones in the area, and she didn't want to mix those connections with her own personal issues. The way forward to solving their problems was not at all clear.

"I worry about you," Miriam said. "You're running yourself into the ground."

Tears sprang to Rebecca's eyes, but she blinked them back. "It's just a crunch time."

"Don't be so stubborn."

Their conversation was interrupted by the sound of Annie clomping down the stairs. "Where did you put my English book, Mom?" she called.

"I haven't seen it. Are you sure you brought it home?" Rebecca answered. Annie gave her a sour look and stormed out of the room. The whole transaction took less than thirty seconds.

Miriam poured herself a final cup of coffee. "Kids," she said.

"It's constant," Rebecca said.

"By the way, have you talked to your father recently?"

"What made you think of him?"

"We're talking about families, aren't we?"

Rebecca looked fondly at her. "It's been a while since I checked up on him. I think he's okay, but it's impossible to tell. He can't be having an easy time with Vicky, but he doesn't talk to me about it."

"Do you miss him?"

"Miss him? That's a curious notion. I have my life and he has his. The last time I saw him was when he and Vicky came here, and you know how that went."

"You could go to California."

"Since when do I have the time?"

"But a father's a father, no matter what," Miriam said. "Even if he's a second- or third-rate one."

"I phone him every so often, but what else am I supposed to do?"

"You're awfully cavalier." Miriam became more serious. "You wouldn't want your kids to treat you that way."

Rebecca sighed. Miriam had this thing about families, that they should stick close together like birds in a nest. She was a smart woman, but she missed the point that separation is sometimes better than disappointment and frustration. "It's just the way it is," Rebecca said. "My dad and I have nothing in common."

"Don't be so sure," Miriam said.

Rebecca felt a sudden weariness. "I'm too busy to think about him. He's background, not foreground. There's so much else going on that seems more crucial."

Miriam patted her arm. "For now," she said.

Soon after that Rebecca was invited to give a workshop at a conference for therapists in San Francisco. She had sent the workshop proposal to the conference committee months before, never expecting it to be accepted, and when it was, she had been elated. She decided that the professional perks were too good to pass by, and the trip would serve a double purpose by giving her an opportunity to check up on her father. She told Stan she was going, and the plans for the trip fell into place, with Miriam agreeing to stay at the house while she was away. Miriam would make sure that Stan kept his temper, the kids got to school on time, and nothing too disastrous happened at Annie's sleepover party, which was planned for that weekend.

In May 2004, Rebecca flew to San Francisco and checked into the grand conference hotel on Market Street. At first she was thinking only about the conference and its glittering possibilities. She settled into a handsome Victorian room with red draperies and a high, inviting bed, and in the closet she hung up the sexy black dress she'd bought especially for the banquet at the end of the conference.

As the conference activities began, she went to lectures and workshops, saw old friends from graduate school, and made new contacts. On the third afternoon she gave her workshop, "Advanced Therapeutic

Listening Skills," to a room of curious, attentive therapists. She felt nervous as she began—she'd never talked publicly about this subject, although it had been the subject of her Ph.D. dissertation—but soon she hit her stride. At the end, when the participants crowded around her with many questions, she answered them with ease.

Her workshop had been a success, and this accomplishment raised her up one more level on the professional ladder. For hours afterward, she was thrilled. But when the next morning arrived, she began to feel restless. The hotel, with its windowless conference rooms and dimly lit hallways, seemed confining in a way she hadn't noticed. Ducking out of a workshop, she wandered through the revolving front door and onto Market Street, which bustled with tourists and shoppers. The day was crisp and sunny, a typical California spring day. As she started along the sidewalk, she caught the scent of sharp spring air through the exhaust of the city traffic. This smell was like no other she knew, and she was flooded with memories of flowering jonquils and daphnia and the fresh green grass that spread like a velvet carpet over the Pacific coastal hills at this time of year.

She had to get out of the city.

She rented a car through the hotel concierge and headed toward Tilden Park, driving east over the San Francisco Bay Bridge and onto the freeway toward Berkeley. She didn't go on freeways much anymore, not since the panic attack, and at first she worried that she'd have another one, but she settled into the rhythm of the road and became more confident.

She exited the freeway at Berkeley and began to wind up the hill on the narrow streets she remembered so well. She took a little detour and swung past the house she grew up in on Glendale Drive. It looked just as she remembered, a small wood-framed home built on a hillside with eucalyptus trees towering over it. The front door was ajar, and a kid's tricycle and a pile of digging toys sat outside in the front yard. The sight of so much family life pleased her. It would be a pleasure to peek inside the house and see what the new owners had done with it, and for a moment she considered stopping and introducing herself, but she didn't have much time, so she decided to move on.

Tilden Park spread over miles and miles of land at the top of the East Bay hills, just above Berkeley. When she got there, Rebecca pulled to the side of the road to take in the view. The Pacific coastal hills to the east were radiantly green and dotted by clumps of oak and pine trees, and they rolled majestically into the distance as far as she could see. The sight, so familiar from her childhood, brought tears of recognition and relief to her eyes. She drove a little farther to a special spot she remembered, and she parked the car and got out. Scrambling down a dirt slope, she followed a trail that wound through tall, fragrant euca-lyptus trees to a clearing, a private meadow. She lay down on the grassy earth, breathing in its smell—so fertile, so fresh—and she felt dizzy with pleasure. This was her rightful place.

After a while Rebecca pulled herself up from the grass. She thought about Charlie and the times they had hiked together through these hills when she was young. He had marched ahead, always the leader, intent on reaching his destination, and she had trailed behind gathering wild flowers—orange poppies, Queen Anne's lace, or yellow mustard. She had felt enveloped by the curve of the hills, the blue sky overhead, and the earth under her feet, and she hardly heard his pleas to move faster.

A few hours remained before she had to be back at the hotel in San Francisco to meet friends to go to the conference banquet. Now, more than anything, she wanted to see her father. She rushed up the trail toward her car and, fortified by the green hills and the rich earth, she drove as fast as she could toward Piedmont.

The house in Piedmont looked even more forbidding than Rebecca remembered. The massive front door had been stained black, or per-haps it had always been that way and she hadn't noticed. She rang the bell, which chimed its long arpeggio. The same dark-haired maid who had been there in 2000 let her in. "You're Maria, right?" Rebecca asked.

"Yes." Maria gave her a bright, sweet smile. "You're the daughter of Mr. Stevens."

"Glad to see you again," Rebecca said, pleased by her warm welcome. "How are you?"

Maria eyes flickered. "I'm okay."

Rebecca wondered if something was wrong, but she might just be having a difficult day. This huge house and its many demands would be enough to wear anyone down. "Is my father here?"

"In his library."

Maria had learned English in the last few years, Rebecca noted. The woman led her down the shadowy hall that was familiar from four years ago and knocked lightly on a door to the right. "Mr. Stevens, your daughter has come," she called.

When Charlie didn't answer, Rebecca slipped into the library. Her father had fallen asleep in his big leather chair, his head drooping to the side, a line of spittle running from the corner of his thin mouth onto his gray sweater. When he'd come to Skokie with Vicky, he'd seemed tired and worn down, but he had been fit enough then, a man who appeared to be about his age. But today he looked like a sick old man, his body frail and shrunken, his skin thin like plastic wrap, and he had dark, hanging pouches under his eyes.

"Dad?" Rebecca said, shocked.

He sniffed and jerked his head. "Wha?"

"Dad, it's me."

Charlie's eyes widened. "Rebecca? What are you doing here?"

For a moment she saw a light in his face, and she kissed him on his forehead. Pulling up a chair next to him, she told him about the conference in San Francisco and the workshop she'd given. "People liked my work," she said, "and they asked a lot of questions, always a good sign."

Charlie nodded sleepily, eyes half-closed, but then he seemed to come to attention. "You sound just like your mother," he said. "Her voice was musical."

"Really?" Rebecca knew from the few photographs she'd seen of her mother that she had inherited her deep brown eyes and impossibly curly hair, but he'd never mentioned this other likeness. "That's so lovely, Dad. I didn't know that." For a moment Rebecca felt a familiar yearning for this mother she didn't remember, and she edged her chair closer to Charlie. "I'd really love to hear more about her sometime."

Her father closed his eyes without answering. He'd never talked much about her mother, and she'd learned only a few sad facts from him in the past. Her mother—Anna was her name—had been his secretary for a short while and then they'd married. Rebecca's birth had apparently come soon after the marriage, and her mother's cancer must have been discovered around then. She'd died four years later. Charlie had never met any of Anna's relatives, and he didn't think she'd had any, or perhaps she'd left them behind when she moved west, just as he had. There was the fact that she was Jewish, although it seemed she never practiced the religion. This is what Rebecca knew, and in this moment, when she yearned for this unknown mother, she wanted to press Charlie for more details, but she did as she had always done before, even as a little child: she pushed away her desire. Her mother was dead, but Charlie was the parent she knew, and he was alive. Today he was in a worrisome condition, and she needed to attend to him.

She looked around the room at his mahogany desk and leather furniture, and at the plaques on the wall. From the piles of business magazines and papers on his desk, she could see that he spent many hours here, an aging man with a home office instead of the downtown suite she remembered. "How's your health these days?" she asked.

"Okay."

"Are you keeping busy?"

"There's a project up north," he said in a halting way. "In Red Bluff." He fell silent.

"And?" she prompted.

"We'll see," he finally answered.

Charlie had never been an articulate man, but he'd opened up enough in the past about things that interested him. His real estate projects were always at the top of that list, but now it seemed that he didn't have the energy or the spirit to talk even about that. Rebecca filed away this observation. "Where's Vicky this afternoon?" she asked.

"Out to get her hair done. She'll be back soon."

"Looking gorgeous," Rebecca smiled.

"Yes." Charlie's voice perked up for a moment.

Rebecca wanted to use this time before Vicky returned to find out more about him. "How's everything going, Dad?" she asked, leaning forward, inviting him to confide in her therapist's way.

"Fine."

"You and Vicky are doing okay together?"

"Sure. Why not?" His body stiffened.

"What is Vicky really like?" she asked. "I know you love her, but I haven't gotten to know her."

He sighed, looking into his lap. "She's capable. She's smart."

Rebecca paused for a long moment. Her father was less self-revealing than most clients. "That's admirable. But tell me, is she good for you?"

He glanced up uncertainly. "What do you mean?"

She caught his eyes with hers. "Just that. Does Vicky treat you right?"

For several moments Charlie didn't speak. As though in slow motion, all the lines in his face collapsed downward and his eyes filled with tears. "Sure she does," he finally said, his voice breaking.

"What's wrong, Dad?" Rebecca asked, alarmed. "Tell me."

His tears streamed down his cheeks and his lips quivered, but he didn't answer.

She suddenly felt afraid. "I want everything to be okay for you," she said in a rush. "I want you to be happy."

He was silent.

"If you need me, just let me know," Rebecca said. "I'll drop everything and come. You can count on me." With these words, she vowed to herself to watch over him more carefully in the future.

Charlie wiped the tears from his cheeks with the back of his hand. "I know, sweetheart."

"I'm your daughter," she said softly.

They sat in silence, letting the words settle, and then Charlie straightened up, ready to move on. "Vicky has a daughter," he said in a clearer voice. "She's a little younger than you, but not by much."

"I remember. Her name is Lana, right? How do you get along with her?"

"She and her mother fight whenever she comes to visit from Los Angeles. When she leaves, Vicky is in a terrible state."

"That must be hard for you."

"I hate to see Vicky hurt," he answered. "She feels so bad. Sometimes she goes into the bathroom and I hear her screaming and crying."

Rebecca remembered how her father had always grieved over injured dogs and cats, caring for them until they healed. The image of Vicky as a creature in pain flashed before her; she certainly didn't see her that way, but if Charlie did, it would only strengthen their bond. "There's nothing you can do about Vicky's fights with her daughter," she said, slipping into her therapist's voice. "It's between the two of them. They have to work it out."

"Right," Charlie said, sounding relieved. "I guess you know something about that from your clients."

"I do," Rebecca said, touched that he remembered she was a therapist. "Does Lana come here very often?"

"No, not really."

"That's good." She began to tell Charlie about Paul and Annie, and for once he seemed to listen. She felt close to him in this library, so much like his old downtown real estate office. When she was five or six, he took her there sometimes, and she'd climb onto his lap while he worked at his desk and he'd twirl her around in this same leather chair. "We're flying, we're flying," she used to sing, "higher and higher," and she'd see the office walls whiz by, the books and the desk, the plaques and the paintings of ducks, round and round until they couldn't go any faster.

Just as Rebecca was getting ready to say good-bye to her father, a door slammed somewhere, heels clicked on the marble hallway floor, and the library door burst open. "Rebecca, what are you doing here?" Vicky asked. Her platinum hair was pulled back tightly from her face into a sprayed French twist.

"I dropped by to visit," Rebecca answered, trying to hold a friendly note.

"Did you call first?"

"No."

Vicky fixed her icy stare on her. "I would have thought you would. That would have been the polite thing to do."

Rebecca stood up now, angry. "I figure I can visit my father whenever I want, Vicky. I don't need to make an appointment. Besides, you're hardly the one to talk about politeness after the way you acted in Skokie."

Vicky stared at her for a moment. "Unlike you, Rebecca, I didn't appear unannounced at your house."

Charlie struggled to rise, pushing himself up stiffly from his chair. "Rebecca's here for a therapist conference," he said to Vicky. "She's going back to San Francisco right now." He forced a smile, as though to show his wife his allegiance.

"I see," Vicky said, moving next to him. Dressed in an elegant beige suit, she appeared to tower triumphantly over him even though she was shorter.

"I'm glad you came, Rebecca," Charlie said in a small voice.

"Me, too," she replied.

Arms crossed, Vicky stared at her without speaking.

Rebecca wanted to fight hard with this woman, tell her what she thought, strike her or hit her, knock her down. For a long moment they locked eyes. But then Charlie coughed, breaking the stalemate, and Rebecca mumbled good-bye and rushed out of the house.

5

When Rebecca got back to the hotel, she was in no mood to socialize, and she left a message for her friends saying she was skipping the conference banquet that evening. The sexy black dress would have to be worn another time. She ordered a chicken sandwich and a glass of wine from room service and collapsed onto her bed.

Her phone rang; it was Stan, asking how things were going. She told him about the workshop, and when she learned that the household was running smoothly under Miriam's firm hand, she was relieved. At least that part of her life was in order. "But I saw my father this afternoon," she said. "He's in terrible shape."

"He's getting old," Stan said.

"The problem is with Vicky, not his age," Rebecca answered. She started to tell him what her dad had revealed to her about his marriage. "He was so distraught that he cried. I've never seen him that way before. I'm worried."

"Maybe he was just in a down mood today."

"Something's wrong with him, Stan."

"So call his doctor."

Rebecca hung up, frustrated with Stan's lack of concern, and she decided to phone Ella, who would better understand. "Hold on a minute while I turn off the TV," Ella said when Rebecca reached her in her Chicago condo. Ella watched the cooking channel to decompress every evening when she got home from seeing clients, a habit that

Rebecca and their other officemates teased her about. She countered by saying that the cooking channel beat throwing dishes against the wall or smashing her car.

But Rebecca was not in a teasing mood tonight. She described what she had seen that afternoon, and Ella asked her a lot of questions. "You'd better watch out," she said. "That woman sounds like a sociopath."

Rebecca felt chilled. "I think she might be," she answered. "I hadn't put a diagnosis on her, but that fits."

"You know how sociopaths can fool you. They can be charming."

"Vicky's never been charming with me," Rebecca said. "But she charms my father. She's smart, and I imagine she knows how to use sex to her advantage. Even Stan seemed impressed by her when they came to Chicago in their RV."

"The problem with sociopaths is that they can be destructive," Ella said. "You know this as well as I do. They're capable of great cruelty and violence, especially when they're emotionally attached to someone. If they feel threatened, they often act out."

"I'm afraid that's exactly what's happening. But what can I do?" Rebecca felt more helpless than she had in a long time. "I live so far away from my dad, and he never talks openly to me on the phone. I just happened to get this information today because I dropped in on him when Vicky wasn't there. I'm the only relative he has, but I feel so impotent."

"It's a bad situation," Ella said.

"I wish you had an answer."

"So do I."

Outside the hotel, the traffic on Market Street continued into the night. Too unsettled to sleep, Rebecca opened the novel she had bought at the Chicago airport. Ordinarily a good book was something to look forward to when she traveled, but tonight she could hardly focus on the words. She lowered herself onto the floor, stretching into a yoga position, but her shoulders and neck hurt and her body felt stiff, and she didn't have the patience to work through the kinks. She climbed into bed and wrapped a pillow over her head.

Many hours later she woke up from a nightmare: She'd been all by herself in the center of a circus ring when a huge, impeccably groomed silver horse, twenty times bigger than her, charged toward her, nostrils flaring. She rushed this way and that, trying to escape, but she couldn't get away, and the horse lunged toward her with crazy eyes and bared teeth.

Rebecca awakened terrified. *Breathe*, she told herself. *It's only a nightmare*. But she tossed in bed until the morning light cracked around the edge of the red velvet drapes.

One more day in San Francisco before returning to Chicago. One more day to figure out what to do about Charlie while she was still in town. The conference was winding down, and now that her part in it was over, she could concentrate on him—but the way forward was a puzzle. She mulled over her conversation with Stan the night before. His idea of sympathy was to tell her not to worry, but maybe his suggestion of talking to Charlie's doctor was worth pursuing. Her father had always been a hardy man, but maybe he had some condition she didn't know about. Every possibility needed to be investigated.

Rebecca called Dr. Moore, who had been her father's doctor for as long as she could remember. She had met him as a child when she was taken to him with the flu; she hadn't liked his curt way and had refused to go back after that. Luckily, the doctor was in his office today and took her call. "Your father came in recently for his yearly checkup," he told her, his words clipped like she remembered. "There's nothing to be concerned about. He's fine."

"But he seems to be deteriorating," Rebecca said sharply. She went on to ask about his heart, his lungs, his digestion, going into as much detail as she could. "What about his blood tests? He looks so pale. Maybe he has a blood disease or something."

"I checked your father thoroughly and he had all the appropriate tests," Dr. Moore said, sounding impatient. "Your father's a tough old bird. Rest assured, Rebecca, there's nothing wrong."

After hanging up, Rebecca was all the more determined to find out why Charlie was ailing. She decided to talk to Jim Hart, who had been her father's lawyer and friend for years. If anyone could help her, it would be this man. Charlie had met him when he'd started his real estate business in California in the sixties, and they had become close friends, playing golf every Wednesday afternoon.

She called Information and got Jim's telephone number, and when she reached him at his home in Berkeley and heard his familiar voice she felt better immediately. Jim and his wife, Fran, had been like family to her when she was young. She remembered the dinners she and Charlie had eaten at their home; Jim, a great cook, had often made a big spread of southern fried chicken, biscuits, and gravy, and when they'd finished eating Fran had played Broadway tunes on the piano and they'd sung along. "I'm in town," Rebecca told Jim. "I need to talk to you about my father."

Jim suggested they meet that afternoon. He and Fran were planning to come to the city to see a play, and they could stop by the hotel before that for drinks. "Fran will love seeing you," Jim said warmly. "And so will I."

Rebecca roamed around the hotel all day, dropping into a seminar on treatment for bulimic girls and another on therapy for teenaged depression. In the midst of analyzing case studies and discussing possible techniques, she didn't think much about her father, but when five o'clock arrived she was only too happy to spot Jim and Fran in the lobby. Jim, tall and gentlemanly in his gray suit, and Fran, dressed in chic red and black, made a striking couple. They'd never had kids, and when she was young Rebecca had often dreamed of being their child.

"There's our girl," Fran called in her trilling voice. She rushed over to Rebecca and clasped onto her, Jim following.

Rebecca happily led them to a table in the hotel bar, settling between them. "We'll get to your father," Jim said in the Tennessee drawl she had always loved and tried to imitate as a teenager. "But first tell us about you."

Rebecca talked about her kids, and her work, and her success at the conference. "You always were ambitious," Fran smiled.

"I wanted to be somebody."

"You didn't get much help from Charlie, as I remember." Fran arched an eyebrow.

"That's not fair, Fran," Jim said. "Charlie did the best he could."

"Oh, I know, but he left her alone a lot, and there were some things he couldn't talk to her about. Like birth control. Remember, Rebecca?"

"You called up Planned Parenthood and made an appointment for me when I was sixteen," Rebecca laughed.

"Oh, god, I think I even drew a map for you to get there."

"Your dad was intimidated by having a daughter," Jim said. "He didn't know what to do with you when you started to grow up."

"It took me a long time to figure that out," Rebecca said. "I always thought he just stopped liking me."

"Not true," Fran said. "Charlie was devoted to you, but he's the most awkward, inept person I've ever known." She paused. "Also, you weren't the easiest teenager."

"Me?" Rebecca smiled.

"His delightful little girl turned into a person with a mind of her own. You were always on his case about one thing or another. I remember you telling him he shouldn't be so racist. And you pouting and sulking around the house."

"I was angry at him for ignoring me."

"I understand," Fran said. "But you did give him some hard moments."

"I know." Rebecca sat thoughtfully for a moment, sipping her glass of wine. "Now that I'm a mother, I have more sympathy for him," she said. "But speaking of Charlie, I'm afraid we have a serious problem."

She went into detail about what she'd observed at his house and what he had told her.

"I haven't seen your dad in months," Jim said. "Every time I call, he says he's busy with Vicky. We haven't played golf since he moved to Piedmont. I miss him."

"Something strange is going on," Fran said.

A plan was made: Jim would drop by the Piedmont house unannounced in the near future. "But watch out, Vicky doesn't like those kinds of visits," Rebecca said.

"She'll be a lot nicer to Jim. He's a man," Fran said. "An attractive man."

Jim gave her a fond glance. "I'll see what's happening and I'll let you know. Maybe Charlie will speak honestly to me. But what I really hope is to get that old guy out on the golf course again."

Two weeks later, the bedroom phone in Skokie rang and Rebecca dashed to get it. She had been taking her time drying off after a long, hot shower, getting ready for bed. The day had been difficult: two new clients had showed up at the same time, throwing her schedule off course, and she'd had a fight with Paul about not taking out the garbage, his job.

It was Jim, reporting on his first visit to Charlie's house. "You were right," he told Rebecca. "Your dad doesn't look good. He certainly doesn't have the same old zip. He seemed glad to see me, but Vicky hovered around the whole time."

"Did she get on your case for dropping by?"

"A few dirty looks, but she was well-behaved. But she wouldn't leave us alone to talk."

"That woman gives me the creeps." Rebecca wrapped the towel tighter around her.

"I don't like her either, but she's Charlie's choice. We have to respect that," Jim said.

Rebecca sighed. "You're more gracious than I am."

The conversation ended on an unresolved note, with Jim saying he'd continue to drop by to see Charlie.

Stan, who had ambled into the bedroom during the phone call, cleared his throat loudly after it was over. "I know how to solve the mystery about your father," he said brightly.

"How?" Rebecca asked, slipping into her flannel nightgown.

"It's easy," he said. "Call up Vicky. Ask her directly what's going on with her husband."

"You're kidding, aren't you?"

"You could try."

Rebecca threw the damp bathroom towel at him. "That's really stupid, Stan," she said. "Go take your shower. Vicky's the most unapproachable person I've ever known. Besides, she hates me."

"Ahem," Stan said. "Are you sure it's not the other way around?

The next afternoon Rebecca took Annie to the mall to shop for school clothes. Her head was throbbing, as it had been all afternoon at the office, and Annie slouched beside her in a bad mood. Annie didn't like wearing anything but beat-up jeans and faded T-shirts, and getting her to buy something else was a fight. She was no longer the sweet-faced child she'd once been. She seemed to be taking after her brother, glaring at adults and complaining about most everything, and she'd dyed part of her hair pink. She was now taller than Rebecca, her body skinny and straight, her breasts starting to fill in. As they walked from store to store, she nixed every suggestion Rebecca made. "Help me out a little," Rebecca said to her, feeling like her head was about to explode. "Just try on this one blouse. Blue looks good on you." But after an hour of this, she'd had enough.

Back at the house, Rebecca gulped down three Advils, wishing she could hide out in her bedroom and nurse her headache, but she had dinner to fix and phone calls from clients to return, and she needed to make sure that the kids did their homework. She also needed to call Charlie. She had been dreading another of those go-nowhere conversations with him, but since she'd spoken with Jim he had been especially on her mind.

When her headache began to ease, she dialed the Piedmont number, hoping that her father would answer. While she waited, she recalled Stan's suggestion last night that she speak to Vicky about her father's condition, and she decided it would be worth a try if the woman answered the phone instead.

A formal voice came on the line: "Mrs. Stevens speaking. Who is calling, please."

"Hello, Vicky, it's Rebecca. How are you?"

"Fine."

"Keeping busy?"

"Certainly."

With those civilities out of the way, Rebecca began to talk about the remodeling they were doing in the downstairs bathroom, remembering Vicky's interest in home decorating. "I chose beige and blue for the walls—" she started to say.

"Mr. Stevens isn't here," Vicky interrupted. "You'll have to call back."

"I'll do that," Rebecca said, nice and easy. "No problem. How is my father, by the way?" She made her tone casual, anything to open this woman up.

"He's perfectly fine."

"Good, glad to hear that." Rebecca tried hard to stay calm. "When I last saw him, he seemed run down. I thought maybe something was wrong that he wasn't telling me." There was no response again from Vicky. "I'm glad I have a chance to talk to you alone," she continued. "I want you to know that if there's an emergency or if you need help of any kind, I'm here. Just call and I'll get on the first plane."

"That won't happen," Vicky said.

"You never know."

"No. I'm telling you. I will not call you."

"What?" Rebecca said. "I'm Charlie's daughter."

"That might have mattered in the past, but it doesn't matter now."

Rebecca gripped the phone hard, trying not to lose her temper. "How can you say that?"

A long pause. "I will be very clear with you, Dr. Rebecca Lev. Your father and I can look after ourselves perfectly well, thank you. We do not need you or want you. Leave us alone. Do not call, and do not come here again to check up on him."

"But surely you don't mean that," Rebecca said with rising desperation.

"I will repeat myself. Stay away from us."

"I know what you're doing," Rebecca yelled. "You're trying to have complete control over my father. You can't bear to have me around because I threaten your plan. But don't think you'll get away with it."

Vicky hung up on her before she was finished.

"The situation's deteriorated," Rebecca said grimly to Stan that night when he came home late from a poker game. She'd been waiting up for him in the kitchen, and the words came out in an angry blast.

Stan threw his jacket on the kitchen table. "Ask me how much I won," he asked, his voice loud and boozy. "I might be able to spring for that TV after all."

"Stan, listen to me. I talked to Vicky about my father, but it made things worse. She ordered me to stay away from him. No calls, no visits. Can you believe that? I'm his only daughter. She's doing something really evil."

Stan came closer to her, reeking of cigar smoke. "Don't be so melodramatic, hon. Vicky's jealous of you, that's all.

"You're disgusting." Rebecca pushed him away. "You can't see a bad situation when it's smack in your face."

"But I can see you're overreacting."

"How would you feel if it was your father? You'd be upset."

"Sure, but I'd put it in perspective."

Rebecca felt like fighting more with him, but she told herself it wasn't worth it, that it wouldn't change a thing. "I don't want to argue," she said. "I just want to figure out how to help my father."

"Okay, I have a suggestion." Stan glanced at her. "Promise you won't jump down my throat?"

"I won't," she sighed.

"Vicky has banned you from that house, right? Respect what she said, and leave Charlie and her alone for a while."

"But it's not like I've been barraging them with phone calls or visits."

"That may be true, but you won't succeed in changing Vicky's mind, at least not right now. Give her a little space and she might be nicer."

Rebecca took a deep breath. She hated Stan's suggestion, but she saw the sense in it. "How much time do you have in mind?" she asked slowly.

"Oh, six months or a year. Whatever it takes for her to calm down."

"But that's so long. What about the danger to Charlie?"

"What danger? You're imagining it. Let's say that Vicky is mean and controlling. That's too bad, but are you going to rush to California and drag your father out of the house? Force him and Vicky into therapy?"

"No," she sighed.

"You're two thousand miles away. Besides, you've told me dozens of times that it's a mistake to get mixed up in anyone else's relationship."

Rebecca had to admit that ever since that last trip to California she'd been frantic about Charlie, maybe too frantic. In reality he'd only gotten himself into a bad marriage, like so many clients who came to her office. She'd guess that his attachment to his wife was so great that he'd hang on and endure her nastiness to the end. "Maybe you're right," she said. "But first I need to talk it over with Jim. He'll have to promise to keep an eye on Dad and report to me if anything's wrong."

"Good decision," Stan said.

"If I stop calling him, I'll write him a letter explaining why. I'll send him a birthday card next month and a gift for the holidays. I want him to know I still care."

"Sure," Stan yawned.

"But Vicky will throw those things out before he sees them. He'll never even know."

"You're probably right."

"How awful," Rebecca said, putting her face in hands. "How very, very awful."

The following morning Rebecca sat in her office, fiddling with a paper clip and waiting for her first client, a nurse with a drug problem, to arrive. Ella stuck her head through the open doorway. "You don't look very happy," she said.

Rebecca gestured for her to come in, and she began to tell her what had happened with Vicky. "I'm considering not calling my dad's house for a while," she said. "That's what Stan suggested, and this time I think he's right."

"That's a big decision."

"I was sitting here mulling it over," Rebecca said. "Will it really help if I stay away from him and Vicky? If only I knew for sure."

"You can't know," Ella said.

"The whole thing frightens me."

"I understand why," Ella said. "But you don't really have any other alternative. Hopefully that woman's antagonism will ease once she's feeling more secure."

"Let's hope."

Ella settled back on the couch, tucking her legs under her. "I went to a psychic for the first time yesterday," she said. "A friend at my yoga class told me about her, and I thought I'd give it a try. It was weird, but she somehow knew that my family is always fighting and I get caught in the middle. I didn't tell her that. She even knew that Gary had dumped me. She said I have a wounded heart."

"That's pretty amazing," Rebecca replied. "Did she say anything about the future?"

"Like there will be a dark and gorgeous man appearing on the horizon, ready to sweep me off my feet? No. But she said I should pay special attention to my nieces and nephews, that they need me."

"That sounds right. I remember the bar mitzvah and you being worried about your nephew."

"After I left the psychic's place, I had this amazing breakthrough. I realized that I can live without having kids of my own. There's plenty of them in my own family for me to love and nurture. I never thought I'd say that."

"Good for you," Rebecca said. "That's worth whatever you paid her." The bell in her office rang—the nurse was arriving in the waiting room—and Ella rose to leave. "I don't believe in psychic powers," Rebecca said to her, "but email me the name and number of that woman. I think I'll give her a call. Who knows, maybe she'll say something that helps me get through this thing with my father."

"Tea?" the psychic asked Rebecca two days later. She was reclining in a La-Z-Boy armchair, her slippered feet stuck out in front of her. A flowered English teapot and cups sat on a table next to her.

"Thanks," Rebecca said, trying to get comfortable on the plastic-covered couch. She looked around at the crocheted doilies set on every possible surface, the artificial flowers in vases, the figurines of little children, the framed homilies. One embroidered picture said, "Life is like a flower, opening to full bloom then becoming dust." *A depressing sentiment*, Rebecca thought, and for a moment she considered leaving.

"Help yourself," the psychic said, gesturing toward the teapot. Two cats wrestled playfully on the braided rug at her feet. "Scat!" she yelled, clapping her hands. "Get out of here."

The cats scampered away, and Rebecca rose, poured herself a cup of tea, and returned to the couch. "You don't need to do anything during this session except shut your eyes," the psychic said. "I go into a trance. When I come out of it, I won't remember what I said."

The woman certainly was strange, and Rebecca felt like laughing, but she was also intrigued. She put down her teacup and closed her eyes. After several minutes, she peeked and saw that the psychic's face was filled with alarm. "Darkness, that's what I see," the woman said. "No light, just thick darkness. A deep hole roiling with darkness."

"It can't be that bad," Rebecca said, not knowing whether to take this seriously.

"It's pulling you in." The woman coughed. "Now I see an old man, pale, balding. Is that someone you know?"

"My father? It must be him."

"He's very still."

"Something is wrong with him, I know it," Rebecca said, her voice rising. "I want to help."

"There's nothing you can do. He's in darkness too."

Rebecca's heart started to race, and she began to tremble. "Is there no way out?" she asked.

The psychic didn't answer right away. "After many years. You have to go deeper into the darkness before you can come out."

Rebecca's stomach turned over in fear and she thought for a moment that she might have another panic attack. "Will I survive?"

"You will."

"And my father?"

"You will leave him behind."

The psychic continued talking, but Rebecca was so stunned by her predictions that she didn't listen. "Do you have any questions?" the woman asked abruptly.

"My children, what about them? Annie. Paul."

The psychic said Annie's name several times, drawing out the syllables, and then she chuckled. "That girl, she has a mind of her own, but she's strong. You don't need to worry about her."

"And Paul?" Rebecca dreaded this answer.

More silence. "He doesn't know who he is or where he belongs. He's hurting badly."

"That's the truth." Rebecca swallowed. "What about Stan, my husband?"

The woman concentrated for a few minutes. "I don't get an image, sorry."

Rebecca had had enough of this session, but when the psychic asked if there was anything else, she ventured one last question: "What is the darkness you're talking about?"

"I don't see it anymore," the woman answered. "That means I've come out of the trance." She opened her eyes and took a sip of tea.

6

It was the spring of 2005, and Paul was in trouble. At fifteen, he was staying out too late on weekends with a crowd of kids Rebecca didn't like, and his grades had fallen to Ds and even an F. He was a smart kid and had managed in the past to slide through school, getting good enough grades without much effort, but now he was disgusted with studying and was threatening to drop out. He withdrew even more from Stan and Rebecca, his face sullen and angry, his eyes hidden under his stringy brown bangs, and he usually didn't answer when they spoke to him. The only person in the family he seemed to care about was Annie, and the two of them spent hours behind the closed door of his room.

Once Rebecca eavesdropped on them, desperate to find out what they were talking about. She heard the murmur of Annie's higher voice, then Paul's loud tone: "The world's a shithole," he said with great feeling. "Nothing good will ever happen."

Rebecca felt frantic about her son. She'd counseled scores of families with difficult teenagers, but this was her own child. She didn't want to be angry with him, but she couldn't stand that he was rejecting her. Surely she deserved better than that after all she'd done for him—although as soon as she thought this, she chided herself for being so self-righteous.

One afternoon she forced herself into his messy bedroom and asked him what was going on. She was concerned about him, she said, trying to keep her voice low-key and friendly. When he didn't answer, she told him she was sorry he was having a hard time, and she only wanted to help. "Stop using that therapist crap on me," he said. "Just leave me alone." Rebecca was stung silent by this, but then she tried another approach, asking him directly if he was so hostile to her because she had married Stan. "That's your issue, Mom, not mine," he retorted.

Rebecca left his room feeling that she had completely failed as a mother. She hesitated outside in the hall. "I love you," she called through the door, gently at first and then with her full heart: "Paul, I love you, I truly love you." There was no answer.

That evening Rebecca talked to Stan about Paul, and when they went to bed, neither of them could sleep. "You've got to take a hard line with that boy," Stan said. "Send him to one of those military schools where they know what to do with kids like him."

"I don't agree," Rebecca replied, infuriated by Stan's lack of understanding. "We need to believe in him. He's going through a hard time."

Stan turned away in disgust. "You always defend him."

"No, I don't," Rebecca replied, although she knew he was right. "But rigid discipline isn't the answer here." Their argument went on and on, and it only stopped when she stormed off to the bathroom at two thirty in the morning, returning to find Stan asleep.

When the high school secretary called to report that Paul had skipped school once again, Rebecca insisted that they have a family conference. Annie and Paul sat next to each other at the kitchen table that evening, their arms folded in front of their chests, looking down defiantly while Stan and Rebecca lectured them about the need to succeed in school. "Life isn't always fun, Paul," Stan said. "It's about time you grow up and take responsibility for yourself."

"You're such a success? You didn't even make it through college," Paul muttered.

"That's just mean," Rebecca said to him. "Shame on you."

"Stop picking on Paul," Annie said, glowering at Stan.

"I'm calling your father," Rebecca threatened. "A few weeks with him this summer will straighten both of you out."

"We won't go," they answered in one voice. The last visit two years ago had been a disaster. Rebecca had driven them up to Wisconsin and dropped them off at Peter's apartment in Madison, but he'd hardly spent time with them and they didn't like his girlfriend, Marcie, who kept telling them what to do. They had called Rebecca in desperation, asking to be picked up early. When she appeared at the apartment, Peter had accused her of alienating the kids from him, and she had been only too glad to drive away.

"Then you'll have to go to summer school to make up your grades," Stan said to Paul, arms crossed.

"Fuck you, you can't force me."

"Oh yes I can."

When Miriam heard about this uproar, she offered a solution, saying she'd take the children to Florida for three weeks that summer. They could stay with her in her friend's condo and spend days at the beach. "We'll have a grand adventure," she told them. "Besides, I want to get out of town." Paul and Annie gladly accepted the plan, knowing that a trip with their grandmother would have its own rewards.

"Miriam will get those kids into shape," Stan said later to Rebecca, upon hearing about the plan. "She won't take any shit from them. When they come back, Paul will be willing to go to summer school and Annie will be much more agreeable."

"I hope you're right," she sighed.

Miriam and the kids left for Miami as planned, and the next morning Stan and Rebecca packed up the car and set off on a three-week camping trip, the first they'd taken together. As they headed west on the freeway, the land stretched ahead as far as they could see, fields of corn and wheat reaching all the way to the horizon, and the sky above was a radiant blue. A perfect day to begin a vacation.

Going away together was exactly the right thing to do, Rebecca thought. After all the tension and fighting, it was a chance for the two of them to become closer. She glanced over at Stan, who was sprawled behind the driver's seat, one hand on the wheel, whistling some song she couldn't identify, and she decided she'd try to be open and see the good in him during this trip. She hoped he'd do the same for her.

They slowly made their way toward the Rocky Mountains, meandering along county roads, staying in small campgrounds along the way. Each evening Stan unpacked the car, set up the tent, and built a fire—he liked doing these things, he said, because they reminded him of his scouting days—and Rebecca sat in the sling chair they'd brought along, sipping a glass of wine, appreciating that he was doing all the work. Away from the kids they got along better. Whenever Rebecca had the impulse to say something about Paul's troubles at school or her concern about Annie's belligerence, she stopped herself, and she didn't mention the tension that had grown between the two of them.

Five nights into the trip they pulled into a diner in a dusty town on the high plains. While waiting for their hamburgers to be served, Rebecca checked her voicemail. There was no word from Miriam or the kids, but there was a message from Jim. Ever since she'd stopped calling her father a year ago, Jim had reported every few weeks on how he was doing. It was reassuring that he was there in California, watching over Charlie. She had thought maybe her father would try to contact her, but she had heard nothing from him in all this time—no letter snuck to the post office, no secret call when Vicky went out shopping. She felt disappointed that he'd let her disappear so easily, but she was also relieved; the obligation to stay in touch with him these past years had brought her nothing but great frustration.

Rebecca listened carefully to Jim's soft, drawling message: "Sorry to bother you on your vacation, Rebecca, but I saw your father today. He has a big ugly bruise on the side of his face. When I asked him how he got it, he wouldn't answer." Jim ended his call by saying that this wasn't an emergency and Rebecca shouldn't worry, but he wanted her to know.

When Rebecca told Stan about this, he brushed aside her concern. "Everybody gets bruises from time to time, hon. You should see me in the workshop, always knocking against something."

"But my father doesn't have a workshop."

"Maybe he's been outside playing with those dogs."

"In his state? Those days are over, Stan."

"All I'm saying is that we don't know what his bruise means. And since we have no way of finding out, let's assume that your father is just fine. It's our vacation, remember?"

"Always the optimist," she said, forcing a smile. "Okay, I'll drop it."

The next morning they drove into northern Colorado, its purple, jagged mountains rising in the distance. Stan flipped on the radio, trying to find the news, and settled on a station playing country music. Rebecca stared out the window, mesmerized by the shifting yellows and greens of the landscape and the odd gnarled trees that appeared every so often, standing alone like sentries, and she took pictures of all this in her mind.

When they stopped later for a picnic lunch in an isolated spot off the road, Rebecca brought out her camera to photograph the far-off mountains in the west, and then she focused her lens on Stan, who was trying to balance on a fallen log. "Let me take your picture," he said when she'd finished. "Do something sexy."

Rebecca thrust out her ass and pulled back her shoulders, posing like a model, and then she pulled her shirt over her head and unhooked her bra. "Go ahead, I dare you," she laughed, feeling the warm air on her nipples. This was a side of herself she kept hidden from Stan, a freedom that showed up in her dreams and fantasies, and it excited her to reveal it even for a moment. Soon they were making love in the thin mountain sunlight.

"That was good," Stan grinned in the car a little later, and Rebecca smiled back. But then she began to think about Jim's unsettling message and decided she needed to find out more about her father's bruise.

She tried to call Jim on her cell phone, but there was no reception, so she slipped into a telephone booth the next time they stopped for gas.

"Tell me more about Charlie's bruise," she said when she reached him.

"It isn't right." Jim sounded discouraged.

"Maybe it's from medication?" Rebecca said. "Certain ones can cause it."

"I asked, but he said no. He's taking remarkably little medication for a man his age."

"If nothing is wrong with my father's health, what's happening most likely has to do with Vicky," Rebecca said to him. "How about investigating her? Maybe we can get some information that will help us make sense of what's happening."

Jim hesitated. "That's pretty farfetched, but we can't just sit around and watch him go downhill."

"We should hire a detective," Rebecca said. "Maybe she has a history of running older men into the ground and taking all their money."

"I'll find an agency," Jim said. "Or better yet, I'll investigate her myself. I have the time now that I'm retired."

"Great idea," Rebecca smiled, imagining this courtly man taking on the task with his usual doggedness. Jim had a wide net of contacts from the past, and he'd figure out a way to use them.

"Okay, we're set," he answered. "When you get back to Skokie, you'll have a report. And if you don't, you can fire me."

After two weeks on the road, Rebecca could hardly believe how invigorated she felt; she vowed to find more time for herself when she got home. She would schedule a few hours every weekend for photography, as Miriam was always pushing her to do, and she would exercise regularly, take a Pilates or yoga class or even start running.

Stan and Rebecca finally spoke honestly about the tension between them, acknowledging how strained and unhappy they'd become. As they were beginning the long drive back to Skokie, Stan went even further: "I feel like I'm on the bottom of the list of people you love," he said.

Rebecca was stung by the starkness of this image, and she reached over and touched his arm. "I'm sorry," she said, feeling guilty.

"The children come first, and even your dad is more important to you than I'll ever be."

Rebecca's impulse was to contradict him or make light of what he was saying, but she had to admit to herself that he was speaking the truth. Even though she felt closer to him on this vacation than she had in a long time, he'd never captured her heart or her imagination in the way he'd wished. She'd become withholding and critical of him, and she chided herself for that. "But I do love you," she said. "I love you a lot."

"I wish you'd changed your last name to Felder," he said. "You go around with Peter's name instead of mine."

"But we agreed it's best because the kids have that name and that's how people know me professionally."

Stan sighed. "I know. But it rankles."

"Poor Stan," Rebecca murmured. "You're the one I'm married to. That's what counts." She vowed to herself that she would give him more love and attention in the future, something he surely deserved. She'd just have to make the effort, which in this vacation state of mind didn't seem so hard.

Stan and Rebecca arrived home with a few days left to themselves before the children returned. When she went through the piles of vacation mail, Rebecca spotted a Priority Mail envelope that had arrived from Jim. "Don't open that yet," Stan said. "It will just upset you."

"It won't," she said, although she knew he was right.

The harmony she and Stan had achieved on the trip was in her mind as she began to look at the report from Jim. She intended only to scan it then put it aside, but she couldn't help herself—she read it in depth, and she became more and more agitated as she read.

"What does it say?" Stan asked, drawing closer.

"A lot of biographical stuff about Vicky," she answered. "She grew up in Jefferson County, Oklahoma, the oldest of nine kids. After high school, she ran away to L.A., hoping to break into the movie business."

"How did Jim learn all this?"

"He tracked down her younger sister Pat, who still lives in Oklahoma. Apparently the family lost contact with Vicky after she left and then she resurfaced a decade later, bringing her baby, Lana, home for a visit. Nobody knew who the father was. There was a huge fight, and Vicky stormed off. They haven't heard from her since then."

"Any idea about how Vicky supported herself before Charlie?"

"Well, she didn't get into movies. But she's no dummy, and she held down a series of administrative jobs in the corporate world."

"You should be reassured," Stan said. "She sounds like an ordinary person, trying to make a life for herself and her daughter."

"I thought there'd be something more dramatic," Rebecca said slowly.

"Like she's a con artist or a murderess?" Stan clapped her arm. "Now you can drop the subject. You can let it go, once and for all."

Jim had ended his report by saying that he'd uncovered nothing alarming about Vicky. She'd been married twice before, short marriages ending in divorce, and she'd had a series of boyfriends, but that was to be expected. No arrests or convictions, no excessive drug use. With a record this clean, the matter should have been closed. "But I've been a therapist too long," Rebecca said to Stan. "I've had clients who seem like righteous citizens, but the secrets they hold would shock you. Like the teacher who gets off on pornographic photos of young boys, or the lawyer who has an obsession with cutting herself, or the high city official who locked his teenage daughter in her room for a full twenty-four hours when she came home late."

"Come on," Stan said. "You're jaded from the people you treat. Your stepmother has a lousy personality but she makes your father happy."

"She's not my stepmother." Rebecca paused. "And I don't agree that she makes my dad happy. Not after what he told me."

"Stop it, hon."

"Okay, okay. I'll call Jim one last time to thank him, and then it's over."

When Rebecca reached Jim at his home later that evening, he told her that Vicky's sister, Pat, had been only too happy to complain to him. Vicky had been a mean child, stealing her jewelry, forcing her to do her chores. "That sounds like her," Rebecca said. "But it doesn't mean anything. Sisters talk like that."

Jim paused. "But the saga isn't over yet. I stopped by your father's house yesterday, and now he has a big gash over his right eye. It's swollen pretty bad. I couldn't tell if he needed stitches, and when I offered to take him to the emergency room, Vicky said absolutely not."

"What's going on there?" Rebecca cried. "I feel so powerless."

"Yup, well, that's two of us."

"I'm not even in communication with him anymore." Rebecca could hardly contain her agitation. "What if he really needs me?"

"There's nothing you can do," Jim said. "Except be there when he reaches out for help from you. Charlie's a proud man. It's his life, and he has to live it as he wishes."

"I've told myself that a thousand times," she said. "But when you go to his house again, do me a favor. Take him aside and talk to him away from Vicky. Tell him one more time that I love him. And remind him that he should call me right away if he needs help."

"Sure, I'll do that," Jim said softly.

The children returned home from Florida in better shape than they'd been, and the family moved into the second half of a humid July with Paul enrolled in summer school and Annie registered for a course in wildlife preservation at the nearby nature reserve. During this time, Rebecca and Miriam met for lunch at a deli, as they did every few weeks. Miriam described the Florida trip, making the kids sound like ideal traveling companions rather than the problem Rebecca had recently considered them to be. "You bring out the best in them," Rebecca said. "I don't know how you do it."

Miriam took a bite of her corned beef sandwich. "They're good kids."

"Did they talk to you about what's bothering them?"

"You think I'd let them be silent?" she laughed.

Rebecca stabbed a piece of lettuce with her fork. She felt envious of Miriam; if only the children would open up to her, it would make things so much better. "Did you learn anything I should know?" she asked wistfully.

"They're trying to figure out who they are. Like all other adolescents on this planet."

"I wish they'd let me in."

"You're their mother, what do you expect?" Miriam said. "It's easy being a grandmother. A lot easier than being a mother. Hasn't Stan told you how I failed at that?"

Rebecca had heard many stories about Miriam's sharp tongue and how she'd used it on Stan when he was young, making him feel worthless and unloved. He still seemed intimidated by her, although Rebecca knew he'd never admit it. "Nobody's perfect," she said, forcing herself to eat the bite of lettuce.

Miriam shrugged. "I'm not, that's for sure. Speaking of parents, Stan tells me you worry too much about your father."

"He refuses to see the seriousness of the situation with Vicky."

Miriam wiped her mouth. "You're right to be concerned. I'm on your side about this. I remember hearing about how that wife of his acted when she came to Chicago."

"I think Vicky's harming my father," Rebecca said, feeling her breath quicken as she spoke. "I mean serious harm. First a bruise, now a gash—what is going on?"

"Are you afraid she might kill him?"

The two women looked soberly at each other for a long moment. "I wouldn't say that. But maybe. Maybe. Tell me, am I being paranoid? Stan thinks I am." Rebecca's head swam with anxiety.

Miriam sighed. "I don't know. But you've got to get your father out of that house."

"But how? I can't force him to leave. Or throw her out."

Miriam lowered her gaze. "No, but there must be some legal thing you can do, some court order."

"I've investigated that already. Jim checked out the laws in California thoroughly as soon as we knew we had a problem. It turns out I'd have to prove that Charlie is incompetent or get him to file a restraining order against Vicky." Rebecca paused. "He'd never do that. So we can forget that approach."

"Too bad." Miriam was quiet for a moment then she brightened. "I've got it. You could go there and kidnap your father. Take him out for a drive and never bring him back."

Rebecca smiled sadly. "It's a good idea, but I don't think it would work. He'd hate it. He's a prideful man who wants to control his own life. I understand that about him. I wouldn't want anyone to kidnap me either."

"He'd adjust," Miriam said firmly.

Rebecca put down her fork, leaving most of her salad untouched. "No, he wouldn't."

Two months after the lunch with Miriam, Charlie telephoned Rebecca. It was an early fall evening; the leaves hung golden on the maple trees in Skokie and the air smelled like sawdust. Rebecca had taken Ruckus outside for a walk, but Paul called her back into the house, acting more animated than he usually allowed himself to be: "Hurry up, Mom, I think it's Grandpa Charlie on the telephone."

Rebecca ran inside to the phone. "Dad? Is that you?"

A thin voice came over the line. "Rebecca?"

"Dad, are you okay?" Silence, then she heard a terrible wheeze, as though someone had whacked him on the back. "What's wrong?" she shouted. "What's going on there?"

"I'm okay." His voice was so feeble that she could hardly bear it.

"Where's your wife?" Rebecca asked. "Is she there with you?"

"She's out."

"Oh, good." For a moment she had imagined Vicky attacking him while they spoke.

"There's going to be a divorce," Charlie said, his voice gaining strength. "I'm ending this."

Relief flooded through Rebecca. "Oh, Dad, I've been so worried about you."

"It'll be over soon."

"What has been happening?" Rebecca asked. "I heard from Jim about those terrible bruises. Has Vicky been hurting you?"

"Yes," Charlie said, his voice faint again.

"What? Tell me, Dad. Please."

"She gets mad and hits me."

"My god, I was afraid of that!" Rebecca yelled.

Suddenly Charlie drew in a sharp breath. "I'm in here, Vicky," he called, fear in his voice. "I'm on the phone. I'll be finished in a minute."

"She's back?" Rebecca said. "Watch out."

"I've got to go. Right now." With that, Charlie hung up.

Rebecca paced around the kitchen. With a fifty-fifty chance he'd pick up the phone if she called him back, she dialed his number. "Charlie Stevens," he answered faintly.

"Are you safe in that house with Vicky?" she asked, her voice frantic.

"Thanks for asking, Bob," he answered. "Yes, we're set here. I don't need any more firewood."

"Are you sure you're okay?" she asked. "Tell me the truth."

"No problem."

"Isn't Vicky a danger to you?

"No, I don't think so." His voice trembled with bravery.

"Do you need me to come there?"

"No, not at all."

"I could take you away from Vicky," Rebecca said. "Please let me do that. I can catch a plane tonight and bring you back here to Skokie with me tomorrow. You can live with us until this whole thing gets settled."

"Thanks, Bob, but that's not necessary. I don't need your help. As I said, I'm set. I'll call you if something comes up."

"Okay," Rebecca said. "I won't rush out there. But promise me you'll send an SOS if things with Vicky get too bad."

"Sure. I will."

"I love you, Pa," she said. "I love you so much."

"Me, too," Charlie answered softly. "Good-bye."

7

The call Rebecca had been dreading came from Jim on December 3, 2005 at the worst possible moment, in the middle of another crisis with Paul. The trouble began earlier that evening when Rebecca passed by his bedroom and saw him snorting cocaine with a friend. "What's going on here?" she yelled, rushing in, knocking the paraphernalia off the table. "Goddammit, you're really screwing up!" The friend sidled out of the room, and Rebecca stood over Paul, who had a smirk on his face. She raised her arm and fist as though to hit him.

"Go ahead," Paul said. "I dare you."

Her arm dropped and she stared at him, not knowing what to do. Within moments, Stan was hovering over her shoulder. "Coke? In my house? You fucking shithead, you're grounded for the next six months, and that's final."

"Whatever." Paul continued to smirk, but Rebecca could see fear in his eyes.

"I'm sending you to see Dr. Fletcher," Rebecca said. "He works with kids like you." Jerry Fletcher was a psychiatrist who'd been successful in diagnosing and treating underlying depression, which she feared was Paul's real problem.

"I won't go."

"Yes, you will."

Annie, by this time, had rushed into Paul's room as well. "Nothing's wrong with Paul," she said. "He doesn't need a psychiatrist."

"Stop being his defender," Rebecca said. "If you cared about your brother, you'd know he's destroying himself. He's snorting coke, for god's sake."

Annie crossed her arms, glaring at her. "So what? It's not like he's a drug addict or something."

In the midst of this, the telephone rang. Everyone froze, and then Rebecca picked up the receiver. "I'm at the hospital," said Jim, his voice hoarse. "Your father's in a coma. I dropped by his house an hour ago and he wasn't there. Maria said he'd been rushed to the hospital, so I came right over."

"Oh god!" Rebecca yelled. Stan and the children stared at her.

"According to Vicky, he had an accident," Jim continued. "She says he slipped on the marble floor in the entry hall and hit his head. The doctors say he has a cerebral hemorrhage."

"What time did this happen?"

"Eleven this morning."

That would be one o'clock in Chicago, just when she'd ushered a new client into her office—a man who'd been picked up for his second DUI and was facing jail time. She hadn't even been thinking of Charlie then. "They rushed him to the hospital in an ambulance?" she asked, trying to make sense of what was happening.

"Yes, and now he's on life support."

"He can't breathe by himself?"

"That's right. Dr. Moore says he's dying."

Rebecca sank onto the kitchen chair, no longer able to stand. "I'm coming right away."

When she hung up the phone, Annie put her arms around her, hugging her. "I'm so sorry, Mom," she said. Rebecca buried her face in Annie's chest and let out long, gulping sobs.

"I'll go online and make a plane reservation for you," Stan said.

Rebecca wiped her eyes. "Paul, while I'm gone I want you in school every day. I can't be worrying about you."

For a moment he looked sheepish, then he nodded. "He's still grounded," Stan said. "That means no going out and no friends coming over to the house."

This crisis, which had filled Rebecca's whole horizon only ten minutes earlier, hardly mattered anymore. "It's up to the three of you," she said. "You'll have to figure it out."

Stan drove Rebecca to O'Hare Airport, and she managed to find her seat on the half-empty flight to San Francisco. After the plane took off, she stared out the window and into the dark, formless night, stunned. The woman sitting next to her had a nasty cold and was coughing in her direction, but she didn't have the will to turn away or change seats. Everything within her was shutting down; when the flight attendant brought around the drink cart, she couldn't even find the voice to ask for water. The only thing that mattered was getting to her father before he died.

It was after midnight by the time she rented a car in San Francisco and reached the hospital. She checked in with the guard in the lobby and went up the elevator, through the silent hospital corridors, and past the nurses' station to the room on the seventh floor where Charlie was. The door was half-closed. Inside she heard the sound of a ventilator whooshing in and out like a bellows. Gently opening the door, she went into the room. There, like an exhibit on display, was Charlie, stretched out on his back, connected to a breathing machine. Transfusion lines dangled from his arm and he looked pink, a ghastly reminder of his past vigor. When she gingerly touched his hand, it was burning hot. "I'm here, Dad," she whispered.

Charlie lay silent on the bed, partly covered with a sheet. His eyes were open, glazed. His chest automatically rose and fell with the ventilator. "Dad, it's me," she tried in a louder voice. "It's your daughter, Rebecca. I just flew in from Chicago to be with you." He didn't answer, and tears sprang to her eyes as she felt the horror of his state.

A night nurse came into the room to check Charlie's vital signs. "What's happening with my father?" Rebecca asked. "Why isn't anyone helping him? I thought there would be doctors and nurses scurrying around."

"He's stabilized," the nurse said.

"What does that mean?"

"He's comfortable."

"That hardly seems true," Rebecca said. "My father hates to lie on his back. Can't you turn him over?"

"I'm sorry." The nurse wrote something on her chart.

"Do you think he'll come out of this coma?"

"I can't say. You'll have to talk to the doctor."

She looked around the room and for the first time thought about Vicky. "Where's my father's wife?"

"She was here earlier, but she went home to get some rest."

Rebecca settled into the orange vinyl chair by the hospital bed, planning to stay with Charlie for the rest of the night. She stared at his body, trying to accustom herself to the sight. Once she thought she saw a facial muscle twitching and her heart beat faster; if only he would rise up and ask what she was doing there. But nothing happened, it was just a fantasy, and her heart returned to its normal beat—*whoosh, whoosh*, like the breathing machine. On the left side of her father's forehead was an abrasion, the injury that must have caused the cerebral hemorrhage. It had oozed, soaking through the gauze that covered it, but it was small. How could such a little thing put him in this state, she wondered.

Charlie was hers for the night. "Oh, Dad, what happened to you?" Rebecca whispered. "Did Vicky bash you over the head or did you really fall? I can't believe you'd let yourself die in this way." She wondered if he could hear her. She'd once read that hearing is the last sense to go before death, so she began to talk to him. "Thanks so much, Dad, for all those good things you gave me. The love after Mom died, the games on the weekends, the fishing trips in the Sierra Mountains. Those silly TV programs we watched together." She meant all of this, but her voice sounded hollow and self-conscious, as though she were making a deathbed speech.

"Forget that," she said. "It wasn't all wonderful." *Whoosh, whoosh,* the breathing machine responded. "I was hurt and angry when you started to ignore me." She began to speak with honesty about the past, and she felt the unfairness of it all, that Charlie couldn't respond, that nothing could be done now except to let these words exist, but she also felt a rush of ease, as though something tight in her was beginning to let go. "I know I was a real pain during those years, but I felt so lonely," she said. "It was so sad, living in that silent house, you gone so much. And when you were home, we hardly talked. And then the flight into marriage with Peter, that disaster. I was just trying to find love and survive without you."

Charlie's eyes did not blink. Rebecca saw him anew on the bed, an old man who was dying. Another wave of sorrow passed through her, and she began to weep. "I love you, Dad. I'm sorry I let you get hurt. I'm sorry I didn't protect you. I didn't know what to do." She repeated this again and again. She wished he could absolve her of blame, tell her that he understood, but all that came back was the constant sound of the breathing machine.

After a while Rebecca noticed that her father's body seemed bloated, as though air had been pumped into him. She gently touched the smooth, freckled surface of his arm. "It's okay, Dad, I'm here with you now." She took his burning hand in hers, holding it like a parent would a sleeping child's. "I won't let anything more happen to you."

Leaning back in her chair, she began to remember how Charlie had cared so tenderly for her in the years after her mother died. At night, when he put her to bed, he'd sometimes told her a story, something about the travails of little animals or birds. The stories had always taught the same lesson: that perseverance wins out over misfortune. This was the hope he'd given her. As she'd listened to him, she had felt warm and safe, and she'd known that he loved her. Sometimes he'd sung to her in a scratchy voice, songs from a different era. And when it was time for him to leave, he'd always said, "Remember, sweetheart, don't let the bedbugs bite."

The words of one of Charlie's songs began to flow from her, an offering to what once had been. "You are my sunshine," she began to sing, almost in a whisper. Her voice grew in strength, and she wept, this time without self-consciousness. Her words were punctuated by gasping, convulsing sobs, and then the song diminished, trailing off into silence. She was spent.

The room was lit by a dim fluorescent light on the wall, the night outside black. Rebecca looked at her watch: twenty minutes past three. The time of stillness. She'd noticed with her clients that a feeling of silence often entered the room at twenty minutes past the hour and twenty minutes before. A kind of cosmic softening. Rebecca let the moment sink into her. Charlie and she were part of this larger cosmos: He happened to be dying and she happened to be living, but the difference was inconsequential. The universe would continue no matter what. And in this universe lived Paul, Annie, and Stan, immersed in a crisis that also now seemed small. She reminded herself to call them in the morning, after she met with the doctor, to tell them what was happening. The breathing machine began to sound like a metronome, marking the beats of Charlie's remaining life: one, two, three, four. Her eyes felt swollen and sore from weeping, and she let them close.

The next thing Rebecca knew, a nurse bustled into the room, taking Charlie's temperature, checking his transfusion drips. The woman had an efficient, morning-coffee air about her, and Rebecca sat up, surprised to find herself in the vinyl chair. Light streamed through the window onto the linoleum floor. She glanced over at her father and saw him lying in the same position, his eyes still open, unblinking. "Shouldn't he have some drops in his eyes?" she asked the nurse. "They must be so dry by now."

"Check with his doctor," the nurse replied, straightening Charlie's sheet.

"When is he coming?"

"Probably in an hour."

Rebecca glanced at her watch. It was seven thirty; there was time enough to get something to eat before the doctor arrived. Feeling hungry, she headed out of the room and down the corridor, glad to be away from Charlie's dying body and those unseeing eyes. But then she caught sight of Vicky getting off the elevator. Wrapped in a white ermine coat, her father's wife moved slowly, regally, nodding to the doctors she passed. Rebecca's face flushed and she dashed into the nearby women's restroom, locking herself in one of the stalls.

She hunched over on the toilet for a long time, her stomach clenched. She didn't know if she had the strength to go through with what was ahead. She felt light-headed, like a panic attack might be on the way, and she desperately tried to compose herself. After ten minutes, somebody knocked on the door of her stall—"Are you okay in there?" Rebecca rose and opened the door. "Just getting a little peace and quiet," she said to the nurse aide who stood outside. The woman searched her eyes, and she spoke in a soothing voice: "There's a chapel downstairs, if you want to be alone. You can sit there for as long as you want. It's better than the toilet stall."

Rebecca stepped out into the hall and rode the elevator downstairs. She found the cafeteria, but a leisurely breakfast was no longer possible with Vicky there in the hospital. She bought some coffee and a sweet roll from a vending machine, and she hurried toward her father's room, steeling herself for what was next, reminding herself to stay calm and in control.

The door to the hospital room was shut, but Vicky couldn't keep her out. Rebecca walked into the room without knocking. Right away she noticed that Vicky had draped her ermine coat on the orange vinyl chair, the chair she thought of as her own. She had taken over the space without a thought, even though Rebecca had planted her suitcase right next to it and left her scarf on the seat.

Charlie was in the bed just as he'd been before, flat on his back. Vicky was crouched over him, her hand slipped under the sheet below his midline, moving up and down in a rapid rhythm. "What are you doing?" Rebecca shouted.

Vicky slowly withdrew her hand, a haughty expression on her face. "Your father's gone," she answered, as though she were stating a clinical fact. "He's always responded to my touch before."

Rebecca felt so sickened by Vicky that she couldn't speak. She wanted to grab this woman, rip that cold expression off her face, smash her hard, anything to punish her for her crassness. Instead, she picked up Vicky's ermine coat and threw it on the linoleum floor, and she sat in the orange vinyl chair next to Charlie, claiming her place.

Vicky silently retrieved her coat and then rang the call button. When the nurse arrived, she asked for another chair to be brought to the room. "Immediately," she ordered.

The hospital room became silent except for the sound of the breathing machine. The second chair arrived, carried in by an attendant who placed it on the opposite side of the bed. Ten minutes passed. Rebecca kept her eyes glued on Charlie, still hoping for a movement or a sign of life, but in the light of day, his pink color was turning gray and he looked more like stone. When she glanced up, she saw that Vicky was reading an interior design magazine. "What really happened to my father?" she asked. "What did you do to him?"

Slowly, Vicky raised her eyes. "I didn't do anything, Rebecca," she said.

"Then how did he get that wound?" Rebecca asked this in an accusing way, trying to intimidate Vicky, break through her steely exterior.

"Mr. Stevens fell. Period."

"I don't believe you."

"That's your problem, then," Vicky said, returning to her magazine.

Rebecca stared at her. "You don't seem very upset," she said. "Not exactly the loving wife."

Vicky put down her magazine and stared back at her. "Surely you must have learned at your fancy university that people respond very differently to tragedy. What makes you think I'm not upset? How do you know what I'm feeling?"

Rebecca looked away. This woman was a dangerous adversary. "I can't know what's in your mind," she said. "But I know what you did. You destroyed my father."

"Are you sure?" Vicky asked. "Really sure? Or is it that you despise me? You never wanted to share him with me."

Rebecca looked down at Charlie, who was resting between them. The last thing he'd want is for her and Vicky to be bickering by his bedside. "You're wrong," she muttered.

The two women fell back into silence. Rebecca thought of all the things she wanted to say to this evil woman: how much pain she'd caused by being so jealous and possessive, and how horribly she'd treated her father. But instead she reached over and held Charlie's freckled hand, and those thoughts slowly slid into the background. Her father's hands, square and able. She recalled how he'd used those same hands to plant cucumbers and melons in their yard the year she was nine. She'd been his helper, and while they sowed the seeds, he'd told her how hard it had been growing up on the poor Nebraska farm he was from and how hard he'd worked. He'd hated his fundamentalist father, who had whipped him with a belt at will. There'd been no love in that family, and he'd run away as soon as he could. "Thanks for telling me that much," she said silently to Charlie.

The phone on the bedside table rang, and Rebecca quickly claimed it. "It's me," said Jim. "When did you get in?"

"Last night after midnight," she answered, relieved to hear his voice. Being in the room with Vicky was a terrible strain, and she didn't know how much longer she could bear it. "When are you coming?"

"Later," he said. "Fran has a doctor's appointment this morning. Any change in your father?"

"Dr. Moore is coming soon, and I'll learn more."

"And Vicky?"

"That's happening, too," Rebecca answered.

After she hung up, she began to wonder if Jim had all the information they'd need when Charlie died. She knew nothing about her father's will or his desires for burial. She'd been so far removed from his life that she hadn't even thought about these things. She assumed that his wife would inherit everything: Vicky would have insisted on that, and Charlie would have acquiesced. When he had given Rebecca the gift of stock when she was twenty-one, he'd made it clear that it was her inheritance ahead of time. The money had made her life easier, something she'd appreciated, although she'd never told him that. "That gift really helped me through some rough times," she silently said to his body, hoping that somehow he'd receive the thought. "I used it for the house in Skokie, and it's there to help with the kids' college education. I'm so sorry I never properly thanked you."

The door to the room opened, and Dr. Moore bustled in and nodded to the two women. His eyes were owlish, his lips pursed, and he looked like he was bringing bad news. He glanced over Charlie's charts before speaking. "Mr. Stevens is brain dead. That's clear from the tests that were run on him when he was admitted." He hardly paused long enough for them to absorb this information before continuing. "We can do one of two things. Keep him on life support, or take him off."

Rebecca froze. She'd been sitting by this shell of a father for almost twelve hours but hadn't once thought of stopping the breathing machine. She'd adjusted to him being in this state, and it had seemed that he could go on this way forever, a different incarnation of the man she'd known all her life. "Take him off the life support," Vicky said without emotion. "He didn't want it."

"How do you know?" Rebecca asked sharply.

"He told me."

Dr. Moore stepped in: "He gave me the same instructions, Rebecca. I'm sorry, but I have a letter, signed by him, stating this desire. Of course, it's up to Mrs. Stevens, as the appointed agent, and you."

The matter was closed. If that was what Charlie wanted, that's what he'd get. Besides, the prospect of him continuing in this coma suddenly seemed unthinkable to Rebecca now that the alternative had been introduced. "Okay," she said. "But give us some time alone with him to say good-bye."

"Of course," Dr. Moore said.

"You go first," Rebecca said to Vicky.

In the hallway Rebecca walked restlessly back and forth, disturbed by the speed with which her father's death was approaching. Once he stopped breathing, he'd be gone forever, something that didn't seem possible or real. Sooner than she expected, Vicky came through the door. Rebecca scanned her face and saw fatigue and strain but no trace of tears.

Rebecca returned to her father's bedside, and she stared at him, hardly knowing what to say. "Good-bye, Charlie," she began, but she didn't want to make a speech. A funny lightness, like laughter, came over her. "Thanks for the goodness," she smiled at him. The ventilator whooshed back. "Remember this: I love you, I'll always love you." Charlie already seemed far away, somewhere in the outer stratospheres. But then, in a final burst, she said something she'd never said before: "I've been bitter about you too long, holding things against you, and now it's over." Her words flew from her lips like a song, sweet and easy, and she was ready to say good-bye. She kissed Charlie one last time on the top of his balding head, above his wound.

Rebecca, too, had taken only a few minutes with her father, and her eyes were dry when she returned to the hallway. Dr. Moore explained that he should be alone with Charlie when he removed the life support, that this was not a sight for them to witness. He directed the two women into a cramped private waiting room, telling them he'd be back in a half hour.

Rebecca and Vicky sat on opposite sides of a little table. Vicky closed her eyes, and Rebecca picked up a magazine and flipped through the pages without seeing anything. She imagined what Dr. Moore was doing to her father: The ventilator would be turned off and the tube removed, and he would take a few last gasps and then stop breathing. It all seemed so deceptively simple and so very sad.

Soon Dr. Moore returned to the waiting room. "It's over," he said. "You can see Mr. Stevens once again before his body is removed."

Rebecca decided in that moment that she'd already said good-bye. "There's a final matter," Dr. Moore continued, his voice solemn. "An autopsy has to be performed by the medical examiner."

"But my father died here in the hospital," Rebecca said. "I thought autopsies were done only when there was no doctor around."

"We have to ascertain the cause of the injury that killed him," Dr. Moore said. "That is required by law."

"Oh," she said, suddenly alert. What a relief it would be if the medical examiner found out what had really happened to Charlie.

"Do you understand why we have to do this?" the doctor said, looking back and forth between the two women, emphasizing his words.

"I understand," Vicky said in a hard, controlled voice, as though she had been expecting it.

"Good. You can have your husband's body after it has been released. You'll want to make arrangements with a mortuary."

As the doctor left the room, Vicky slid into her coat and Rebecca gathered together her belongings. "What did my father say he wanted done with his body?" she asked Vicky. Why hadn't she talked to Jim a long time ago to get these matters straight?

"Cremation," Vicky answered. "He was very clear about that."

"I'd like to pick out the urn."

Vicky shrugged. "Go ahead."

"What about a funeral or some kind of service? Did he leave instructions?"

"Nothing I know about," Vicky said, opening her purse and taking out her car keys.

"Do you have a plan?"

"No." Vicky turned away.

"I think he'd like a memorial service of some sort," Rebecca said.

"But there's so much to arrange. Somebody has to put the obituary notice in the papers. Then there's the minister for the service, the flowers, the caterers . . ." Her exhausted, confused mind started to spin. "Who's going to handle all these details?" she asked.

Vicky glanced back at her. "You are," she said. "You're his daughter, aren't you?"

8

It rained during the week after Charlie's death, a steady down-pour that knocked the autumn leaves off the trees and turned the California earth into mud. The rain mirrored Rebecca's mournful mood. Those hospital scenes at Charlie's bedside, so tidy in their own way, had been only the beginning of her grieving, and she wanted to escape somewhere and weep.

But she had too much to do. She took on the task of her father's arrangements with grim determination. She would prove to Vicky and everyone else that she was a responsible and dutiful daughter. Setting aside her feelings as best she could, she arranged for Charlie's cremation and met with Reverend Purdy, the new minister at the local Methodist church where the memorial service would be held. At night in her hotel room, she called Stan and the kids to give them the head-lines of what was happening and to check up on them, and then she collapsed into bed for a few hours of fitful sleep. When she awakened before dawn, her mind raced with all the details left to organize.

Charlie had died on Monday; on Thursday night Rebecca drove to Jim and Fran's home in the Berkeley hills. As she sat on the couch next to Fran, she told them about her frustration with the upcoming memorial service: Reverend Purdy was too young and jovial for her taste—he hadn't even known her father—and the church caterers had a scheduling problem. There was no cellist available for the service, her first choice, and they'd have to make do with the church organist.

"Each step of the way seems so difficult," she said. "And then there's the matter of getting a room at my hotel for the kids to stay in when they arrive tomorrow night with Stan. It's iffy."

Jim nodded sympathetically. "Has the cremation taken place?"

"Today," Rebecca said. She paused for a moment, imagining her father's body thrust into the burning oven. "I can't stand it."

"I'm sorry," Fran said, pulling her close and hugging her.

Rebecca was soothed for a moment by Fran's touch, but then she straightened up, too tense to take in more comfort. "Did Dad leave any written instructions for what to do with his ashes?" she asked Jim.

"No, but he told me he wanted them scattered in the wilds."

Tears sprang to Rebecca's eyes. "He always loved the outdoors."

"About fifteen years ago, your dad and I went trout fishing in a stream in the Sierras, close to Lake Tahoe," Jim said. "He brought along some fancy new flies, and we tried them out. It was so beautiful in that spot with the clear water rushing by and the leaves of the birches and ash trees just beginning to change color. Nobody else was there. Out of the blue he said he wanted to end up in a peaceful place just like that. I thought he meant when he retired, but he said, 'No, when I'm gone.'"

"That's about as clear as Charlie ever got. How do we arrange for that to happen?"

"Somebody will have to talk to Vicky. She's in charge of the ashes since she's the widow."

"Damn. She's ended up with everything," Rebecca said. Jim had called her the day after the memorial service to tell her that Charlie's will listed Vicky as the sole beneficiary of his estate, including the house.

"I'm sorry about that," he said. "It's not fair."

"I don't need his money, but I really want his ashes," Rebecca said. "Maybe Vicky will be generous for once. Will you talk to her?"

"Of course he will," Fran said.

Rebecca smiled wanly at the two of them; they were such a reliable pair. "By the way, how is Vicky doing?" she asked.

"That woman's tough," Jim said.

"You mean unfeeling."

"Is she alone these days?" Fran asked.

"Her daughter, Lana, is here now from L.A. Or at least that's what she said when I called her on Tuesday."

"I can't get over my feeling that Vicky caused my dad's death," Rebecca said. "It haunts me. That abrasion so easily could have happened by her bashing him with an iron skillet or something."

"Let it go," Jim said. "Even if she was culpable, it can't be proven."

Rebecca turned to Fran. "Do you agree?"

"Your father is dead. That's a great tragedy, but I agree with Jim," she answered. "Let it go for your own sake."

The evening ended early, but before Rebecca left, she and Jim went over the checklist of arrangements. Now that the memorial service was planned, the flowers ordered, and the obituaries placed in several newspapers, it seemed that everything was taken care of and she could get away to the ocean the next day. What better spot than a rainy, lonely beach to have another good cry before Stan and the kids arrived.

As Rebecca headed back to the hotel through the stormy night, she turned on the car radio and scanned the stations until she landed on a Beethoven violin concerto, one she loved. The sound filled the car and the wipers flapped back and forth in a soothing way. *Let go of your suspicion*, she told herself.

But then she gripped the steering wheel so hard that she almost lost control of the car. She had forgotten to find out about Charlie's autopsy. It had taken place right after his death, before the body had been released to the mortuary, and Vicky must have been informed about the verdict. But what was it?

When Rebecca reached the hotel, she rushed inside, past the gurgling water fountain and the receptionist's desk and the artificial philodendron, and up to her room to call Stan. "I didn't ask about the autopsy," she wailed when he answered the phone.

"It must have gone okay if you didn't hear," he said.

"I don't even know what the medical examiner said."

"I'm sure he declared that the death was accidental. But call the funeral home tomorrow and find out. That's easy."

"Yes, but that's not the problem." Rebecca struggled to voice what was bothering her. "I should have told Dr. Moore or the medical examiner about those bruises on my father's face these last few months. I should have said that Vicky had been hitting him. I missed my chance."

"You had so many other things to handle. It's been such an upsetting time." Stan's voice was reassuring. "Besides, it wouldn't have mattered. An autopsy could not have determined whether your father's death was accidental or not. They could only tell if the abrasion caused the hemorrhage. They wouldn't know how he got it."

"How do you know? They have such sophisticated tests these days."

"Just think about it."

Rebecca sighed. "I guess the hemorrhage could have been caused by Charlie falling or being hit."

"And if Vicky said it was a fall and nobody else was around, who's going to question that?" Stan added.

"But I want to know the truth."

"You never will." Stan's voice was firm. "You have to accept that."

She heard his words, but they were all wrong. "I can't."

Rebecca hung up the phone and sat on the bed, weeping. It was all her fault that the mystery of Charlie's death would remain unsolved. If only she had contacted the authorities, if only she had not let herself get sidetracked by those hateful memorial service arrangements. Charlie's poor body was now a few pounds of dust, and nothing more could be done to investigate the wound on his head. But she couldn't— no, she wouldn't—live with this uncertainty over his death for the rest of her life. That was unthinkable. In a moment of what felt like clarity, she promised to herself that someday, somehow, she would find out the truth about what had happened.

Saturday arrived, the day of Charlie's memorial service—a fine winter day, sunny and cold. From the hotel window, Rebecca stared east over the glittering water of the San Francisco Bay to the silver buildings of the city beyond. "Cheer up, hon," Stan said, slipping his arm around her. He and the kids had arrived the night before, and the hotel had managed to find space for them after all. "This nightmare will be over soon."

"It won't," she replied. "Not with so many questions unanswered."

"Get a grip," Stan said. "The funeral home people told you that Charlie died from accidental causes. The medical examiner determined it, and that's what the death certificate says. You wanted an answer? You got it. Accidental causes. You have to accept the verdict."

"Leave me alone," Rebecca said. Ever since Stan arrived, he had been telling her what to do, vying for her attention, trying to joke her out of her grief. Her last nerve was being stretched by his presence. "Go someplace nice for breakfast, Stan. Enjoy the city. The kids will be fine hanging around the hotel. I've got things to do. Just be back here and ready by one o'clock so we can leave for the church on time."

"Oh, good. You know how much I love churches," he laughed.

"Stop it," Rebecca said sharply. "You might feel uncomfortable in Christian places, but what do you expect? Charlie wasn't Jewish, and his memorial service belongs in the Methodist church."

"I'm just kidding."

"Maybe, but this memorial service is not about you." She grabbed her jacket from the closet and angrily put it on.

"Do you want me to come with you to get Charlie's ashes?" he asked, still grinning.

"I'll do it alone."

"Have it your way," he said. "Your way or the highway."

"I won't even ask you what that means," Rebecca said. "Just make sure you have your suit on by one o'clock."

On her way out of the hotel, Rebecca knocked on the kids' door and Annie cracked it open; through the slit she could see that Paul was still sleeping. She gave her daughter a quick hug. "Go back to bed, sweetheart. Just make sure you and Paul get something to eat at the coffee shop downstairs, and be ready by one o'clock."

Rebecca drove to the funeral home, preparing herself to receive Charlie's ashes. To her relief, the transaction turned out to be uneventful: she walked into the office, the efficient woman attendant handed her the heavy copper urn, and she signed the final papers. "Is that all?" she asked, fingering the urn's smooth, cool surface. The attendant nodded.

Rebecca carried the urn to the rental car with great care, as though it might spill open at any moment. She set it beside her in the passenger seat and strapped it in so that it rested upright on the seat. The urn had a simple, stately look—tall and rounded on the sides, with a cap at the top that screwed on tightly. She had chosen it out of all the others on display because it had no decoration or words written on it and its copper color reminded her of the reddish color her father's hair had been when he was younger. "We're going for a ride, Dad," she said.

She needed to buy some Kleenex, so she headed toward a nearby outdoor shopping mall built in the '70s, one of her father's most important real estate projects. He had brought her there to see it when she was thirteen, proudly explaining how he had put the deal together. She'd been quiet that day, confused by his sudden desire for her company when he'd hardly talked to her for the past year, and she had sat sullen and resentful in the backseat of the car. But that was then, and now she felt almost giddy. "This is your chance to say good-bye," she said. "You should be proud of what you accomplished."

She spotted a drugstore as she pulled into the parking lot and decided to go there for the Kleenex, but it felt strange to leave the urn alone in the car. If someone broke in and stole it, her father's ashes would be gone forever. She reached over for the urn, nestled it under her jacket, and held it close to her. As she walked toward the drugstore, she described what she was seeing to Charlie: "The mall still looks good, though it could use a paint job and some better landscaping. But it seems to be thriving. All the shops are rented out, a good sign in this terrible economy." Talking like this seemed to her the most natural thing to do.

The urn stayed with Rebecca after that. On the car ride to the Methodist church later that day with Stan and the kids, she cradled it gently in her lap. "What do the ashes look like?" Annie asked from the backseat. She was wearing a dress at Rebecca's insistence but wasn't happy about it. Stan was in his best suit, his hair greased down, and Paul was presentable in jeans and a sweater, looking more like his tall, skinny father as he grew older.

"They're like any other ashes, I imagine," Rebecca answered.

"Can we take a look?"

"Brilliant idea," said Paul. "We'll open the urn, turn on the AC, and then Grandpa Charlie can blow all over us."

"Ha, ha," Annie said. "You're so funny."

"That's gross," Stan said, stopping at a light.

"I thought you liked jokes," Paul said.

"I do. But it seems weird to cremate a family member and carry around their remains in a little jar."

"I think it's fine," Annie said. "Better than putting their bodies in the earth, where they just rot."

"Dust unto dust," Stan said. "Isn't that the way it's supposed to be?"

"Charlie wanted to be cremated," Rebecca said.

"Do you think he wanted to die?" Paul asked.

"I doubt it."

He was quiet for a moment. "Do you think Vicky killed him?"

Rebecca had tried to shield Annie and him from her suspicions, and she wasn't about to stop now. "Let's assume the best case scenario," she answered wearily. "That he died of natural causes."

"I can't believe you're saying that," Stan laughed. "You, of all people?"

"Stop it, Stan," Rebecca said angrily. He shouldn't be mocking her like this in front of the kids, especially on the day of her father's funeral.

The family rode in silence the rest of the way to the Methodist church, an ivy-covered stone building in a residential neighborhood in Oakland. A sign outside the church announced Reverend Purdy's next sermon topic, "Forgive Those Who Trespass." *An apt title*, Rebecca thought, except that she'd never forgive Vicky. She remembered this little church with its moldy smell and the heavy cross behind the altar, and how Charlie used to drop her off at Sunday school even though he never set a foot in the building himself. She had never understood why he insisted on her going, and when she asked, he'd just shrugged. One more mystery, although she supposed it had something to do with him trying to be a good father. He'd been raised with religion himself, although he hated it.

Rebecca saw a group of people gathered outside the church, chatting to one another. She scanned their faces and recognized a gray-haired woman—Liz, Charlie's secretary from years ago—and several business cronies and hunting buddies, now old men. She felt overwhelmed for a moment by her memories of being Charlie's little daughter and knowing these people. She didn't know if she could face them without breaking down, and yet it also pleased her that they were there. Charlie would have a decent send-off after all.

After Stan parked the car, the family entered through the big doors of the church. People nodded sympathetically in their direction, and a few old Berkeley neighbors approached them, whispering their con-dolences. They silently walked down the aisle to the front pew, Rebecca still clinging to Charlie's urn, and she slid in next to Jim and Fran, with Stan on her other side. The organist played a quiet medley of hymns, standard funeral music. Rebecca had worn a soft blue suit, nothing too somber or formal, and she rubbed the urn, talking in her mind to Charlie, telling him who she'd just seen: *All your friends are here, Dad. You should be pleased.*

But Vicky was missing. Two o'clock arrived, time for the service to begin. Rebecca turned to see a hundred or more people waiting patiently in the pews behind them. Young Reverend Purdy stood at the rear of the sanctuary in his black robes, rocking back and forth on his heels, looking impatient. "We should wait a little longer for Vicky," she whispered to Stan. "Go tell the minister. Please."

The heat in the church had been turned up high, and the organist continued playing. Several minutes passed. "Aren't you going to put the urn on the altar?" Jim whispered to Rebecca.

She rose slowly, approached the altar, and set the urn gently among the roses and ferns. As she returned to her seat, she glanced toward the back of the church. Through the open church doors, she saw a black limousine parked at the curb. Two women were climbing out, one draped entirely in black. Vicky had arrived.

The organist ended with a final flourish, and the congregation waited expectantly for the minister to appear. But instead, Vicky started slowly down the aisle, her head bowed. Her black veil trailed almost to the floor, and she clutched a black lace handkerchief in a black-gloved hand. She was an eerie, ghostly presence. "It must have taken her weeks to put that outfit together," Rebecca whispered to Jim. A younger woman in a black suit followed Vicky down the aisle, her long blond hair and composure marking her as Lana, the daughter. Gliding along on four-inch heels, she had a tense little smile pasted on her face. Vicky slid into the pew across the aisle from where Rebecca sat with her family, and Lana followed.

Reverend Purdy appeared in the front of the church. He began the service in a soaring voice, thanking God for Charlie's life. He extolled his goodness, calling him "a man of great virtue and wisdom," and he prayed for comfort for the grieving widow "whose husband was plucked away from her before his time." Rebecca grimaced up at Stan. "And please, God, don't forget Charlie's beloved daughter and son-in-law, and the two young grandchildren whom he cherished so much." Stan raised his eyebrows.

Rebecca felt like an alien in this sanctuary. The man being spoken about wasn't the Charlie she knew, and God had nothing to do with her life as far as she could tell. But the service went on, with the soprano soloist singing "Abide With Me," which brought surprising tears to her eyes.

Rebecca brought out the Kleenex and passed some along the row as Jim walked up to the pulpit and started his eulogy. "I've got to speak honestly," he said. "Charlie was a hard guy. Complex and unknowable in many ways, and so very proud. But he was my friend, probably my best friend." In his soft drawl, Jim went on to describe how he remembered Charlie at the golf course, Charlie talking about business in a lively way, Charlie and his little daughter Rebecca coming over to their home for dinners. "I'll really miss him," he said, his voice breaking. "Nobody's perfect. Good friends can't be replaced."

The service concluded with some Bible readings that were meant to be comforting to the mourners. As the organist played the final hymn, Rebecca stared ahead, sniffling, trying to compose herself for the reception. The minister, now his hospitable self, said a quick benediction and invited everyone to the social hall for some refreshments. People waited for the bereaved family to leave first, and Rebecca quickly led Stan and kids down the aisle. "Why so fast?" Stan whispered.

"I want to get out of here before I have to face Vicky," she whispered back.

They headed toward the social hall, where the caterer had set out coffee, lemonade, and trays of cookies and little sandwiches. "I'd give anything for a beer," Stan said.

"Sorry," Rebecca smiled, for the first time that afternoon. "It's a church, remember."

"You don't have to tell me."

Her irritation with him faded. He'd bothered her through the last two days, but at least he had shown up, and his presence in this moment brought her a measure of comfort. "Thanks for being here," she said.

Stan grinned. "Sure. Sure thing."

As the people filed into the social hall, Rebecca greeted them, shaking their hands, listening to their condolences. She didn't feel up to the task, but she liked hearing their stories about Charlie. He'd helped a lot of employees and friends in his lifetime by paying doctors' bills and school tuition fees, and she felt proud of him.

When the last few people drifted away, Rebecca was ready to leave. "Where did Vicky go after the service?" she asked Stan. "Did you see her climb into that limousine?"

"Her chariot, you mean?"

"I bet she rushed home to take off those outrageous widow's weeds," Rebecca laughed.

"Let's get going," Stan said. "Maybe we can catch a movie tonight, or do something fun."

"You deserve it," she answered. "And so do I."

After Rebecca paid the caterer, they started toward the car, to which Paul and Annie had retreated an hour earlier to listen to music on their iPods. "The ashes," Rebecca suddenly remembered, turning back. "I'd better get them."

She threw open the church door and walked into the sanctuary. The overhead lights were still on, and now that the room was empty, it looked small and dingy, the beige paint on the ceiling beginning to peel and the green carpet frayed. Rebecca climbed the steps to the altar, going to where the red roses and ferns had made a beautiful cradle for Charlie's copper urn.

But the urn was not there.

Rebecca stood before the altar, hardly believing what she saw. Before the service, she'd envisioned the flowers and the urn together, making a perfect whole, and it didn't seem possible that one could exist without the other. But of course Vicky had taken the ashes away, it was her legal right. She'd waited until everyone left the sanctuary, and then she'd ordered Lana to go up to the altar and retrieve the urn. Hiding it under her black veil, she'd silently and triumphantly walked down the aisle, out the front door, and into the waiting limousine. There was nothing anybody could do about it.

"That bitch!" Rebecca yelled. Her voice echoed throughout the empty sanctuary, heard only by the caterers packing up the leftovers.

Part Two

2011

9

Six years later, the telephone in Rebecca's office rang during a break between clients. "Dr. Rebecca Lev speaking," she answered in her usual professional way. Nobody was on the other end of the line, or perhaps it was a client too wrought up to speak or a would-be client too anxious to ask for an appointment. "Can I help you?" she tried again. "You've reached my therapy office."

"This is Lana Rogers. We haven't met," a low, crisp voice emerged.

"Hello," Rebecca said, surprised. There had been no contact with Vicky or her daughter since the memorial service.

"I've called to inform you that my mother died from a heart attack last month," Lana said.

"My god, I wasn't expecting that," Rebecca said.

"Neither was I, but there it is," Lana said. "I'm putting the house in Piedmont on the market. Is there anything you want from it?"

Rebecca thought quickly. "My father's urn. Your mother kept it in the RV, behind the house. Or at least that was what I was told."

The copper urn had been a sore matter for Rebecca for the past six years. After the memorial service Jim had called Vicky to ask if Rebecca could have it, and Vicky had answered absolutely not, the urn belonged to her. Jim had then asked her where she was keeping it, thinking that Rebecca could view it when she next came to California. "In the RV, if you must know," Vicky had answered. When Rebecca heard about this, she was outraged. Her father surely deserved a more respectful resting place than the RV. She imagined Vicky slipping into the passenger seat and glancing over at the urn she'd probably put in the driver's seat. "Let's go, Charlie," she'd order in that cold, cutting voice. When there was no response, she'd lash out about all the things he'd ever done wrong.

"I'll ship the urn to you," Lana said.

"It might get lost," Rebecca said. "I don't want that to happen. I'll come for it as soon as I can."

A long pause, then Lana replied, "If you wish."

After the conversation was over, Rebecca collapsed onto her swivel oak chair. A piece of string left over from the morning newspaper sat on her desk, and she wrapped it around her finger, pulling it as tight as she could. When the tip of her finger turned purple, she unraveled it and threw it into her wastebasket.

She had done her best to forget about Vicky over the past six years. There had been so many other problems that needed her attention, and when Vicky came to mind, she'd told herself to let her go, there was nothing she could do about her. All this time she had pushed her existence out of her mind, and she had mostly succeeded.

Rebecca glanced over at a cartoon on her desk that she had torn out of a magazine and brought into the office today. "Denial works," the caption said. A woman was sitting in an armchair, calmly drinking a cup of coffee, while a ghostly figure hovered above her. Rebecca had chuckled when she saw the cartoon, and she'd planned to tack it up in the building's shared kitchen for her officemates to see. But it didn't seem so funny anymore. Lana's call threatened to dispel the denial she'd been carrying all these years, and she didn't know what would emerge.

Rebecca dropped her head into her hands—something she often did these days. She felt overwhelmed and frightened. Inchoate thoughts about Charlie, Vicky, and the past rushed through her head, and she felt like they could take her over. But then she straightened up and told herself to stop it, she didn't need to think about this, at least not now. Not when she had so much else that weighed on her mind.

She took a sip of leftover coffee from the pottery mug on her desk, and she began to think about Paul and Annie. The problems with the kids were fewer now that they had moved out of the house, Annie to college and Paul to an apartment in Chicago, but they still existed, and that depressed her. She was sure she had failed as a mother—an indictment made by her, the judge, and her, the jury, with no room for extenuating circumstances. In the past, when the kids were younger, she'd told herself there was time left to fix what was going wrong, but now that they were all grown up—older than she'd been when she left her father behind—and even though they seemed to be doing well enough, the hope of setting things straight between her and them had slid away.

She remembered the upset two nights ago with Annie, who was home on spring break from her college in Colorado. She had announced in a defiant way that she had just come out as a lesbian and was happier than she'd ever been, that she had finally embraced her true identity. Rebecca, who'd had three glasses of wine by that time, blurted out that she wasn't pleased with this news. "Why not?" Annie's voice was sharp. "What's wrong with being a lesbian?" Rebecca muttered an apology, knowing she was handling the conversation all wrong, but her mind was dulled by alcohol and she couldn't figure out how to recoup. Annie just stared at her. The situation got worse when Stan learned about Annie's announcement from Rebecca and told her she was just going through a phase and she'd get over it.

In the kitchen this morning, before Rebecca left for work, Annie had hardly spoken to her. All this tension was too much, and now there was Vicky's death, which once again raised the unfinished business about her father. Rebecca felt like she was pinned against a dartboard with darts coming from all sides.

The telephone rang again, and she picked it up. Stan's big voice bounced over the line: "My car's ready at the garage. Do we have money in the joint account to cover it?"

"Just charge it," Rebecca said. She didn't feel like talking to him, but he needed to hear the news about Vicky. "Vicky's dead. Lana, her daughter, just called."

Stan was silent for a moment. "What's happening to the house?"

"Lana's selling it. It's hers."

"That's not fair," he began. "You and the kids should have inherited your father's money, but Vicky finagled it away. You got screwed."

"Is money the only thing you care about?" she said. "We've had this conversation a hundred times already."

Stan sighed. "At least this whole episode is finally over."

Rebecca now remembered with great clarity that rainy night in the hotel in California when she'd vowed to find out the truth about what happened to her father. She hadn't done anything about it since then, but in that moment she made a decision to change that. "You might think it's over," she replied, "but there are too many questions hanging out there. I can't ignore it any longer."

"What are you saying? Vicky is dead."

"I can still investigate."

"That doesn't make any sense. How are you ever going to find out anything new now?"

"A little support would be nice," she said, hanging up.

She glanced at the clock and saw that she had only ten minutes left before her four o'clock clients arrived. With all that was going on, she probably wouldn't be much use to the couple, who had been warring for weeks about whether to adopt a child. She considered canceling their appointment, but they were already on the way to her office, driving through traffic, and they had to make a decision today about whether to move forward with the adoption plan.

Her eyes were burning, and she went down the hall to the restroom to put in some eye drops. Looking in the mirror, she frowned at herself. Little lines puckered around her mouth, the worry lines between her eyes had deepened in recent years, and she looked like she was aging fast. Disgusted, she ran her finger over the tiny raised brown spot on her forehead. It was called a beauty mark, but she looked anything but beautiful.

Back in her office, the clients arrived on time, their faces set in anger. Rebecca sat in her swivel chair, trying to pay attention. The woman had a voice like a pecking hen, and she began to complain that her husband never took her needs seriously. He slouched back, an unpleasant grin on his face as he countered her accusations.

"'Never.' 'Always.' You use such absolutes," Rebecca said to them. Her comment was ignored. After a few more minutes, she had had enough. "I'd like you to listen to how you're talking to each other. Is this really how you want to be?" The couple fell silent, and she continued. "It seems that fighting is easier for the two of you than making important decisions, like you have to do today." Her tone was kinder than she felt. The couple got her point, and with her help they finally decided to pass on the adoption—a decision she thought was wise, given how precarious their marriage seemed to be.

At five o'clock Rebecca closed up her office and started the short drive home. The last session had been successful enough, but she had gone through the motions as a therapist rather than feeling deeply with these clients. One more case of her heart no longer being in her work. This was happening all the time these days, and she questioned whether she should consider another line of work. But the idea of giving up her profession was so monumental that she pushed it aside, telling herself she'd have to deal with it later.

Her thoughts turned instead to the evening ahead. Paul was coming for dinner tonight, a big event since she didn't see him much anymore. During the years when he'd been doing drugs and cutting classes, she'd thought she had lost him for good, but—thanks to a hardcore rehab program—he had turned himself around. He'd earned his GED, and now, at twenty-one, he was delivering pizzas and taking classes at the city college, planning to get a degree in videography. Rebecca still worried that he'd fall back into the frightening hole he'd been in, but he seemed steadier and more predictable these days.

Annie would also be home tonight. She'd offered to cook lasagna for dinner, and Rebecca had been relieved since her own interest in cooking was just about nonexistent. But now that Annie was angry with her, she might forget what she had promised. Thankfully, a pot of Miriam's chicken soup sat in the refrigerator if the lasagna failed to materialize.

But when Rebecca came through the kitchen door, there was Annie, busily stacking up layers of pasta, ricotta, and tomato sauce in a bright casserole pan, singing along with a woman's voice that was blasting from her iPhone. Tears sprang to Rebecca's eyes at this glimpse of her daughter working away, her blond hair sticking up in spikes, her sweats dotted with tomato sauce, her surprisingly throaty voice blending with the music. "Hi, sweetheart," she said. "Who are you listening to?"

Annie glanced up, and Rebecca saw her eyes become immediately wary. "Tracy Chapman," she said. "She's a lesbian."

"That's nice."

"Don't be condescending, Mom."

Rebecca felt herself slump. Would these tensions with her children never cease? But the table needed to be set and a salad had to be made, and she busied herself with these tasks as Annie finished the lasagna and popped it in the oven. She opened a bottle of red wine and poured herself a glass. The thing to do, she decided, was to talk about Annie's lesbianism as a given in their family rather than tiptoe around it. "Does Paul know you're gay?" she asked her over Tracy Chapman's voice.

"Of course," Annie answered. "He's known forever."

Of course, Rebecca thought, turning away so that Annie wouldn't see her eyes welling up once again with tears. Her two children were close in ways that cut her out, a bond forged in a childhood they no doubt found lacking. "Do you have a special girlfriend these days?" she asked, trying again.

"Nobody special. But a lot of really cool hook-ups."

"That's good," Rebecca said, wondering what a really cool hook-up was, exactly.

Annie eyed her and then began to smile. "Keep on trying, Mom."

When Paul arrived an hour later, looking older with new, hip glasses and a cotton shirt instead of a sweatshirt, smiling and ready for an evening of family relating, he and Annie immediately began to laugh together. "Mom's so straight," Annie said to him. "When I told her I was gay, she really blew it."

"What did you expect?"

"But she must have gay clients."

"It's different when it's your own kid," Rebecca broke in, not liking being the object of their speculation. "I'm happy for you, Annie, but give me a little time to get used to it."

At that moment Stan burst into the kitchen with a bouquet of yellow daffodils. "For you," he said, laying the flowers in front of Rebecca.

She picked them up, examining the straight stems and yellow petals. "Thanks, but what's the occasion?"

"The deli by the store had a special."

"The flowers should go to Annie since this is her coming-out party," Paul said.

Rebecca fished a blue glass vase out of the cabinet and arranged the bouquet. "They're for all of us," she said. "Especially Annie. Right, Stan?"

"They're for the whole world," he muttered.

Rebecca scooted her chair over to make room for him at the table. "Sit down with us," she said. "Annie made lasagna."

But Stan and the kids had never recovered from their battles. "Gotta go," he said. "I'm already late for my tennis match." He began to sing in a falsetto: "I'm late, I'm late, for a very important date. No time to say hello, good-bye . . ."

He rushed around to find his tennis racquet, and as he dashed out of the house, he waved it at them. Paul shook his head. "He's cornier than ever."

"He hardly ever acts like that anymore," Rebecca said.

"He can't resist it when we're around."

"How can you stand it?" Annie asked.

Rebecca shrugged and poured herself another glass of wine. Annie brought out the lasagna and salad, and they dove into the food. The kids talked about college and friends, their laughter filling the kitchen, and Rebecca didn't think about the phone call from Lana during dinner. But afterward, when they were eating the chocolate cake she had bought on the way to the office that morning, she told them about Vicky's death.

For a moment, they just stared at her. "Here today, gone tomorrow," Paul said. His edge had softened, but he still led with sarcasm.

"Vicky killed Grandpa Charlie, right?" Annie said.

"I'm not sure," Rebecca replied, surprised to hear Annie say this. In the past she had clung to the idea that his death was an accident.

Paul's gaze settled on Rebecca. "Well, we know at least that Vicky was hitting him. Why didn't you stop that?"

Even after all these years, she felt unnerved by his question. "I didn't know how."

"There must have been something you could have done," Annie said. "There's always something."

"My father and I had a long-standing pact to never intrude in each other's lives," Rebecca said.

"You could have broken it."

"Seriously, Mom, you know how to intrude. You did it with us," Paul said. "Remember that time you forced me to go to the psychiatrist?"

"It was different with my dad. I was afraid I'd lose him completely. He was a proud man, and he wanted to make his own decisions." Rebecca saw from her children's faces that they didn't understand. "I can't explain it any better than that."

"Anyway, he never amounted to much as a father or a grandfather," Paul noted.

"What a terrible thing to say."

"Be real, Mom. I don't think he even knew our names."

"I'm touchy about this subject," she said. "He was my father, remember? I loved him."

Paul paused. "You're not over his death yet."

"I guess not. When I left California after the memorial service, I didn't give myself time to mourn. And then the mystery of how he died . . . I never have reconciled myself to it."

"Poor Mom," Annie said.

"But today I had the idea of looking into it again. Stan thought I was crazy."

"You're not," Paul said. "At least, most of the time you aren't."

"It's about time I find some peace," Rebecca said.

Annie turned to Paul. "Remember that time Grandpa Charlie and Vicky visited us in the RV?" she asked. "We got Ruckus to do all his tricks. He liked that. We were such dumb little kids back then."

"And look at us now," Paul smiled.

When dinner was over and Paul said his good-byes, about to leave for his job at the pizza parlor, Rebecca felt like throwing herself on him, begging him to stay. And then Annie went upstairs to her room and shut the door. Rebecca started up the stairs after her, wanting to weep in her arms, but she stopped, afraid that Anne would resent her all the more. She crept back to the kitchen and collapsed into a chair.

She took a deep breath, sighed, and poured herself another glass of wine. She glanced over at the refrigerator. Ever since they'd moved into this house, she'd had the habit of scotch-taping photos onto the refrigerator door, a living scrapbook showing the kids at different ages and stages. Everybody in their family was there, except for Charlie. She thought of the times she could have photographed him but didn't make the effort. One more failure.

The daffodils on the table caught her attention, and she remembered she hadn't put the packet of preserving powder into their water. As she pulled the green vase toward her, it tipped and spilled, and she rushed to mop up the water with a dishtowel. She felt like smashing the vase onto the floor and watching it break into a hundred pieces, even a thousand, but she lugged it to the sink, poured more water into it, and scattered in the powder. At least the daffodils would live a few days longer, although then they'd die.

Stan had been thoughtful to bring the daffodils tonight, not his usual way. Now that the kids had left home, the two of them were like roommates with different schedules, even more distant than they'd been before. She was used to this, and it gave her a certain amount of freedom, which she liked, but she had a gnawing hunger for something more intimate and honest, something more revealing.

She might have found the closeness she craved with someone else, but when men approached her, she turned away. The spark between her and Kyle, the therapist upstairs, had died long ago, and they had settled into a friendship. During breaks in the office, he confided in her about his marriage collapsing, and she was the first person he'd told when he'd decided to file for divorce. He'd now begun to date other women, but every so often he'd look intently at her and say, "Sensible Rebecca, when are you going to take off the wraps?"

Later that night, Rebecca staggered up the hardwood stairs, holding tight to the banister, making sure each step landed where it should. How many times she'd come this way, tired after a day's work, liking the solitude of being alone but keeping an ear out for Stan's return. People spoke about the satisfaction of long-lasting marriages—she, too, had encouraged clients to stay together through difficult times—but where was the pleasure for her? She thought back to Paul and Annie's talk during dinner about the exciting things they were doing. They were at the beginning of their lives, and she was in the middle, trapped in so many ways of her own making.

The problem wasn't just her marriage. It was also her feelings about her work. She had tried to talk with Ella and Karen about this a few days ago when they'd gone out to lunch at a nearby cafe, taking a break from the intensity of seeing clients. Rebecca had blurted out, apropos of nothing else, "I'm sick and tired of listening to so much pain and sorrow. The thought of doing this for the rest of my life is enough to make me want to shoot myself."

"You're just going through a stage," Ella had smiled. "It's burnout. How many therapists do we know who get that? It comes with the territory."

"It's something larger," Rebecca had answered. "This work isn't right for me anymore. I'm serious. I chose it when I was younger because it was a pathway to success. I wanted to be somebody. But now it no longer fits."

"But you like healing people," Karen said slowly. "And you're so good at it. You have more clients than I'll ever have."

"That might be so, but that time is over."

Ella searched her face. "Is this depression talking? You've never gotten over your dad's death. You couldn't save him, and now you want to stop trying to save other people? Is that it, or is it that your lousy marriage is getting you down?"

"Those are just theories," Rebecca said impatiently.

"Yes, but something is causing this shift in you. Maybe the problem is perimenopause. You're the right age." Ella suggested more exercise, perhaps a daily run, and vitamin B capsules. "Last year, when I was so depressed, it turned out that perimenopause was part of the problem. Those things helped me," she said.

"The state of your body really affects your mood," Karen added. "Take me: now that I'm past menopause and all that hormonal upheaval, I'm a lot more positive."

"You'll come out of this slump," Ella said.

Rebecca had only nodded. Clearly Ella and Karen didn't understand the depth of her despair.

Rebecca made it up the last two stairs. If her closest, most sympathetic friend and her well-meaning officemate weren't able to fathom the extent of her unhappiness, something surely was wrong. In the bedroom she flopped onto the bed, her head spinning from the wine. She remembered how she'd made herself dizzy as a child, turning round and round until she could stand up no longer. That had been pleasurable, but tonight she held her face in her hands, not knowing whether to laugh or to cry. It seemed she could go in either direction.

Her thoughts went once again to Charlie's urn. She'd need to claim it soon. She feared if she didn't go right away it might be given to Goodwill or thrown out. She imagined the trip to California, perhaps a weekend squeezed in between other commitments. But no, a weekend trip to California would be way too short. Not only did she need to claim the urn, she had to try to find the answers to the questions that still haunted her. She began to think of another scenario: She'd spend several weeks in California. Or even better, the whole summer.

Stan banged into the house through the kitchen door, and she could hear him rummaging around in the kitchen. The refrigerator opened and closed, and the microwave started to hum. In a few minutes the heavy aroma of lasagna reached the bedroom. She rose from the bed, pulled off her black slacks and sweater, her usual work outfit, and threw them in a heap on the bedside chair. She wanted to get into the bathroom before Stan appeared.

She heard him clomp up the stairs. "Where are you?" he called.

"In here."

"Where's here?"

"The bathroom. Where else would I be?" She took her time cleansing and moisturizing her face and rubbing lavender lotion on her dry skin. She couldn't stop thinking about the summer ahead. The vision began to coalesce in her mind into one thrilling whole. She would leave Stan at home and take the trip by herself, a well-deserved break from the stultification of work and the monotony of marriage. She could afford to do it; she had enough money saved. Her practice would survive her absence with Ella and the other therapists in the building covering her for emergencies.

The idea excited her more than anything had in a very long time. She'd travel light, bringing only what she needed, and she'd be free from her therapy clients, free from the Skokie house and its demands, free from Stan. And shedding the layers of age and professional station, she'd even be free from herself and all that she had become.

Rebecca wrapped her kimono around herself and walked softly into the bedroom. Stan was stretched out on the bed, his thick arms sprawled on both sides, waiting for his turn in the bathroom. "How was your day?" he asked her.

"Fine," she answered. "And yours?"

10

When Rebecca told her clients she would be away for the summer, they were not pleased. Stan, too, didn't like the idea, and he threatened to take time off from work and drive to California with her. She spoke to him as she would to an unhappy child, telling him that she needed to make this trip alone, that he had to stay in Chicago, that he would survive just fine without her. For the next few days, he studiously avoided her.

The malaise she'd been feeling recently had been intensified by the demands and pressures on her, she was sure, and once she was out of town she'd return to a state of better balance. The California summer stretched ahead with its many possibilities, and she dreamed of brisk ocean air, foggy nights, and rolling hills covered with tall, golden grass. But before she left, she needed to organize the household and office finances, arrange for the lawn to be mowed and the house cleaned while she was gone, stock up the pantry, and take Ruckus to the vet and buy his pills for the arthritis he'd developed. She decided she would bring her laptop along with her —she couldn't imagine being without it—but she didn't want to be burdened with email, so there were colleagues and organizations to notify.

Hardest of all was dealing with the clients whose problems intensified as the time for leaving grew near. One mother's teenage son ended up in juvenile detention for dealing drugs and another's daughter was diagnosed with childhood diabetes. These families, and several others, were in crisis, calling and emailing nearly every day, it seemed. "I'll refer you to one of my colleagues for the summer," she told them guiltily. "I realize my leaving is hard on you."

Rebecca couldn't wait to get away from these people who wanted and needed so much from her. The last night before she left Skokie, she and Stan had sex, something they hadn't done for what seemed like years, and in a quiet moment afterwards he said he was afraid she wouldn't come back to him. "Don't worry," she said, moved by his fear, but her answer sounded tentative to her own ears.

In the third week of May, Rebecca packed up her black Audi and began the two-thousand-mile drive to California. She felt giddy with freedom, and she sped west along I-80, darting around the slower drivers, skimming over the countryside like a bird or a dragonfly. So great was her pleasure that she had no fear of having a panic attack, or an accident, or a sudden bout of regret.

On the second day of the trip, in the flatlands of Nebraska, it was unseasonably hot, and she stopped for lunch at a little cafe outside of Sidney, a small farming town. Somewhere around here Charlie had grown up. The farm had always been mythic in her mind, a place with an evil man beating his son and a mother who did nothing to stop it. There had been a much older, unmarried brother in that household, or so Charlie had said, but he hadn't intervened either, and Charlie had left him behind along with his parents.

Rebecca paid for her sandwich and coffee and asked the server if she could see the local telephone book. She skimmed through the names under S, looking for Stevens. It was a common enough name, and she wasn't surprised to find four entries. For a moment she considered calling these people, asking if they were related, but then she decided against it. They had never come looking for her, and she had gotten along without them all these years.

The car was hot, certainly over a hundred degrees, and sweat dripped down her sides. She switched on the air conditioner. She, more than anyone she knew, had a family of missing persons. All those relatives of Charlie were unknown, and on her mother's side there was a huge hole. Someday she'd try to find out more about her mother's background—as far as she knew, there were no aunts or uncles, but surely there must be second cousins somewhere—and she'd discover more people to populate her family.

But for now, her hopes were set on Lana, this mysterious stepsister she'd seen across the aisle but hadn't spoken to at her father's memorial service. She'd be meeting her in person for the first time now, all these years later. Rebecca imagined the two of them becoming friendly over the summer, exchanging confidences, becoming close. Perhaps Lana could even be an aunt to Paul and Annie, something they'd never had.

The pleasure of this fantasy carried her along the interstate for the next hundred miles.

Two days later, Rebecca drove down the block toward the Piedmont mansion. A high stucco wall had been built in front, closing the house off from the world, and at first she thought she was on the wrong street. She parked the Audi, passed through a gate in the wall, and went to the front door, noticing that the ivy was growing up the pillars and weeds had sprung up everywhere. The exterior of the house looked dingy and unloved, with paint peeling off the window trim. Vicky had let the place go.

Rebecca rang the doorbell. The chimes were familiar, but a note was missing from the arpeggio, making it sound strangely syncopated. Maria, the same maid she'd met during her last two visits, opened the door, smiling: "Lana will be back soon. Come in." Maria had on jeans and a T-shirt rather than the white uniform she'd worn in the past, and her short black hair was free from a maid's hairnet.

Rebecca was reassured to see this familiar face, and she came into the entry hallway. She had made arrangements to meet Lana in a half hour, and she was feeling nervous. Her desire to get along with Lana had intensified along the interstate, but in this peculiar, intimidating house, with all its reminders of Vicky, she wasn't so sure it would happen. Even if it didn't, she told herself, Lana would be an important source of information about Charlie.

"When did you get to California?" Maria asked.

"I stayed in Reno last night and drove in today," Rebecca said, looking at her with interest. "What is your last name, Maria? I don't think I ever heard it."

"Gomez. Maria Leonora Gomez."

"You've been working here for a long time."

"Mr. Stevens hired me in 1997."

"That's fourteen years," Rebecca said. "I guess you saw a lot." This woman would be the other person who could tell her something about Vicky and Charlie.

Maria glanced away. "You can wait in Mr. Stevens' library," she said. "Lana will come soon." With that, she disappeared down the shadowy hall.

Rebecca surveyed the barren gray walls of the entryway, marked by nail holes where a painting had once been hung. This was the place where Charlie had had his fatal accident, or so Vicky claimed. She reached down to touch the cold marble floor, imagining a skid by an unsteady old man and a tumble toward death. It could have happened that way, but then again, perhaps it hadn't.

She drifted down the hallway to her father's library. Stripped of his books and plaques, with only a few pieces of furniture remaining, the room had a lonely feel. Charlie's favorite leather swivel chair was jammed into a corner; she pulled it out, spinning it around. As she waited for Lana, she felt suspended between the past and the present, remembering that last disturbing visit with Charlie when he'd revealed how Vicky had been mistreating him. Shaking off her feeling of guilt for not watching over him more carefully, she imagined Charlie alive and content in this room, writing at his desk, talking on the phone in his soft voice to a reluctant client. She could almost hear him say, "I have a great project for you. It's in Martinez, a town that's growing fast." He'd listen for a while, then end the conversation by saying, "Well, think about it. No pressure at all."

Surely there must be something personal of her father's left in the room besides the little bit of furniture. She went to the desk and searched through the drawers, but they were empty except for a few paper clips. She tucked the clips into her pocket just as Lana came through the door, calling her name. Rebecca jerked back as though she'd been caught stealing.

"How was the trip?" Lana asked. She was beautiful, with blond hair halfway down her back, slanted green eyes, and a long, slender body.

"It was okay. Uneventful, actually," Rebecca answered. "I was afraid my car wouldn't make it—I have way over a hundred thousand miles on it—but it did. Obviously." She gave an anxious little laugh.

"Come with me," Lana said in a crisp, commanding tone, "and we'll get something to drink in the kitchen."

Lana's stiletto heels made a sharp, echoing sound as Rebecca followed her down another long hall toward the kitchen. She realized how little of this house she'd been shown, unwelcome visitor that she'd been. Glancing into the rooms they passed, she noticed stacks of boxes neatly taped. "You've been busy," she said to Lana.

"Maria agreed to stay in the house a little longer to help do all this. Mother never threw anything out."

In the kitchen a radio was playing a Mexican ballad, and Lana turned it off and poured glasses of iced tea. The two women sat at the table in the corner. "This house is so huge," Rebecca said. "And the high wall outside, that's new."

"It was built after your father died."

"And the yard, it's so different."

"You mean it's a mess," Lana said sharply.

"You could say that." Rebecca gave another nervous laugh.

"Mother wasn't much for keeping up the grounds."

Rebecca took a sip of iced tea. "Did your mother entertain very much?"

"Never," Lana answered.

"That's hard to believe," Rebecca said. "I thought she'd have big formal dinner parties in this house after my dad died, with servers passing around platters of hors d'oeuvres."

Lana looked away. "But she didn't."

"It must have been hard for Maria, cooped up here in this house all those years," Rebecca continued.

Lana shrugged, her mouth becoming tight.

"Charlie would have been good to her," Rebecca said. "What about your mother?"

"I don't know. I wasn't their watchdog."

Lana seemed impenetrable, a disappointment, and Rebecca tried a different tack. "Do you still live in Los Angeles?"

"I moved up to the Bay Area five years ago."

"And you've been living here with your mother?"

Lana's green eyes narrowed. "Never. I have a house in San Francisco." She rose, her face set. "I'm heading back to the city. Make yourself comfortable, the house is all yours. I'll see you tomorrow."

Rebecca suggested they go out to dinner together the next night and Lana agreed, although there was no enthusiasm in her voice. Rebecca watched out the kitchen window as she drove away in her white Mercedes convertible, her hair hardly ruffled by the wind. Like her mother, she had a whiff of Hollywood about her.

After Lana left, Rebecca began to wander through the house. It was stuffy and claustrophobic, and she considered throwing open the windows to air it out, but it would take days to get rid of that stale odor. Everything looked clean and in place, ready for the arrival of potential buyers. On the second floor she discovered the master bedroom suite with two huge bathrooms, mirrored on all sides, and a dressing room with enough closet space for dozens of suits, dresses, and gowns. She wandered into the master bedroom, flipped on the light switch, and saw heavy gold brocade draperies drawn over the windows. A bed with an imposing faux-French headboard dominated the room, and a Chinese rug covered the floor. She imagined Vicky trailing through this room in a creamy transparent negligee, her nipples showing through. Charlie would be in bed, entranced by the vision, and she'd make him wait, exciting him all the more until she'd finally let him touch her.

Rebecca fled from the master bedroom, slamming the door behind her. On the second floor there were other bedrooms, furnished like expensive, impersonal rooms in a modern hotel, ready for guests that apparently never came. She continued down the grand winding staircase and returned to the library, the most familiar place in this mausoleum. She tried to feel her father's presence there, but he had disappeared long ago. Sitting again in his leather chair, she shivered.

She couldn't sleep in this creepy house, that was clear. Before leaving Skokie, she had phoned Jim, telling him of her plan to come for the summer, and he had invited her to stay with him. Fran had died two years before from liver cancer, and he said he'd appreciate her company, a break from the sorrow of living alone. She decided to take him up on his offer.

But before leaving Vicky's house, she had one more task: claiming her father's ashes. In the overgrown yard behind the house, she found the old silver RV, just as Jim had told her she would. A wild plum tree spread above it, spilling its purple fruit on the roof, and vines grew around the tires. She peered inside the RV, looking for Charlie's urn, but the windows were cloudy with age. She rattled the door, but it was locked, and she couldn't find a way to enter the van.

"Maria?" she called, going back to the kitchen. "Do you know where the key to the RV is?"

"Lana has it," Maria replied.

"I'll get it tomorrow, then." Rebecca sat down at the kitchen table and watched her polish a silver pitcher with a felt rag. "Where will you go when you're finished at this house?" she asked.

"My brother lives in Oakland. I can live there."

Rebecca wondered what kind of job Maria would have next. The economy was a disaster, but with her English-speaking ability, she should be able to find something better than doing housework for another demanding woman. If Charlie had been alive, he'd have made sure that she ended up in a good place. "My father, was he a kind man?" she asked.

"Oh, yes. Mr. Stevens helped me a lot. He was very good."

"And his wife?"

Maria's face quickly closed. "Not so good."

"Why do you say that?"

Maria shrugged, and continued polishing.

"Tell me, please."

"Mrs. Stevens got very angry," Maria said. "Yelling. Hurting."

"Hurting you?" Rebecca's voice rose.

Maria's black eyes showed a hard anger. "She slapped. She hit. Sometimes she locked me in my room."

"She did that?" Rebecca said, her voice rising.

"She's a bad woman."

Rebecca felt sickened by this, and she searched for the right words. "How disgusting. How horrible," she said, although these words couldn't convey the depth of her feeling of outrage. "Why did you stay on in this house?"

Maria hesitated for a few moments, as though deciding whether she could trust Rebecca, and then she sighed. "I'm not legal here. Mrs. Stevens said she'd report me to Immigration if I left. They'd put me in jail or send me back to Mexico."

"Oh, Maria, I'm so sorry. I should have known that was happening."

"It's over now."

"Yes." Rebecca stared at her. All these years this woman had been cowed by Vicky and tricked into being her slave. "I've heard about situations like this, but I never imagined it going on here in this house." She paused. "Did you get a salary, working here?" she asked, already knowing the answer.

"Mr. Stevens, yes. Mrs. Stevens, no."

"We'll make it up to you," Rebecca said in a rush. "I'll talk with Lana."

"I don't need help."

Rebecca straightened up. "Tell me, were you in the house when my father had his accident, before he died?"

"I don't know anything about it," Maria answered.

"But he fell down and hit his head. That's what his wife said. Did you see it happen?"

"I don't know," Maria said again.

"But maybe you do."

"No."

A woman who had the strength to survive Vicky wouldn't speak about this matter until she was ready. "Some other time," Rebecca said. "That woman can't hurt you anymore. She's dead."

"I know that."

Rebecca rose, ready to leave. "I'll be back tomorrow," she said. "Will you be here?"

"I'm not going anywhere," Maria answered. Her face softened and she flashed a sweet, broad smile. "Bye, bye."

The next day Rebecca awakened early, still on Midwest time. She threw open the window of Jim's guest bedroom and breathed in the sharp, tangy scent of the sea, so different from the humid Midwest air she'd left behind. The fog had rolled in during the night, blanketing the city and the bay, causing the temperature to drop by twenty degrees. For years she had dreamed about this summer fog, and she loved watching it twist and turn, hiding whatever it encountered, bringing down the heat of living. Charlie used to call it the best air-conditioning there was.

Rebecca straightened the single bed and covered it with the diamond-patterned quilt Fran had pieced together years ago. She felt a sudden exhilaration, and she flung her arms overhead and stretched, opening to her good fortune: she'd gotten herself to California, and she had the rest of the summer ahead of her.

Last night, her first night there, she and Jim had settled in together over a dinner he'd made, his specialty of fried chicken. He told her about Fran's death—Rebecca had missed the funeral because it was the same day as Annie's high school graduation—and they reminisced about the good times they'd had with her. "She was my great love," Jim said softly.

Rebecca reached for his hand. "She was the best."

They both choked back tears, but then Jim started to stack the dinner plates. "How did it go in Piedmont?" he asked.

Rebecca told him about meeting Lana and seeing Maria, and she ended with a full account of Maria's enslavement. "I still can't believe that happened," she said.

"It's criminal." Jim's lips pursed in anger. "Vicky should have been prosecuted."

"How did we miss it? I feel terrible about that."

He just shook his head. "We had no control over what happened after your father died. It's not our fault."

"But we could have predicted it."

Rebecca helped Jim clear the table and they began to stack the dishes in the dishwasher. "I haven't been to that house for years," he said. "How does it look?"

"It's a dump outside. And inside, it's really depressing. It seems that nobody came there to visit. Vicky was more of a recluse than I ever would have expected. I thought she'd let loose after my father died. Entertaining, parties, travel, affairs. She had the money and the looks to be the belle of Piedmont."

"You never know," Jim said. "Did you meet Lana?"

"I can't quite figure her out. There's something remote about her. Not nasty like her mother, but not very friendly."

Jim began to smile. "You should get her to tell you about her life."

"What do you know?"

"You'll find out."

When Rebecca was young, Jim had teased her this way, leading her on until she begged for an answer. "Tell me, Jim," she said, remembering how much they'd both loved this game. "Come on."

"Lana has quite a history. Of course, we can only imagine what it was like to have Vicky as a mother. But even so, Lana ended up in Los Angeles, partying with judges, politicians, studio heads, guys like that. Lots of drugs, booze, sex for money. To her credit, she managed to break away and start a career in business. She's apparently a whiz at marketing."

"How did you find this out? It's not the kind of thing that shows up on Google."

"A lawyer friend of mine in Los Angeles. I thought you'd be interested."

"I wonder if anyone told Charlie."

"He was pretty shrewd. I'm sure he figured it out for himself."

Rebecca felt a surge of fondness for Jim. "You old gossip," she laughed.

Later that day, when Rebecca arrived, the white Mercedes was sitting in the driveway of the Piedmont house. She walked into the house and found Lana busily sorting through her mother's Wedgwood china and sterling silver on the dining room table. "What will you do with all this?" Rebecca asked, surveying the bounty.

"Sell it." Lana put a final plate on a stack of china. "My mother liked expensive things, but I can't keep most of them. The estate appraiser gave me a decent bid, so they'll go to him."

Lana would make a lot of money out of this house, Rebecca thought bitterly. Money that she didn't deserve, money that should have come to her and the children. There was nothing she could do about it, but Stan was right, this wasn't fair. "I want my father's leather chair," she said firmly. "I'd like it shipped back to Skokie."

"Anything else?"

"His belongings. I want everything of his."

"Mother got rid of his things after he died," Lana said. "But maybe Maria knows more than I do."

It turned out that Maria had saved two boxes of Charlie's possessions for Rebecca, and she carted them out. "I hid them from Mrs.
Stevens," she said triumphantly. "I kept them for you."

"You're so kind," Rebecca said in a rush. "That means so much. I'll
open them later."

After she carried the boxes to the Audi, she returned to find Maria
busily wiping down the kitchen cabinets. "What happened to the
dogs?" she asked her. Rebecca hadn't thought about them yesterday,
but in the middle of the night she had remembered they were still alive
six years ago.

"They're dead."

"Did Vicky take care of them after my father died?"

Maria shrugged. "I tried, but they got sick."

"That's too bad," Rebecca said guiltily. She should at least have made
sure they received good care in their last years, maybe even brought
them to Skokie. Another lapse on her part. But now her greatest concern was claiming the urn, and she headed into the backyard, Lana's
key in hand. The lawn had grown high and the bamboo by the dog
kennel had spread far past its boundaries, swaying in the breeze. She
stopped for a moment by the kennel, remembering how excited the
children had been about the dogs that day they first visited Piedmont.

When she reached the RV, she slipped the key into the lock. The
creaky door opened, and she climbed inside. To her shock, the RV
looked like a bordello, with glittery mirrors, red walls, and a plush red
carpet. This was Charlie's and Vicky's secret palace of pleasure. Satin
bathrobes were draped on the bed, his and hers, a whip and mask
were in the corner, and sex toys sat on a shelf. A bottle of champagne
with two crystal flutes rested on the little table, ready for an intimate
celebration. Rebecca gazed around this playground, feeling like an
intruder.

In the driver's seat, just as she had imagined, sat Charlie's copper
urn, gleaming in the sunlight. Her heart lurched. She'd dreamed
about this moment for so long, and now it was finally happening. She

started to pick up the urn, but stopped. It seemed wrong to disturb the arrangement that had been there for those six years.

The urn commanded the space around it, and a baseball cap had been hung on the cigarette lighter, "Captain of the Ship" stitched on the front. Rebecca sank onto the passenger seat. Suddenly the placement of the urn didn't feel like something done out of hostility and disrespect. Maybe Vicky had been so devastated by her husband's death that she'd not been able to let go of him, and keeping his ashes here, in this place of intimacy, had been an act of attachment.

Rebecca let herself picture a distraught Vicky turning the RV into a special memorial for Charlie, a hideaway where she came to remember what had been lost. The sex toys revealed a certain kinky bent, but perhaps she'd had the best sex of her life with this husband, or she'd discovered some tenderness that had been missing, or she'd loved him more than anyone had known. Perhaps she had experienced more passion with Charlie than Rebecca ever had with Stan, a disturbing thought.

Rebecca had a moment of sympathy for Vicky as she sat there in the passenger seat of the RV, but it didn't last long. Vicky had been crazy, that much was clear. If she had been attached to Charlie, it would only have fueled the intensity of her violence and her anger, causing her to strike out at him. Every therapist knew that.

She imagined her father and Vicky locked in an embrace on the bed, their naked bodies filling the RV with their pungent sexual odors. She felt nauseous and began to gag. Thrusting open the door, she stuck her head outside and took gulps of air, but that wasn't good enough, she had to get out of there. She took one last look at Charlie's urn sitting on the driver's seat, and she fled.

11

Layers of orange and red clouds stretched across the San Francisco Bay that evening and a thick bank of fog threatened to roll across the water. "I'd forgotten how beautiful the sunsets are here," Rebecca said to Lana as they sat across from each other at Skates, a Berkeley restaurant overlooking the bay.

Lana raised her wine glass. "To the sunset."

"I'm glad we came to this restaurant," Rebecca said. "I can't get enough of that view. At home we have Lake Michigan, but I hardly ever get over there, and there's nothing inspiring about it, not like this beautiful bay."

Lana was looking around the room, obviously not interested. "The service here is really slow."

"Are you in a hurry?" Rebecca asked.

"I have other commitments."

Several men sat at a table nearby, finishing up dinner, and Rebecca saw them eye Lana. She'd changed into a tight black sweater and pants and spiky black heels, and with her long blond hair she looked like she was straight from a fashion magazine. Rebecca felt shabby next to her in the jeans and blouse she'd been wearing all day. "Everyone must tell you how beautiful you are," she said to Lana.

"It happens."

"I suppose people expect certain things from you because of it.

That must be hard sometimes." Rebecca was sounding like a therapist, something she had vowed not to do, and she told herself to stop.

"I never noticed."

Rebecca buttered a piece of sourdough bread. "Your mom was beautiful, too," she said.

"Charlie certainly thought so," Lana answered.

"He really loved her. At least at first."

Lana glanced up. "At first? They were quite the lovebirds until he died."

"Except when they were fighting," Rebecca said. "I got the impression they fought a lot."

Lana didn't answer, and Rebecca nibbled at her bread, gazing out the bay window as the red and orange streaks on the western horizon faded into darkness. Small waves lapped against the restaurant pilings below, and she heard the cry of a seagull over the restaurant noise. "Charlie and Vicky had big problems," she said.

"No, they didn't," Lana replied. "They got along well. I only ever saw them laughing together."

"I got a different impression," Rebecca said, determined to hold her own.

"Well, you're wrong."

Rebecca settled back in her chair, deciding to change tactics. "Tell me about your mother," she said. "I never got to know her."

"You didn't miss much. She was quite the bitch, bossing everyone around." Lana's voice finally had more expression. "I wouldn't stand for it. We were forever battling, even when I was young."

"That must have been difficult."

"It was." Her voice returned to its monotone. "Now, what about you? Happily married, I assume. Good career, good kids, and all that?"

"Yes and no," Rebecca answered. "Everything seems up for grabs right now." Lana didn't question her about this, and she didn't feel like offering details. "I understand you have a marketing job with a software company in San Francisco," she said.

"Where did you hear that?"

"A family friend."

Lana's eyes narrowed. "How the word travels. Then you probably also heard other things about me."

"No," Rebecca stammered. "Well, sort of."

Lana fixed her gaze upon her. "I know my way around the world. And there is one thing I know for sure: Charlie and Vicky got along just fine. It wasn't a problem."

"Okay, I hear you," Rebecca said glumly.

The waiter brought their entrees and another round of wine to the table. Lana picked at her food while Rebecca ate hungrily. When she finished, she began to question Lana about the RV and what she planned to do with it. "Have you been inside that thing?" she asked. Lana shook her head. "It supports your theory about Charlie and Vicky being lovebirds." She remembered she hadn't returned the RV key to Lana, and she pulled it from her jeans pocket and slipped it to her. "Take a look in there. But I have to say," she continued, "I heard a different story about my father's relationship with your mother from him. He was really miserable toward the end. Vicky frightened him. I'm sure he would have divorced her if he had lived."

"He must have been exaggerating."

"I don't think so."

Leaning across the table, Lana spoke brusquely. "After Charlie died, my mother never recovered. She stayed in that house all those years, living like a recluse. It was because she'd lost your father. I never would have thought she was capable of such devotion."

Rebecca would not win this round. "It's hard to know the truth," she said softly.

Lana stared at her. "That's right."

When Rebecca returned to Jim's house, she slumped onto the couch, disgruntled and weary, and told him about her disappointing evening with Lana. "We didn't even get around to talking about compensating

Maria for her years of work," she said. "Things were that tense. Lana had an edge, and I guess I did too."

She described the strange, disturbing scene she'd discovered in the RV. "I'm so confused about what it means. The deeper I get into this, the more I don't know," she said. She rambled on, going around in circles, expressing her frustration about not having answers.

Soon Jim had had enough. "Stop it, Rebecca. You have to let go. You'll never find out the answers to all these questions."

"I owe it to my father to try."

"No, you don't. You're a broken record." Jim shook his head. "It's six years. Vicky's dead. What's done is done. You can't change that."

Rebecca stiffened, hurt by his lack of support. "You sound like Stan."

"Maybe he's right."

"I'll find out the truth," she said. "I think Lana's lying, or she misunderstood what was going on between the two of them."

"She'd probably say the same thing about you."

"Whose side are you on?"

"Yours," Jim shot back. "I don't want to see you wasting your time on something that's going nowhere."

Rebecca said goodnight coolly to him and made her way into the guest bedroom. Even though Jim had been her comrade through those final months of Charlie's life, tonight he'd come on too strong. But maybe he was right that she should let go of this obsession; it too easily could get in the way of her summer's pleasure. In the bedroom she threw back Fran's quilt and slipped between the sheets. Still discouraged by the day, she picked up her novel. *Read*, she commanded herself.

Her cell phone rang in the living room, where she had left it when she came back from the restaurant, and she dashed to answer it, thinking it must be Stan calling to check up on her. "Yes?" she answered.

"I'm leaving town, Rebecca," Lana's voice came over the line. "I've just made arrangements. I thought you should know."

"What does that mean?" Rebecca paused. "I won't see you at the house tomorrow?"

"I'll be away for the rest of the summer."

Rebecca jaw clenched. "That's too bad," she said.

"Maria will get your father's chair crated up and sent to Illinois," Lana continued. "I think that's all you need."

"But Charlie's ashes are still in the RV. You have the key. I returned it to you tonight."

"I'll drop it off in Piedmont tomorrow before I leave, and you can stop by the house later to get the urn. I'll tell Maria you're coming."

"So I won't see you again?"

"No."

"Have a good summer," Rebecca said angrily, hanging up.

Jim came into the living room with his laptop; he had gotten into the habit of playing solitaire in the evenings. "So much for Lana," she said darkly to him. "I should have known."

He clucked sympathetically. "It wasn't a match made in heaven."

"I guess not." Rebecca felt more disappointed than she could say. "It's Lana's loss, but it's mine, too. We could have been something to each other."

Back in her bedroom she kicked the jeans that she'd dropped on the floor. "Shit," she yelled. But then she told herself that Lana's leaving wasn't a huge event and she should accept it in a calm way. That would be the most sensible approach, since it was already clear that they would never be friends. But then a rage rose within her and she felt like fighting Lana as best she could. Lana was the closest thing to Vicky, and she wouldn't let her get away so easily. Back and forth her feelings went, and her breath became shallow. She felt fragmented and off-balance, just as she had before leaving Skokie.

She rushed into the living room, retrieved her phone, and went back into the bedroom, calling Stan. "You're there?" she said.

"It's after midnight," he grunted.

"Sorry, I just needed to hear your voice. Go back to sleep. I'll call you tomorrow."

"Okay." As she hung up the receiver, Rebecca imagined Stan stretched out in the queen bed they'd bought ten years before, the mattress pressed down and lumpy on his side. She wanted to buy a new mattress, but he liked it the way it was.

She returned to bed and picked up her magazine again. "*Read*," she commanded herself.

When Rebecca arrived at the Piedmont house the next day, Maria handed her the key to the RV. "It's too bad that Lana's leaving town," Rebecca said, still outraged about Lana abandoning her.

Maria looked surprised. "Leaving town?"

Rebecca stared at her. "She said she'll be away for the rest of the summer."

"Oh."

"She didn't tell you?"

"Not yet." Maria turned and left.

On the mahogany table in the entry hall Rebecca noticed some papers from Coldwell Banker Realty, and she flipped through them. The house, it seemed, was going on the market in two weeks, with an asking price of just under three million dollars. Once again Rebecca felt a surge of anger that she had been so irretrievably cut out. She couldn't imagine who would buy this monstrous house in this economy, but maybe some rich person would come along and set Lana up for years to come.

In the upcoming weeks there would be a lot to do to get the house ready for the market. Lana would hire a stager, but she still needed to be around to make decisions about what to sell and what to keep. The outside of the house needed a major cleanup and replanting, and she'd have to organize that. Obviously she had lied to Rebecca when she said she'd be away for the summer. But why? It could be that Lana didn't want her around, asking uncomfortable questions, getting in her way. Or perhaps she feared that Rebecca would start legal proceedings against her to get part of her wealth—although she must have already consulted an attorney and learned that Rebecca didn't have a case. Or perhaps Lana simply didn't like Rebecca. Whatever reason it was, Lana had gotten rid of her like yesterday's garbage.

In the entryway, standing on the same marble floor where her father had supposedly fallen, Rebecca made a decision: she would not let Lana get away so easily.

She stomped out the back door to the RV. Yesterday she'd been stunned and confused, but today she grabbed the urn off the driver's seat. "Let's get out of here, Charlie," she said sharply. "This is not a good place for you or for me." Checking to see if there was anything else she wanted, she claimed the Captain's baseball cap that hung on the lighter. Let Lana figure out what to do with all those sex toys.

"Here's the key," she said to Maria, back in the kitchen. "And thanks again for saving those boxes of my father's things."

"Did you open them yet?"

"I'm waiting for the right moment." Maria was finishing up the job of washing out the cabinets and it was time for Rebecca to leave, but this might be her last chance to get more information. "It was very sad when my father died," she said.

"Very sad," Maria agreed.

Rebecca came closer to her. "I never knew what happened to him. Isn't that terrible?"

"He fell down," Maria said quickly. She seemed nervous, twisting the cleaning cloth in her hands.

"Maybe he did." Rebecca waited a moment. "Or maybe he didn't. I think his wife hurt him."

Maria looked away. "No."

"She was capable of it. I think she bashed him with something really hard. He was very weak then, and that would have been enough."

Maria looked frightened. "No, no," she said. "Mrs. Stevens didn't do that. She hurt me, but not Mr. Stevens."

"I don't believe you, Maria," Rebecca said. "I know she hit my father sometimes. He had those bruises. Come on, tell me the truth."

"Mr. Stevens fell down a lot," she said stubbornly.

"And what else?" Rebecca pushed.

"Nothing."

"Oh, Maria," Rebecca sighed. She wanted to do something to make this woman talk, but if she threatened her, she would be as bad as Vicky. "Okay, I guess that's it. I won't be coming here anymore. Now that I have my father's ashes, there's no reason. But I'd like Lana's address, if you'd give it to me."

Maria rushed off and returned with Vicky's pink address book, decorated with flowers and little mirrors. Rebecca held the book for a moment, thinking it might contain a key to understanding who Vicky was and what she had done to Charlie, and she considered dropping it into her bag and leaving. Maria wouldn't be able to stop her. But when she flipped through the pages of the book, there were no addresses or phone numbers for anyone except Lana, a few doctors, and some tradespeople. She copied down Lana's address on a scrap of paper in her purse and handed the book back to Maria. "How can I find you after you move?"

"I'll give you my brother's telephone number," Maria said, and she scribbled it under Lana's address.

"Good-bye," Rebecca said. "Thanks for your kindness to my father."

Maria smiled at her. "No problem."

"And one more thing," Rebecca said. "When you next see Lana, tell her that I'll be looking for her."

As she opened the front door to leave, she saw Maria standing there, her dark eyebrows raised.

12

The next morning Rebecca drove to Lana's townhouse in San Francisco. The narrow, tall building sat on a side street in an expensive district in San Francisco, and it was painted white with black trim, unlike the pastels of the surrounding townhouses. The windows were heavily draped, and the townhouse had a metal-gated front door. Rebecca insistently rang the doorbell, determined to get a response. "Yes?" Lana's voice finally scratched over the intercom.

"I need to talk to you. It's Rebecca."

"I'm not available."

"You lied to me about going out of town," Rebecca shouted. "You're avoiding me because you're afraid I'm going to ruin the good deal you have now that your mother is no longer around."

"Go away."

Rebecca kicked the cactus pot on the doorstep, stubbing her big toe. "Damn!" she yelled. A man walking his dog past the townhouse glanced suspiciously at her, and she nodded at him in what she hoped was a reassuring way. "You can't get rid of me," she said, turning back to the intercom.

Lana didn't answer for a moment. "There's nothing more I can do, Rebecca. You have your father's urn, and Maria gave you the boxes of his things. Surely that should satisfy you."

Rebecca was even more infuriated by her patronizing tone. "It doesn't," she shouted. "I want to know what happened to my father. You could help me."

"You're wrong."

"Let me into the house so we can talk."

"Absolutely not."

"Dammit, Lana!" Rebecca screamed.

"You're harassing me, and I won't stand for it," Lana said. "I refuse to talk to you, and that's my right. If necessary, I'll get a restraining order. It won't be the first."

Rebecca tried to return to civility. "All right, I won't bother you anymore. But think about it. I can't hurt you. I just want to know the truth. What's wrong with that?"

She waited a moment for Lana to answer, but nothing came over the intercom. "Think about it," she said again. "I'll be back."

Rebecca felt like shouting atrocities at Lana's townhouse, but instead she rushed to her car and peeled away from the curb, past the man with his dog. By the time she got three blocks away, her anger had turned into tears. She'd failed with Lana. What a huge disappointment that was. Gone was the dream of a stepsister, gone was the hope of Lana helping her find the answer to her father's death.

She pulled over to the side of the street and wept over the steering wheel. Suddenly she heard a crashing thud that sounded like a two-ton crate falling on the Audi. She jumped, her heart racing, and opened her eyes to see two boys catching a soccer ball that had just bounced off the roof. "Get away from my car!" she yelled at them. They looked at her with surprise, and she saw herself in their eyes, a woman out of control, an enemy of fun and games. One of the boys mouthed that they were sorry, although she couldn't hear his words, and they scampered down the block.

"Pull yourself together," she said to herself in a shaky voice. She looked at her face in the car mirror, at the snot running from her nose, the red, blotchy skin and puffy eyes. "You're a mess."

She started the car and turned onto a busy thoroughfare. A truck cut in front of her, and she leaned on the horn, blasting the driver. But this wasn't how she wanted to be. She'd arrived in beautiful California to have a beautiful summer, and this rage had no place there. If some driver wanted to pass by her, what was the problem? She wasn't in a hurry, she reminded herself. She had no obligations, no reason to rush, and she could drive around the city like a tourist if she wanted.

In fact, she could do anything she wanted this summer, and nobody could stop her. The sensible plan would be to stay in the Bay Area, take photography classes, and make contact with colleagues, but she had no stomach for doing this. In her state, she didn't even know if she could carry it off. Instead she'd go away by herself, she decided—wander up north and stop where she wanted, and when she'd had enough of one place, she'd move on to another. If Stan or someone else didn't like it, that was their problem.

For the next hour Rebecca drove aimlessly around the city, relishing this plan, and she ended up in front of Lana's townhouse again, although that hadn't been her intent. She looked to see if there were signs of life, but there weren't any, and she continued down the street. Then she spotted a familiar white Mercedes convertible racing toward her from the opposite direction, unmistakably Lana's car. As Lana passed by, her face unreadable, Rebecca buzzed down the window and waved wildly at her. "See you later, sister!" she yelled. With that, she burst into hysterical laughter.

The next morning Rebecca packed up the black Audi with all her possessions. In the trunk went the boxes of her father's things, still unopened; Charlie's tall copper urn rode along in the passenger seat, strapped in by the seat belt. "That looks mighty strange," Jim said with a concerned look. "Are you sure you want to do that?"

She kissed him good-bye, glad to be leaving behind his inquiring glances. Last night he'd asked her several times if she was all right—and she hadn't even told him about the argument she'd had with Lana over her intercom or her behavior in the city. "Something's going on," he said. "You're not acting like yourself." She'd gazed innocently at him, daring him to go further, but he'd retreated. Afterward she felt unsettled by his comments and wished she'd been honest, telling him how overwhelmed she was by her emotions and how afraid she felt of falling apart, but she was ashamed and didn't want him intruding. Better that she go through this alone—whatever this was.

Rebecca headed over the graceful, five-mile Richmond–San Rafael Bridge toward the busy freeway that stretches from the south of California to the north, Highway 101. She'd bought a map and some guidebooks, but these were just for backup. Next to her was the urn, and she touched its smooth surface. "It's you and me again, Charlie," she said. "We're off on an adventure, just the two of us." Having his ashes there felt just right, and she was full of love for this father who had reappeared after such a long absence. "I'm so glad to have you back," she said brightly. It seemed so natural to talk to him this way that she hardly noticed it, even though any other therapist would have considered it a worrisome sign.

She was already feeling better than she had for days. The Audi drifted along the freeway, past the turnoffs for the suburban towns north of San Francisco and into the open countryside. Here there was no fog, and the temperature rose into the high eighties. Rebecca opened the car windows, letting in the scent of manure and hay. After an hour of freeway driving, she began to see acres of vineyards stretching over the valley floor and up the sides of the foothills. The leaves of the plants were light green in the morning light, the trunks twisted and brown like ancient carvings.

She'd traveled this road long ago with Charlie when she was eight, before these vineyards had been planted, but she hardly remembered that drive. She'd been fidgeting in the backseat, too impatient to reach Clear Lake, their destination farther north. They'd gone there for a week, the best vacation of her childhood, and she remembered a beautiful lake with crystal blue water. "Guess what, Dad?" she said, touching the urn. "We're going to Clear Lake. That's our first stop." As soon as she said this, the plan seemed right; Clear Lake was the only place in the world where she and Charlie could go on this sunny June day.

Rebecca laughed at how easily the decision had been made. The summer would be just like that, and she only needed to let it unfold. She turned on the radio, found a classical music station, and sang along with what sounded like a Brahms piano concerto, blending her voice with the instruments. The soaring music matched her mood, and she felt ecstatic, like she could drive off the face of the earth and into the sky.

Soon the music fuzzed out, and she switched off the radio. Stan never would understand what was happening to her. She'd phoned him last night, telling him that she planned to head north, and he had asked for an accounting of where she'd be. When she said she didn't know, he asked her to keep her phone on at all times so he could reach her. But he'd be calling too often, saying the same things over and over, and she told him to forget it. "What about emergencies?" he'd asked irately. "What if something happens to me or one of the kids?" She'd agreed that in that case he should text her or leave a message and she'd get back to him quickly, but otherwise she'd call him every few days.

"The truth is, I didn't marry Stan for love. It was for security," Rebecca said to Charlie's ashes as the car breezed along on Highway 101. "I needed someone there with me while I worked and raised the kids, and he was willing, at least for a while. He's a decent guy, but I can hardly talk to him. Truthfully, I wish I wasn't married to him." The copper urn gleamed in the summer sunlight, and Charlie, now her confidant, absorbed her words. "One of the best things to come out of that marriage was Miriam," she continued. "It's too bad you didn't meet her when you came to Chicago. She's the mother I never had."

The image of Miriam in her crowded old house, surrounded by her paintings and her animals, made Rebecca feel like singing again. Miriam had understood why she needed to get away for the summer, and she'd argued her case with Stan. The night before Rebecca left for

California, she had come by the house to say good-bye. "Take good care of yourself," she'd said, fixing her eyes on her. "I hope you find what you're looking for."

"So do I," Rebecca replied, sobered by her intensity.

"You'll always be my daughter," Miriam said. "Remember that." Rebecca hugged her cushiony body longer than usual that night.

"Miriam's really intuitive," Rebecca said to Charlie. "But leaving Stan is not an option. I left one marriage, and I can't imagine leaving another. I don't have the energy or the fortitude." Her voice had returned to its habitual tightness. "I don't want to hurt Stan. In fact, I don't even want to think about him right now. You're the important one, not him."

Satisfied with this, she straightened the seat belt around Charlie's urn. The terrain had become hilly, and Rebecca spotted a small river running next to the road. She considered stopping for a swim, but it was already past two and she had farther to go. The freeway narrowed into two lanes for several miles, and she finally cruised into the little town of Hopland, a good place to find something to eat before climbing east over the mountains to Clear Lake. She pulled into the parking lot of a deli and turned off the ignition, but it seemed wrong to leave Charlie in the car in full view of anyone who passed by. She slipped the urn under her jacket in the back seat. "I'm hiding you, just in case," she said.

Rebecca lifted her face to the sun, eager to receive its warmth. Her body felt cramped after sitting behind the wheel for so long, and she stretched and shook out her legs. In her jeans and tank top, her hair tussled by the wind, she felt free, no longer the buttoned-up therapist doling out Kleenex and care.

A battered van turned into the lot, parking next to the Audi, and a man with a scraggly red beard and wild eyes jumped out. As he passed by, he scanned Rebecca up and down, giving her a long look of approval. "Where you headed?" he asked. She turned away, flattered by his attention but unsettled by his appearance. "How about a beer? The Keg next door is open."

"I'm driving," she said.

"You sure?"

It had been so long since someone had come on to Rebecca in such a direct way. "I'm sure," she said.

The man walked toward The Keg, but just before he entered, he called back at her, asking her once more to come. She turned away, feeling more vulnerable than she had in years. She stood uncertainly in the parking lot and considered putting on her sweatshirt to hide her breasts from view, but it was hot and the man had disappeared. Instead she unlocked the car door and retrieved the urn, wrapping it under her arm. "You're with me," she said softly to Charlie. "That's your job."

After lunch Rebecca drove east from Hopland, into the mountains of Lake County. When she and Charlie came this way long ago, the road had been barely passable, but now it was paved. She saw no other travelers, only oak trees, scrubby bushes, and an occasional turkey buzzard circling overhead.

After twenty slow, twisting miles into the mountains, Rebecca reached the summit and pulled over to see the view to the east. The majestic mountains spread out before her, covered with golden grass and dark patches of trees, and nestled far below was Clear Lake, sparkling and blue. A rich, warm feeling flooded through her—this was the place of her dreams—and she got out of the car and took several photographs of the sight to mark this grand moment of arrival. She and Charlie had stayed at a little family-run motel by the lake for their vacation, and how fitting it would be if she found that same place to sleep that night.

She began the long, winding drive down to the lake. The trees and undergrowth on the sides of the road were so dense that she could hardly see what was ahead, and she felt as if she were venturing farther and farther away from civilization. But after a few final turns the curving road stopped abruptly at the foot of the mountain at a traffic light on a four-lane highway. She'd thought of Clear Lake as hardly populated, but almost forty years had gone by and this had changed. Cars and trucks bustled on the road in front of her.

The traffic light turned green, but she didn't know which way to go. At the last minute she decided to turn left, and she drove a mile before coming to the first exit, which was for Lakeport. She faintly remembered this town, and she expected to see a charming town square and a lakeside marina. Instead she ended up on an unsightly main drag jammed with fast food restaurants and auto lube shops. "What's going on here?" she said aloud to the urn. "What happened?"

The ugly sprawl of the town stretched ahead as far as Rebecca could see, and she pulled over, too confused and disappointed to continue. She glanced at her hands on the steering wheel: they looked mottled and veiny on top, like they belonged to an old woman, but when she turned them over they were pink and hardly lined, the hands of a young child. She rubbed them together, feeling their warmth, and then she pulled back into the traffic.

Soon she spotted a sign for a boat landing, a good omen. She made a sharp right turn and drove quickly down a residential side street toward the lake, yearning to get close to the cool, refreshing water. At the end of the street, she parked the car and ran onto the concrete boat landing. To her horror, mounds of garbage were piled there, and the water was green and murky, not the blue she remembered. When she dipped her hand into it, it felt greasy and smelled of motor fuel. But this was a boat landing, she told herself, a place that could be expected to be dirty. Surely there must be cleaner areas nearby.

A teenage couple wandered past, smoking and joking around. "Excuse me, where do people swim here?" Rebecca asked them.

"Swim?" the girl laughed in a friendly way. "Nobody swims in this lake."

"I got sick from it once," the boy said, hitching up his baggy pants. "I won't swim there again."

Rebecca stared at them. "Aren't there beaches?"

"No," they said in unison.

"What happened to the lake?"

"It's filled with algae from the fertilizers that run off the fields," the girl said. She lit another cigarette from her boyfriend's, and took a deep drag. "And some mining company put a lot of garbage into it before then, or something like that."

"How awful," Rebecca said. "Nobody swims here, really? Not anyone you know?"

The couple eyed her with what seemed like concern. "Sorry," the boy said.

The kids sauntered away to join a group of tattooed bikers hanging out at the corner, and Rebecca fled back to the car. "I can't believe it. It's shameful what they've done," she said to Charlie. "Remember when we came here, how beautiful this lake was?"

She pictured herself rushing down to the pier as a child and leaping into the clear blue water, happily dogpaddling around. Charlie was there, too, with his fishing gear, and after a while they loaded up the little boat and rowed toward the fishing hole nearby. This was a pleasing memory, but then she remembered that one day he wanted her to go with him to a business acquaintance's house in the countryside, something about a prospective real estate deal, and she refused. The time alone with him was too precious to share with someone else. After his scolding, she finally got into the car, but she sat there with crossed arms, refusing to speak. "I wasn't the most agreeable kid," she said to the urn. "But then again, you shouldn't have dragged me to that business meeting."

She pushed away this discordant memory and drove the car to Lakeport's main street, deciding to venture farther into town. Soon she came to the center, an area with a museum and a town hall, more like what she had imagined. As the church clock struck five, she spotted a Visitors' Information sign in front of a shabby white building with geranium pots, and she decided to see if she could get some help.

Inside, an officious-looking woman with dyed black hair glanced up from her desk when she entered. "I'm looking for a motel I used to stay in, but I don't know its name," Rebecca said. She tried to describe the place, but she was tired from the day and she felt herself tremble with the effort of speaking.

"Sounds like one of those on the northern end of the lake," the woman said. "But they're mostly gone now. You wouldn't want to stay there, anyhow. They're pretty dilapidated."

"That doesn't matter."

"I suggest you find a room at one of the newer motels. You could drive around the lake to the other side, where there's a Travelodge."

"No, thanks," Rebecca said. "Tell me, what happened to Clear Lake? Why is it so polluted?"

"Is it?" The woman began to tidy a stack of pamphlets on her desk. "Clear Lake is a beautiful lake, and a lot of people vacation here."

"But nobody swims in it."

"You're wrong. People water ski, and that means they swim."

"That's a stretch," Rebecca said.

The woman looked at her watch. "I'm closing in a minute," she said. Handing her a map of the lake, she coolly wished her a good vacation.

Back in the car, Rebecca felt drained by the encounter, and she didn't know if she could go much farther. "I hate it," she said to herself. "Why can't things be easier?" She glanced down at the urn, still in the passenger seat: "It's all your fault," she said to Charlie. "It's because of you that I'm here." But then she heard herself and began to laugh in a harsh way. "What a sorry flop I am. I can't even find my way to the motel."

With this, she quickly drove ten miles to the northern end of the lake, searching for the motel she remembered. She passed by trailer parks and little cottages and ranch houses that were strung along the shore so close to each other that she couldn't even see the lake. "I can't stand what they've done here," she cried to Charlie. "They've ruined it." She tried to picture the motel where the two of them had stayed. Hadn't it been surrounded by big pine trees, and hadn't there been grass and a swing in the front and a wide view of the lake?

On she drove, straining to find the motel, but the woman in Lakeport had been right, there was nothing like it anymore. Rebecca heard the roar of a pack of motorcyclists coming from behind, and she screamed. It was as though these bikers were coming for her to push her off the road and make her crash. But they zoomed past, and she was left shaking and breathless. She slowed down to a crawl, trying to steer the car straight, but it wobbled along.

After a few miles, she saw a police car's flashing red light in her rearview mirror and heard the whine of a siren. "Oh, shit," she shouted, pulling over to the side. She quickly threw her sweatshirt over Charlie's urn and found her license in her purse. A young police-woman approached the car. "You're from out of state, I see," she said.

"I'm a tourist," Rebecca said, hoping that would gain her some favor. "I'm sorry I was driving badly, but I was spooked by a gang of motorcyclists that came up behind me. They were so noisy and then they darted so quickly around me. I just got confused."

The officer looked her over carefully. "Are you okay, ma'am?"

"It's been a long day." Rebecca tried to smile, but couldn't make her mouth do it right.

The officer handed her back her license. "I'm not giving you a ticket, ma'am, but you need to get off the road. I don't think you're in any shape to drive."

"I'll go just a little farther to the Travelodge," Rebecca said. "I understand there's one up ahead."

"Sounds like a good idea."

"I'll get something to eat and a good night's sleep," Rebecca said, "and then, you'll see, everything will be fine in the morning."

13

In the Travelodge that night, Rebecca had a nightmare. She was suspended high in the air, trying to balance on a tightrope wire that looked as thin as a thread. Ahead there was a place of safety, a landing, but when she looked down she saw a huge dark hole ready to suck her in. The hole seemed to grow, and a harsh, rumbling sound came from within it. She took several panicked steps on the wire, trying to reach safety, but the wire began to swing back and forth, threatening to buck her off. Her legs shook, her mind splintered in a thousand directions, her strength disappeared, and she struggled to find her balance. But it was no use—she wobbled wildly and began to fall.

She jerked awake from the nightmare, screaming. Every muscle in her body was rigid, and she clenched the thin motel blanket for protection. But the shadows in the room seemed to grow larger and larger, threatening to overcome her. There was no safety anywhere.

When morning finally came, she dragged herself out of the tangled sheets and opened the thin curtains. The Audi was in a far corner of the parking lot below, away from the other cars. She faintly remembered arriving at the Travelodge last night and driving around, worried about where to leave it. And then she'd stumbled into the lobby, where a snotty man—or it could have been a woman—took her registration. At first she couldn't find her credit card, and she'd become so panicked that she felt like passing out and almost started to cry, but then there it was, in her wallet as usual. All of this had been too much, and when the receptionist said there was no food service in the facility, only drinks in the vending machines, she'd felt like throwing herself on the floor and refusing to move. "But I haven't eaten for hours," she'd wailed to the snotty receptionist. "How can you not have food?" The reception just turned away.

Rebecca's body ached from the long night. She shook out her arms and legs, but they seemed like unfamiliar appendages. Nothing seemed real in this impersonal room, neither the king bed with its flowered spread nor the tan plastic armchair. The TV on the wall seemed to be floating in the air. The air smelled stale, like somebody had been smoking, but there was another smell, too, a smell of decay.

Her stomach growled. She hadn't eaten since Hopland, almost a whole day ago. She rummaged in the bag she'd brought up to the room and found a Power Bar and an apple. Not much of a breakfast, but it would do for now. She heard a vacuum cleaner down the hall, a reassuring, everyday sound, housekeeping up and running. But that meant she'd soon have to check out of the room. Unless she decided to stay, which was unthinkable.

But where would she go? She was in no shape to get on the road again, but finding a place and making arrangements here at Clear Lake seemed way beyond her capabilities. *Breathe*, she told herself, *you can figure it out.* Vacation rentals, yes, that was it, the category she needed to investigate if she was going to find a place to stay. In the drawer of the bureau was a local telephone book, and she opened it to the Yellow Pages and looked under Realtors.

She called the first realty office on the list, but the brisk hello on the other end of the line intimidated her and she slammed the phone down. *I can't do this*, she thought, but she braced herself and called the number again, managing to navigate the conversation although her voice echoed in her head while she talked. The first few offices had no vacation rental properties, but finally she reached a woman who told her about a secluded little cabin on Clear Lake, available for a price she could afford. The woman went on about the owners, a nice couple that used the cabin for weekends but who were on the East Coast this summer and wanted to rent it to someone responsible to get a little income since the woman had lost her job. To stop the realtor from talking so much, and because she couldn't think of anything else to do, Rebecca arranged to see the cabin immediately. She carted her gear to the car, drove to the realtor's office, and picked up the key.

As soon as Rebecca saw the A-frame wood cabin from the outside, she knew it would be perfect. The cabin sat on a small piece of land that jutted out into the water, and it had a feeling of solitude and separateness about it, so different from all the other homes that were crowded around the lake. Here she could be utterly alone. And the lake looked more appealing in this spot, with clumps of reeds along the shoreline hiding the slimy, green water.

Rebecca unlocked the door of the tiny cabin and stepped inside. The walls were paneled with warm brown pine, and the room felt homey and comfortable with its little couch, two-person kitchen table and chairs, mini-refrigerator, and hot plate. In a cozy alcove there was a double bed covered by a bedspread that looked homemade. Best of all, the cabin had a private wood deck on three sides that extended directly above the clumps of reeds and water. It looked clean and well-loved, with chintz curtains, colorful pottery, and games and puzzles stashed away in a cupboard.

Rebecca called the realtor to tell her she'd take it, and she threw open the windows, preparing to move in. "Good news," she sang to the urn. "I've found us a home. Not where you and I stayed before, but it's every bit as good. Even better." It didn't take her long to carry in her belongings and unpack. "Perfect, perfect," she kept saying, her voice high and shrill. "Just right, just right."

But now she needed to drop a check off at the realtor's and get supplies, enough for a few weeks. One more time of talking with people before shutting the door of the cabin. She could do it, she told herself. She drove back to the realty office and left a check—that chatty woman thankfully was out of the office—and then she went to the general grocery store three miles away. There she loaded up on canned tuna and salmon, dried fruits and nuts, carrots and tomatoes, brown rice and eggs, cheese and crackers, tea and coffee, and bottled water and juice. No more unhealthy chips or candy. She passed by the shelves of wine, but her desire for alcohol seemed to have faded. There was a display of candles, and at the last minute she bought several boxes to light up the room at night.

Back at the cabin, she slowly put away her supplies, exhausted by her efforts. She dragged the cushions from the couch out to the deck and made a comfortable nest for herself where she could sit undisturbed. The lake cast off a faintly stagnant odor, but it bothered her less than she would have thought possible. She sighed deeply, her whole body letting down. This was exactly where she'd wanted to be, although she hadn't known it before she arrived.

All semblance of internal order fell away. Rebecca stayed on the deck that day for hours, staring into the distance without really seeing anything. Mountains and lake and trees merged into a blurry mass, and fragments of thought ran through her mind but none stayed. It was as though her life's course had brought her to this moment, and there was nothing to do but dwell in it.

And then she began to weep, long sobs that seemed to come from the core of her being. She grasped onto the urn, and her body convulsed in waves. "Oh, Charlie," she cried. "Oh, god." She continued weeping as though the well of sorrows was infinitely deep.

After a while a feeling of fear began to race through her, and she suddenly imagined that she would lose her balance, her sanity, everything she'd worked for. She tried to pull back to safety, but then she looked down at the putrid waters and wept some more. "So much sadness," she wailed. "So much loneliness and emptiness." She wiped her runny nose on her arm, and the tears flowed even more, sliding down her cheeks and dropping onto the deck.

The afternoon passed in this way. Rebecca did not notice the sun moving from one side of the deck to another, or the family of ducks that paddled by, or the spider crawling next to her nest of pillows. Finally she got up, her legs hardly holding her, and staggering inside, she collapsed on the bed and slept soundly for fourteen hours.

Rebecca did not leave the cabin for the next three weeks. She hardly bothered to bathe or change her clothes. Her hair became tangled, and she didn't attempt to brush it out. She was becoming a wild woman. That professional Rebecca—so far away—knew that she was breaking into pieces, but it didn't seem frightening anymore. It was only what she needed to do. All thoughts about the past or the future, all concerns about family and clients, dropped away, and she stayed in the little cabin in a dreamlike state, sometimes weeping, sometimes sitting in the nest of pillows on the deck. The hours came and went without her looking at her watch. She slept as long as she wanted, ate when she felt like it, and, at night, when the sun set, she lit the candles she'd placed around the cabin, filling the corners with warm yellow light.

Charlie's urn sat on the kitchen table. Rebecca talked to him often, telling him the things that were in her heart. "Daddy, I love you. I want you back," she cried like a little child. Sometimes she spoke in an older voice: "You were really boring when you talked about all your business deals. I could hardly stand to listen." And in an even older voice: "That time you came to Skokie, what a disappointment. How pissed off I was, how I couldn't understand why you let Vicky boss you around." Sometimes she descended into the pain of his death: "I'm so sorry I didn't protect you better, Dad," she sobbed. "I should have done more. I wish I had."

As the days passed, speech fell away. She and her father began to coexist in silence, beyond words, beyond even thoughts. This silence felt good, as though something had been added rather than taken away, and she realized how long she'd been yearning for it. All those words she'd had in her head her entire life, all those words she'd said during her therapy sessions, all those words with friends and family, all those words on the TV and the radio and the Internet. They were no longer with her. Now, in this state of stillness, away from words, she knew what she had never acknowledged—that within her being was a place of safety and peace.

Rebecca ventured into language only when she called Stan every few days. "It's me," she said reluctantly, fulfilling her part of the bargain they'd struck. Her voice sounded odd after all the silence.

"Where are you? Why haven't you called?" Stan asked. "What are you doing? Are you okay?"

"Yes." She couldn't say more. "How are you?"

Stan would begin telling her the details about his most recent basketball game or the TV program he'd watched earlier that evening, and then he'd move on to what had happened at work. "Oh," she'd answer, or "Really?" Out of kindness and guilt she'd encourage him to speak, knowing how hard it was for him to be by himself in the house with only old, arthritic Ruckus for company.

"Talk to you later, hon," he'd finally say, breezing off the line.

"Bye," she'd answer, hanging up with relief.

One day Annie texted Rebecca: "Need to talk. Now."

This was an unusual request from a daughter who hadn't asked for much in recent years, and Rebecca quickly phoned her. "I'm scared," Annie said, her voice higher than usual. "I don't know if I can handle everything. Summer school is a bitch, and I'm working almost full-time at the mall. The woman I've been seeing, Karina, is freaking out."

In the past Rebecca would have flipped into her wise-mother role, trying to help Annie sort through the complications, advising her to follow her best instincts, but she couldn't do it now. Her daughter's issues seemed so far from her, and she sputtered, "Honey, I don't know what to say."

Annie paused. "Mom, are you all right?"

"Yes."

"You sound weird."

"Do I?" With great effort Rebecca forced herself to think about the questions at hand, but their conversation floundered and Annie ended it with a quick good-bye.

After that, Rebecca decided she wasn't going to talk anymore. The silence, so delicious, so precious, was worth protecting, even if it meant cutting off from those closest to her. Choosing times when she thought Stan, Annie, and Paul would not be answering their phones, she called and left messages saying that she needed to take a break for the next week or two, a retreat of sorts, and that she would get back to them afterward, although of course they should text her if there was an emergency.

To celebrate, Rebecca decided that evening to open Charlie's boxes. This would be a big moment, one she had been anticipating. She dragged them out from under the bed where she'd stored them and tore open the tape on the first box, peering inside. There, on top, lay a black leather wallet. Rebecca rubbed its slick surface, but it seemed new. It was empty inside except for a photograph of Vicky in a Hawaiian muumuu, smiling coolly. The wallet must have been a present from her just before his death, and Rebecca quickly closed it and set it aside. She continued rummaging through the box, finding tailored shirts, an Italian suit, and fine leather shoes, clothing that reflected Vicki's taste rather than her father's. She felt unmoved by these contents; they could have been anyone's.

Then she turned to the next box. Here were more shirts folded in plastic laundry bags and several new pairs of socks with their labels still attached. Under the clothing was a bundle of papers, but they weren't personal, only assorted statements and real estate transaction documents. At the bottom of the box was a plaque honoring Charlie Stevens for his contribution to the Bay Area Real Estate Association. She held it up to the light, wondering what this honor meant to him after so many years of effort. She'd never know the answer: even if her father were alive, he wouldn't have the language to tell her.

Rebecca didn't care as much that the boxes revealed so little as she would have even a week before. In this unexpected journey to Clear Lake, her father had become less form and more spirit, and she didn't need concrete reminders of him. Even his ashes didn't matter so much anymore. She was moving beyond him, beyond the old, familiar sorrow of his death, to an internal freedom.

She threw open the door to the deck, letting in the cool breeze. The frogs in the water had begun their nocturnal song and their croaks filled the darkening room. She glanced at the kitchen table, the comfy sofa, and the pine walls, this magical space that she'd come to love. Everything looked just right—except for the mess from Charlie's boxes scattered all over the floor. Quickly cramming his things back together, she pushed the boxes back under the bed and began the task of lighting her nightly candles.

July arrived. The speedboats at the lake multiplied and buzzed over the glassy surface in the distance, pulling tiny figures along in their wakes. Sometimes the boats headed toward the cabin, veering sharply away when they got too close to the reeds. The sound of firecrackers now filled the air, reminding Rebecca that other people lived nearby although she never saw them. On the Fourth of July she perched on her deck, watching the cascading stars and bursts of color above the lake, and when the fireworks were over she heard the cheering of her neighbors up and down the shore.

Despite Rebecca's intentions, she was being drawn back into the world. She began to notice more about her surroundings: the ducks honking at each other in the reeds, the pear shape of Mount Konocti in the distance across the lake, the faded reds and oranges of sunset, the scummy algae on the water. Everything around her seemed more distinct and three-dimensional, filled with infinite possibility, so different from the flat surface that had been the background for her tumultuous feelings during these past weeks.

One hot afternoon Rebecca began to feel restless. This cabin, which had held her through so many states of being, felt confining, and she decided to venture outside. Her sneakers, which she hadn't put on since she arrived, felt tight and uncomfortable as she wandered down the two-lane road that bordered the northern end of the lake. In the distance she could hear the noise of traffic on the main highway, but the neighborhood seemed empty and quiet, people staying indoors, out of the heat. She walked past mobile homes clustered together in parks with names like Water View and Sunset Hill, and on the lake side of the road were ranch houses and fixed-up cottages, the typical Clear Lake residences she'd noticed that first day. Seeing them wedged together with any hardly space between, she realized again her good fortune in finding her private little cabin.

Soon she came upon a narrow park running down to the lake. A rickety pier extended into the water and Rebecca walked to the end of it, ignoring the sign that warned of risk. The water below looked unappealing and murky without the reeds to hide it, and she gazed at a dead bird caught on a woodpile and a beer can floating a few yards beyond reach. With all this garbage and pollution, she thought that the lake was the ugliest she'd ever seen, yet in the weeks she'd been there, she'd come to love it with the feeling of one who is drawn to disrepair.

As Rebecca headed back toward the cabin, she passed by an old man limping slowly down the street, leaning on a twisted wood cane. She nodded at him, not yet ready to talk to anyone, but she couldn't help but wonder who he was and what had brought him here. A few feet away she heard the man cry out, and when she turned around, he looked as if he were about to topple over. She rushed to his side, steadying him.

"Thanks, darling," he said.

"Can you make it home okay?" she asked. These first words sounded forced, but she settled into them.

"I could use a little help."

The man grasped tightly onto her arm, and they made their way to a tiny cottage down the street, where an equally ancient woman stood at the door, hands on hips, glaring at him. "Didn't I tell you?" she shouted. "Get in here right now."

"This nice young lady helped me home," the man said.

"She should have left you in a ditch."

"Well, she didn't."

The woman stomped onto the porch. "You're too damn much trouble."

"Not as much as you," the man said. "Ha, ha."

The woman beckoned toward Rebecca, her face mottled with despair. "Do you want him? Take him, he's yours."

The couple's nastiness was too much for Rebecca, and she walked away. A little farther down the road, she looked back and saw them on their porch, still arguing. For one moment she considered rushing back and rescuing the old man, but she continued on her way without a feeling of guilt.

It didn't take her long to return to her cabin. After this first entry into the neighborhood, the room looked smaller and more cramped, even a little dark. A few colorful flowers would brighten it up, she decided. She hadn't seen any growing wild in the neighborhood, so she'd need to buy some in town at the grocery store. That would mean breaking her silence even more, but she knew she was ready. Besides, she'd had enough of the Spartan food she had bought when she first arrived, and she was hungry for something better. A crusty loaf of French bread and a chunk of brie would be just fine, with slices of fresh, ripe peaches to finish off the meal.

Rebecca poured herself a glass of cold water from the refrigerator and sank into the cushions on the deck, weary from the walk. Tonight she'd tackle that puzzle of Monet's *Water Lilies* she'd found in a cupboard, but in the meanwhile, a feeling of satisfaction settled over her. Raising her glass of water, she sang out: "Here's to Clear Lake."

14

In the weeks that followed, Rebecca left the cabin more often. She went for walks in the neighborhood, and she ventured farther away on a nearby dusty trail, winding into the mountains past manzanita bushes and oak trees. The grass on the slopes was bleached from the sun and it waved in the wind, making a soft rustling sound that she loved. One day she found a mammoth rock standing alone at the top of a nearby mountain with a ledge just big enough to hold her. She climbed onto it and sat there for a long time, gazing at the view before her. The mountains rolled far into the distance and the sky above was crystal blue, as Clear Lake should be. She returned to this peaceful spot, her own special place, often, and she brought along water and lunches of fruit, cheese, and bread. The effort of climbing into the mountains made her stronger and more surefooted, and her body hardened into a new, smaller shape that pleased her. Her belly was flat and her thighs had lost their flabbiness, and she felt healthier than she had in years.

The evening hours were her favorite. She sat on the deck, watching the shifting colors of the sky after sunset, relishing the quiet that descended on the lake, and when it became dark she lit the candles in the cabin and slowly got herself something to eat—a bowl of vegetable soup she'd made on the hot plate from the fresh summer harvest, or a plate of pasta, mushrooms, and tomatoes, sprinkled with fresh Parmesan cheese. Sometimes she simmered ears of corn she'd bought at a nearby farmer's stand, and she savored the berries and melons she found there. She tasted each distinct flavor, letting them linger on her tongue rather than gulping down her food as she had done for years. Later in the evening, she read a book or worked on the *Water Lilies* puzzle that now covered the kitchen table.

One late July afternoon, Rebecca left the cabin to go to the drugstore to drop off the discs from her Nikon. She was taking her camera everywhere with her now, and she wanted to see prints of the photographs she'd taken in recent weeks. Her photographer's eye was drawn less to the beauty around her and more to shabbiness—the scum on the lake, the rickety pier, the falling-down cottages. She envisioned a book of Clear Lake photographs, black and white, gritty and moving, paradoxical in tone.

The drugstore was crowded inside, and she waited in line behind a man with softly graying blond hair. When he glanced back her way, she noticed the crinkly laugh lines around his eyes, and they nodded to each other. As she left the drugstore she had a sudden craving for something sweet, the first she'd had in weeks, and she went into the Kafe Kup, a café nearby: a bowl of ice cream would cool her off on this sweltering summer day as well as satisfy her sweet tooth.

She ordered chocolate ice cream and settled into a booth at the rear of the café. She intended to read the newspaper she had bought, the *Lake County News*, but she hardly got beyond the front page before she felt a presence above her. "Mind if I join you?" asked the man she'd seen at the drugstore.

She looked up. "If you want."

He slid into the booth across from her. "I'm Daniel Cohen," he said. His eyes were turquoise blue, a startling color, and he looked at her with interest.

She hesitated for a moment, but then she introduced herself and they shook hands. His handshake was firm and easy, she noticed, and his fingers were beautifully tapered.

"What are you doing at Clear Lake?" he asked.

"I'm a tourist." This was the first thing that came to her mind, although once she said it, it sounded abrupt and not quite right. "I've been traveling around this summer and landed at Clear Lake," she added.

"Why here? There are so many better places to go in California."

She shrugged, wishing she had a quick, clever answer to give.

"A woman of mystery," Daniel smiled. "I respect that."

"Tell me about you," Rebecca said.

He ran his fingers through his hair. "I'm working on my novel here. A friend is letting me use his cottage this summer since I'd never get it done at home." He went on to tell her that he taught history at San Francisco State University, and his three little boys stayed part-time with him. "When the kids are around, it's complete chaos. Just before I left the city, one of them rammed his bike into a wall and I had to rush him to the emergency room, dragging along the other two. That was a day I was supposed to be seeing students at the university."

"Was he okay?'

"They're always okay. Those boys are made of rubber."

Rebecca noticed a short scar on Daniel's arm and had the sudden impulse to reach out and trace it with her fingertip, but instead she took another bite of ice cream. "You're ambitious to be writing a novel," she said.

"Or foolish," he said. "I'm not sure I can pull it off." He fixed his eyes on Rebecca. "I've been talking so much, but I'm curious about you."

"I'm a therapist," she said. "I live near Chicago with my husband. I have two kids, so I know something about family chaos, although they've grown up and gone off on their own. I came to Clear Lake by myself a few months ago, intending to stay a few days, but I had a breakdown and didn't leave."

Daniel leaned back. "I didn't expect that."

"But now I'm on the other side of it."

"That must have been something to go through," he said. "A lot of people stay buttoned up tight and wonder why they feel so miserable."

"I see clients like that every day. I just didn't acknowledge that I was one of them." Rebecca wiped her mouth with a napkin, feeling more comfortable now. "What about you? Are you buttoned up tight?"

"Repression is not my thing," he smiled.

"I had to get away from work and everyone I knew before I could let myself go through it," she said.

"What was your breakdown like?"

Rebecca closed her eyes. "A horrendous storm, but with its own beauty. And then it subsided."

"Sounds dramatic."

"Clear Lake was a good place for it." Rebecca pushed her bowl of ice cream over to Daniel. "Here, have some."

Daniel took a bite and pushed the bowl back. "Everything happens in Clear Lake," he said.

"Like people polluting the water," she said. They began to talk about the state of the lake. "It's hard to understand how people can live here and not be bothered by the destruction," Rebecca said.

"They're not like us."

He was thinking of them as an "us," Rebecca noted. She was flattered, but his familiarity made her uneasy. "I like it here," she quickly said. "It suits me."

"A good place to have a breakdown," Daniel said.

"And write a novel. You don't have to worry about people dropping by."

"Except for my kids. They've been stuck with their mom all summer, and I promised them they could come up for a week. I can't imagine what they'll do here."

"They'll find something."

Daniel studied Rebecca's face. "I need to get back to work, but why don't you come to my place tonight and we'll continue our conversation over a glass of wine? I have a 2009 Syrah that I picked up at a vineyard close by."

Rebecca hesitated. "No, thanks," she said. Even though she was drawn to this man, she relished the tenderness of being alone in the evenings and didn't want to break it too quickly.

"Are you sure?"

"I'm sure," she smiled. "But I'll be back here tomorrow afternoon about this time. I need to stop by the drugstore. If you're around, we can talk over coffee."

In the days that followed, Rebecca and Daniel continued to see each other at the Kafe Kup. The locals came and went—not many tourists bothered to visit the area—and they sat in the back booth, undisturbed. At first they told each other the broad outlines of their lives, but the stories deepened and became more detailed as they came to know each other. "I was drinking too much," Rebecca said after describing her life in Skokie. "I became narrow and self-satisfied, an old lady before my time." It felt so good to be this honest with somebody.

"I haven't been a decent father," Daniel told her. "I don't spend enough time with my kids, and I can't blame anyone but myself."

"I'm bored with being a therapist," she said. "My heart isn't in it, and that affects my work. I'd like to quit, but I'm scared. What else would I do?"

"The breakup with my wife was my fault," Daniel said. "I have to admit it. I was restless, and it drove her crazy."

"Restless?" Rebecca raised an eyebrow.

"Other women. She got tired of it. I don't blame her."

"Wives don't like that kind of thing," Rebecca said. "That's what happened in my first marriage. I left the guy."

"And with Stan?"

"He's rock steady."

"But he doesn't interest you anymore."

"I wouldn't say that."

"But I'm right, aren't I?"

"Yes," she sighed.

They discussed politics—their worries about the rise of the right wing and their discouragement about Obama's accomplishments in a divided Congress—and they talked about films. His favorite oldie was *Citizen Kane*, and hers was *Brief Encounter*. One day they arrived at the subject of religion, and Daniel became especially animated. "My family never had anything to do with Judaism while I was growing up," he said, "but I've always been interested. Through the years I taught myself Hebrew, and I've done a lot of studying. Now I practice Judaism in my own way."

Rebecca, who had been drinking coffee, put down her mug. "I'm Jewish on my mother's side, or at least that's what my father told me, and my husband is Jewish. But I don't know much about it."

"You can learn."

"I don't believe in God," she replied. "I never have."

"What does that have to do with it?"

"The teachers at Methodist Sunday school said you can't have religion without a belief in God," she smiled.

"That's just Christianity," Daniel laughed. "In Judaism, anything goes. I don't do all the things that really religious people do, that's for sure. But I've discovered that there's great beauty in many of the practices. Like Shabbat. It's just what I need."

"Do you go to synagogue on Shabbat?"

"I'm too much of a rebel."

"I've been to lots of bar and bat mitzvahs," Rebecca said. "A friend, Ella, even got me going to synagogue with her several times, but it didn't stick."

"Shabbat at home is entirely different."

"I don't know anything about that."

"Come over to my place this Friday," Daniel said, "and I'll teach you all about it."

"Is that a challenge?" she asked, amused.

"You're pretty feisty for a woman who's just had a breakdown."

"I have nothing to lose."

"That means you're coming?"

"Yes," she laughed. "I'll be there."

Late that Friday afternoon, Rebecca readied herself to go to Daniel's house, putting on a creamy blouse that brought out the rich brown color of her eyes and fell over her breasts in a way she liked. But she felt a nervous tickle in her throat and unsteady on her feet, and at the last minute she decided to stay in the cabin. But that would be terribly rude—she had forgotten to get Daniel's phone number and couldn't call him to cancel, and he was preparing a dinner for the two of them. Back and forth she went, deciding one way and the other until she finally rushed out to the car, already late.

She got lost on the way to his house, taking the wrong dirt road, turning around, trying another. She chided herself for getting into a situation where she felt so anxious. But finally she found the house on a rocky piece of land up the hill from the lake. He'd been right when he told her the house was a dump, and as Rebecca parked in the driveway she noticed the bad paint job and missing shutters.

Through the porch window she saw Daniel working at his computer, completely engrossed. Her anxiety about coming there eased, and a feeling of warmth spread through her. He looked up from the computer, and when he saw her on the porch he smiled and moved with ease across the room to open the door. "I'm so glad you're here," he called. "I've been writing all afternoon—a big breakthrough—and I lost track of the time."

Rebecca looked around the house, noting that it was in better shape inside than out. Daniel, it seemed, was a tidy man, with his books stacked neatly in the bookshelves, papers in file boxes on the counter, and the dining table already set with plates and silverware. In the middle of the table was a bouquet of purple and pink summer flowers. She was impressed.

"I don't want you to lift a finger. You're my guest tonight," he said. "I was planning on having everything ready but I got a little behind schedule. The chicken is in the oven, though, and I have only a few more things to do."

Rebecca planted herself on the couch, thumbing through a book of poetry, listening to him move about the kitchen. The water ran and he chopped something, and there was a clunk of dishes. A few minutes later he appeared with a bottle of wine and a colorful salad of tomatoes and cucumbers and put them on the table. She smiled at him, enjoying being taken care of. "Don't rush for my sake. I'm in no hurry," she said.

"Shabbat starts soon," he answered. "I like to start on time. The rest of my life might be chaotic, but this gives me a sense of order."

The last of the afternoon's light poured through the windows, making broad patterns on the hardwood floor, and she let herself move into Daniel's rhythms. She'd decided before she came tonight that she would be open to wherever Shabbat took her. "I'm showering now," he said, passing through the room. "Then we'll be ready."

Ten minutes later Daniel reappeared in a clean shirt, calmly humming. "Now we can begin," he said, smiling at Rebecca. "The sun is just setting. It's time." He reached out for her hand. "Come."

He led her to the fireplace and slowly lit two white candles on the mantle. Covering his eyes, he sang something in Hebrew with great feeling. Rebecca felt strangely peaceful, and the tightness in her body eased even more, as though the light of the candles was penetrating every part of her. Daniel turned around, his face radiant, and kissed her gently on the forehead. "Good Shabbas," he said. She repeated the phrase back to him.

He motioned for her to sit down, and he began to sing more Hebrew prayers, his voice clear and strong with feeling. Sometimes he clapped his hands, other times he threw his head back. She had no idea what the words meant, but when she closed her eyes, shapes and colors drifted into her consciousness. She felt that she was in a rarified world with this man she was getting to know. "*Sh'ma Israel*," he sang, pressing a hand to his eyes.

The service soon came to an end, and they went together to the table for dinner. "But first we bless the wine and the bread," he said, lifting a cup of wine and a challah, singing something more.

Rebecca took a sip of wine—her first since she'd arrived in Clear

Lake, but this was ritual drinking, not drinking to numb herself—and she broke off a piece of challah and smeared it with honey. She was hungry, but she slowed her pace, the way she did at the cabin, and let herself fully taste each delicious bite. "I found a place in town that makes this challah," Daniel said. "Who would have thought?"

"It's perfect," she said.

He brought a platter of roasted chicken and potatoes from the kitchen, and they slowly ate their meal. "How do you like Shabbat?" he smiled.

"How could I not?" she replied dreamily. She was in the same state of stillness and contentment she had experienced alone in the cabin— but now she was doing it with Daniel. She hadn't known such a thing was possible.

"People call Shabbat an island in time. The idea is to take ourselves out of everyday reality for twenty-four hours. It changes everything."

A soft, warm light bathed the room, and the colors of the everyday objects seemed to have intensified, just as they had in the cabin. The tattered rug became a brilliant purple and orange, the poster of a seascape on the wall a rich blue. And the food on the table, the tastes and textures, the colors and smells, became one vibrating whole. Through the windows Rebecca saw the purplish night sky. "It's so beautiful," she said softly.

"The main point of Shabbat is to be happy," Daniel said. "We're commanded to put aside the work and worry of the other six days and enjoy ourselves."

"It's almost too good to be true," she murmured.

They lingered over their meal and left the dishes on the table. Daniel led Rebecca outside, into the night. Together they gazed at the shimmering sky with millions of sparks of light and a sliver of the new moon suspended above. "Just imagine, people have been looking into the night sky for centuries," he said. "I like to think of that."

Rebecca couldn't answer. She felt caught up in something so much bigger than herself, and she had no words for it, only gratitude. Daniel was showing her the way and she was following, her usual resistance dispelled. And when he began to stroke her face and then her breasts, she melted into him. "Come," he said, and they went into the bedroom together.

15

The next morning Rebecca woke up in Daniel's bed. After intense, satisfying lovemaking, they'd fallen into a deep sleep, and she hadn't thought of going back to her cabin late at night. Daniel was breathing gently next to her, still asleep, and she began to stroke the silky hair on his chest. It was like the grass on the California hillsides that flattened out when the wind blew and sprang up again when it subsided.

"I'm so glad you're here," Daniel whispered, opening an eye.

"Me too," she whispered back.

He leaned over to kiss her and then he pulled himself out of bed, his lithe body gleaming in the sunlight that filled the room. Rebecca watched him slip into his pants. "I'll make coffee," he said, "and then we can study some Torah together if you'd like. It's what I usually do on Shabbat mornings."

Over a breakfast of coffee and challah, Daniel began to talk about the Torah. "Jews all over the world study the same section of the Torah each week," he said. "We work our way through the whole thing over the course of the year."

"One people, connected through Torah," Rebecca said. "That's beautiful. In the synagogue where I went for a while, the portion was read aloud and then somebody gave a little sermon, usually quite dull, and that was that. I got the impression that Torah was something to get through, not something that was inspiring."

"That's so misguided," Daniel replied. "If we take the time to really delve into the words, they open up other realms of understanding."

"Let's do it," Rebecca said, intrigued.

"Today we have one of the most provocative portions. It's about the wandering of the Jewish people in the desert."

They read the text from Daniel's Bible, and they began to study it together, searching the words for hidden meanings, discussing the ideas. Rebecca loved sharpening her mind against Daniel's. Sometimes they had different interpretations, sometimes they agreed. "What do you think Moses meant when he called the Jews a stiff-necked people?" he asked at one point. She answered it probably had to do with exaggerated pride, and he thought for a moment then said it could be anger or stubbornness too. They talked a lot about what it felt like to wander. "I've never felt completely at home anywhere," she said. "There's something in me that feels unsettled." He told her he'd always had a sense of being in exile, that it was an existential fact of his life.

After almost three hours, their conversation came to an end and she suggested they go for a walk. They started down the dirt driveway and onto the road, but soon they passed a house with loud rock music playing and another where a man was using a power blower. "Let's go back," Daniel said. "This is too noisy for me on Shabbat."

In the house they ended up in bed again. Their lovemaking this time was slow and easy, and when Rebecca came it was in waves rather than the sharp, shaking highs of the night before. They fell asleep holding on to each other. Later she opened her eyes and saw on the clock that it was six o'clock, exactly the time she had arrived at Daniel's place the day before.

It had been the most perfect twenty-four hours.

But Rebecca's magical feeling began to fade over the supper of leftover chicken and salad that Daniel spread out for them. She couldn't help but picture Stan puttering around at home, dejected and alone on this Saturday night, trying to fill the empty space with noise from the TV that he had moved into the kitchen after she left. He was still her husband, even though she'd found herself a lover who satisfied her so much more than he ever could. She buttered a piece of challah, but when she took a bite, she couldn't swallow. She'd let herself become involved with Daniel without a thought or care about Stan. "I've got to leave," she said, overcome with guilt. "Right now."

"But why?"

"I've got to think about what I'm doing."

Daniel gave her a long look then nodded. "Okay. I understand. I'll walk you out."

Her desire to get away was so strong that when Daniel asked her to stop to look at the night sky with him one more time before she left, she said she couldn't. He wrote down his cell phone number and told her to call him as soon as she was ready, and he kissed her good-bye. She drove quickly down the driveway to the road and back to the cabin.

But once there, she wasn't able to concentrate on anything, certainly not on her feelings about Stan. Instead she drifted around, daydreaming about Daniel and how he touched her with his long, tapered fingers and kissed every part of her body.

During the next few days, Rebecca continued in this dreamy state. She felt like an adolescent caught up in her first romance. The thing to do, she decided on Wednesday, was to write down her thoughts and feelings about her marriage. That would help her sort them through, which she told herself she should do before seeing Daniel again. She pulled her laptop out from under the bed, plugged it in, and turned it on. She created a new document, "My Marriage," and closed her eyes. "Good things," she typed, intending to make a list, but she couldn't think of what to put there. "Bad things," she tried, but that didn't work either. Instead she started to write about Daniel, and the words flowed.

She couldn't wait to see Daniel any longer, even though she'd figured out nothing about Stan. She called his cell and urgently asked him to come to the cabin. "Tonight, for dinner," she said, and he replied that he'd be so pleased to come. She readied the cabin for his arrival, washing the dishes in the sink and straightening the spread over the bed. Charlie's copper urn still sat in the corner by the couch, and she decided it was time to put it aside. She took it outside to her car, opened the trunk, and slipped it in. Then she set about making a salad with the fresh vegetables she'd bought at the farmer's market that day, and she put out the special goat cheese she'd bought. A pot of potato leek soup simmered on the hot plate, and she sliced the fresh rye bread from the bakery. She hardly noticed what she was doing as she went through these simple chores, so great was her anticipation.

Daniel appeared at the cabin promptly at seven. "So this is where you've been hiding out," he smiled.

They nestled into each other, and Rebecca led him outside to see her view of Clear Lake. The sun was just setting, a moment of stillness before the evening arrived with its familiar sound of croaking frogs. "The lake looks lovely from here," Daniel said. "But it has a certain putrid odor." They laughed together in a familiar way.

Inside the cabin they settled down over the meal she'd prepared. With the candles lit around the room, the pine walls had a warm, intimate glow. Daniel began to talk more about his three sons, "a pack of wolves," he joked. "They have so much energy they run me ragged. I should have had them when I was in my twenties or thirties, not my forties." Rebecca listened as he told her about his guilt about not being a more patient, understanding father.

"It's really hard to raise kids," she said. "I remember when my two always seemed to be fighting. I lost my temper more than I wanted. I'm afraid I wasn't a good mother a lot of the time." The images of Annie and Paul flooded into her mind, and she missed them terribly in that moment. "You're lucky your kids are still young," she said. "You're still important to them. Mine have drifted away."

"You'll always be their mother."

"I know, but still . . . There's not a lot I can do for them anymore, and I miss that."

"My parents are unhappy that I moved so far from New York," he said. "But coming to California was probably the smartest thing I ever did."

"Because?"

"I'm freer here."

"You sound like a New Age ad," she smiled. "But I know what you mean. Things are less moored here."

"Like a boat let loose on Clear Lake," he laughed.

Rebecca put down her fork. "I wish I could stay," she said.

"Why can't you?"

"What would I do?"

"Your photography. Develop your creativity. You could get a day job to support yourself."

"And Stan?"

"You'd figure that out." Rebecca noted appreciatively that Daniel didn't push her for answers about Stan; he seemed to accept her complex feelings and hadn't even mentioned her abrupt departure last Saturday night.

"I guess I would."

"Think about it. You grew up in California, so it would be like returning home."

They had finished the meal, and she got up to clear the table. She hadn't seriously considered staying in California, but Daniel made it sound so easy, just a switch in work and marital status, and then a new life. But that was Clear Lake dreaming, not reality. Reality was making the hard decision to leave Stan and let go of a successful professional practice. If she did those things, maybe Daniel would be there for her, or maybe he wouldn't. She told herself not to even think about the future. Tonight this man was in her cabin, looking at her with the most loving eyes, and she was filled with great desire.

The rest of July passed and August arrived, hot and dry. Daniel and Rebecca spent nights together at his place or hers. He talked to her about his writing and how frightened of failure he was. He'd written nonfiction before—articles and books, enough to get him tenure at the university—but a novel was a different matter, much more intimidating. This one was set in the early industrial period in England, a subject he knew a lot about, but he was still struggling with the plot. Rebecca read what he had written, and she suggested that he heighten the rivalry between the two brothers, the main characters, and sharpen their emotions. He appreciated her support and reciprocated by paying careful attention to her photography. She showed him the photos she'd been taking at Clear Lake, and he thought they captured the atmosphere brilliantly. He suggested other places she could photograph, a garbage dump close to his house, a tree split in two by lightning.

Judaism was a big topic in their conversations; she plied him with questions, and he passed on what he knew. She grew to understand that she'd been hungering for something spiritual in her life for a long time, although she hadn't named it, and she spoke to him about this.

Rebecca tried to keep the affair with Daniel in perspective—he was a summer fling and that was all—but each day she became more attached to him. This both excited and alarmed her. When they slipped into bed at night, she didn't think about being married, but afterward her guilt returned and she felt ashamed. She called Stan every few days, checking in, not saying much, mostly silent like her father had been on the phone. She'd learned the lesson of evasion well. As Stan chatted on, she felt burdened by her dishonesty, telling herself that she had to make a decision about her marriage soon.

One evening she called Ella in Chicago, knowing that she'd be in her apartment recuperating from a long day of seeing clients. "I've met someone here," she told her. She went on to describe Daniel, "a history professor—but so much more, such a beautiful man, you should see him, and he's a writer. We spend a lot of time talking about our creative work—I've never had that before—and sex with him is unbelievable."

"I'm jealous," Ella said. "It sounds like you've really fallen for him."

"It's just an affair." Rebecca said. "But it seems like more."

"You're long overdue."

"You should see my smile." Rebecca felt her happiness stretch through her whole face, into her eyes, through her body. "It's huge."

"So what's the problem?"

"Stan," Rebecca said. "You know."

"Of course."

"Truthfully, I don't want to go back to him."

"Then don't."

"It's not that simple," Rebecca said. She paused. "But maybe it is."

An hour after the conversation with Ella, Daniel called to say that he'd just heard from his ex-wife that Colleen, a mutual friend of theirs, was bringing his three sons up to the Clear Lake cottage for their vacation. Because of this, he wouldn't be able to come to her cabin that night. Rebecca, who'd heard so many stories about these children, was pleased with this news and looked forward to meeting them. "That's great," she said. "I'll come by and see them tonight at your place."

Daniel hesitated. "You'd better wait until I call."

"Of course," she answered quickly, realizing that the boys needed to settle in with their father before meeting his new friend.

"Colleen might stay for a few days," he said. "I don't want her to know about you."

"Why?"

"She'd tell my ex-wife."

"But you're divorced," Rebecca said. "Surely your ex-wife expects you to be involved with other women."

"She'd go ballistic."

"I see." Rebecca didn't see, exactly, but she knew how tangled relationships between divorced spouses could be.

"I'll let you know when the time is right," he said. "It might be a while."

She hesitated. "Okay. I guess."

Two days passed. Rebecca kept her phone on all the time, telling herself that this little break from Daniel didn't hurt. In fact, it felt good to be alone again. Without the distraction of his presence, she settled back into her cabin and returned to her photography project. Recently a family of brown quacking ducks had taken up residence in the water below the deck, and she was fascinated by the sight of their rounded bodies against the straight lake reeds. If she could catch the right light, she'd have a compelling shot.

On the afternoon of the third day, the atmosphere was quiet in the way she'd come to expect. The sky was cloudy, unusual at Clear Lake that summer, but the sun darted in and out, casting long shadows on the water. This would be the perfect day to capture that photograph. She brought her camera to the deck and sat patiently, waiting.

Suddenly there was a loud banging outside the cabin, and she ran to the door and threw it open. There stood Stan, a big grin on his face. She stared at him for a few seconds, hardly believing it was him. "My god, what are you doing here?" she screeched.

"I wanted to surprise you," he laughed. "I guess I did."

"How did you ever find this place?"

"I tracked you down through the check you wrote to the realtor. When I called her and asked for the address, she obliged. I'm your husband, after all." He looked proudly at Rebecca, as though he was pleased with his cleverness, but he also seemed a little hesitant. "Aren't you going to welcome me?"

She kissed Stan's scratchy, unshaven cheek, noticing he smelled like stale airplane air. "I sure didn't expect you."

"I got tired of staying home alone."

"Come on in," she said grudgingly. "Why didn't you let me know you were coming?"

"You've been impossible to reach all summer." Stan plopped down on the couch, wiping the sweat off his face with his sleeve. "Whew, it's hot in here. Don't you have air conditioning?"

"The heat doesn't bother me."

"As I say, it takes all kinds." He snorted at his little joke in the way she'd always found embarrassing.

Rebecca gave him a glass of water.

"Aren't you glad to see me?" he asked.

"No," she said, determined not to lie. "I've relished this time alone and I don't want it interrupted."

"Miriam said that's how you'd feel," he said.

"She was right."

"But I thought that maybe I could persuade you to go on a little trip with me. We could drive over to Mendocino and stay in an inn on the ocean. It says on the Internet that it's really nice there."

For a moment Rebecca wavered, feeling guilty about how she'd abandoned him, but she said, "Sorry, not interested."

"But it's better than here."

"I'm not leaving Clear Lake," she said firmly.

"Well, if you won't, we could have some fun in this cabin," he winked. "Or there must be a good air-conditioned hotel in the area with a bigger room. I don't know why you rented such a small place."

"Because I like it."

"But a bigger place with air-conditioning would be better."

Rebecca drew herself up. "Stanley, stop it."

He sighed, daunted for a moment. "I'm sorry. It's just that I've missed you. Can't I stay for a while?"

"Okay, for a while," she said, softening. "But promise you won't complain the whole time."

"I won't," he smiled. In his excitement he lifted her off the floor, hugging her tightly. "You've gotten so thin," he said. "I can feel your bones."

"Put me down," she said in a loud voice. "Let's be clear. While you're here, I'm working on my photography."

"Okay, that's a deal. But at night we'll eat dinner together, right?" he said. "We'll put a little meat on those bones of yours. There must be some great restaurants around here. California cuisine, and all that."

"Don't count on it," she sighed.

After Stan moved in, the cabin seemed to shrink. He'd brought enough clothes to last for the rest of the summer, and they spilled outside his suitcase and onto the floor. Even when he was fishing off a nearby pier or buzzing around the lake in a rented speedboat, Rebecca felt his presence and recoiled. At night he spread out on the double bed while she curled up on the couch. Whenever he tried to touch her, she pushed him away, making her distaste clear.

The longer Stan stayed, the more annoying Rebecca found him. His big, sweaty body repulsed her even more than usual, and she couldn't stand the way he grinned when nothing was funny. If she let him, he'd follow her around all the time, making stupid comments about how she was setting up her camera, or he'd bore her with talk about this or that sport, or he'd crack silly jokes. The things she had once loved about him—his clumsy grace, his eagerness—were now relegated to the past or completely forgotten.

At one point Stan said, "You're in a bitchy mood these days. I thought we'd have a good time together."

"You thought wrong," she answered.

The only time Stan and Rebecca got along better was when they ate out. Sitting on opposite sides of the table, they managed to return to an earlier state of goodwill, gossiping about people they knew, recounting their trips, remembering the time they'd looked all over the neighborhood for Ruckus but found him stuck in the garage. They talked more than they had for years. Rebecca thought of these dinners as their farewell speeches. "It wasn't all bad, was it?" Stan asked more than once.

Six nights after Stan arrived they drove together to the other end of the lake for dinner at a place known for its good barbecue. Rebecca was especially quiet in the car. Over a week had gone by and Daniel hadn't called, but she knew how distracted he would be with the boys vying for his attention. He wasn't used to having them alone for so many days in a row, and he must be having trouble keeping them entertained. She imagined him taking them for a hike up the mountain or a swim in the town pool, trying to be a good father but resenting every minute they were keeping him away from working on his novel.

Still, it was strange that he hadn't called. With Stan in the cabin, she had worried that he might drop by unexpectedly. There would be an awkward moment, but Daniel would know how to handle it. She could call him, she supposed, but she wasn't sure if she should. Didn't he say to wait until he reached her?

Rebecca pulled up in front of the restaurant and began to park. Across the street, in the evening light, she spotted Daniel. With him was a tall, striking woman dressed in a tight sarong. Colleen, it must be. Three little boys trailed behind them, ignored. Daniel, who looked so familiar with his silver blond hair and long legs, seemed utterly engaged with this woman, his arm tightly wrapped around her, and she was holding onto him, her hand slipped into his back shorts pocket. They were laughing, and she lifted her face to his.

"Oh, shit," Rebecca cried.

"What's wrong?" Stan asked.

"Nothing," she answered, clenching the steering wheel. "Nothing at all."

"Then let's go get some food."

"I don't want to eat here," she said. "I'd rather go back to the cabin. We can get some Chinese take-out."

"Okay," he answered in a bewildered tone.

"Thanks," she said, grateful to him for once.

16

A s they sped back toward the cabin, Stan cracked his knuckles, the sound reverberating through the silent car. "Stop it," she said automatically. "You'll hurt yourself."

"No, I won't."

"Yes, you will."

A few more miles down the road, a deer darted into the road in front of them, its sleek tan body shining in the car lights. Rebecca screamed and jammed on the brakes, and the car veered to the side of the road, scraping against the branch of an oak tree before it stopped. "I can't stand it," she cried.

"At least we didn't hit the deer," Stan said.

Rebecca slid out of the car and tried to assess the damage, but the night was dark and she could only faintly see that there was a little dent and a scrape. She put her head in her hands and rocked back and forth. "What's going on out there?" Stan called.

The sound of his voice roused her. "Leave me alone," she yelled. She felt like a child who had been stripped of everything, and the only thing she could do was feel sorry for herself.

"The Chinese food is getting cold," Stan called after a few minutes.

Rebecca stood by the Audi, looking through the window at her husband in the dim light, seeing his heavy body scrunched into the passenger seat, his hand tapping his thigh impatiently. In that moment, the paralysis she'd felt all summer slid away. She climbed back into the car. "Stan, we have to talk," she said. "Tonight."

He glanced warily over at her. "Okay, sure. But let's eat first."

Back in the cabin Rebecca opened the cartons of cashew chicken and vegetable chow mein. Stan wolfed down his food while she picked at hers. "That was good," he said, wiping his face with a paper napkin. "What did you want to talk about?"

She set down her chopsticks. "Ever since you arrived, I've been angry at you," she said.

"I know that."

"I didn't like you coming here."

Stan tossed his napkin into the empty carton. "You've told me that several times already. I'm not stupid."

"No, you're not stupid," she said. "But you're obtuse. The truth is that I don't want to be married to you any longer. I've felt that way for a long time."

He collapsed back into his chair. "Goddammit, Rebecca."

"It's over, Stan. It's been dead between us for years now. I just didn't have the nerve or the heart to break it off."

"I've been happy," he muttered.

"It's not enough for me. And when I'm honest with myself, it never has been." Rebecca began to tell him about her loneliness and her frustration all these years. She was gathering up steam, presenting her case, and even now, even at this late date, she yearned for him to see it her way.

But Stan's face grew hard. "I've loved and supported you for almost fifteen years, and now you've had enough? What kind of person are you?"

Rebecca eyed him. "I've just been telling you about my unhappiness. Haven't you been listening?"

"There's something more," he said. "I know there is. What happened this summer that made you decide?"

"Nothing."

"I don't believe you."

She glared at him for a long moment. "Okay, I'll tell you," she said. "I had an affair. It made me see how much I've been missing. But that's not why I want to split up. The affair was just a symptom, not the cause."

He turned away furiously. "Who's the guy?"

"Nobody you know."

"You planning on staying with him?"

"The affair's over, for what it's worth," Rebecca answered. "And so is our marriage. I mean it."

"You want to get rid of me?" Stan jerked up from the table, his face filled with rage. "Okay, I'll be a good boy. I'll leave."

"Come on, Stan. Don't be like that."

"I hope you don't mind if I pack my suitcase first."

"Before you go, we need to talk about arrangements. The house, money, all that."

"You bitch," he yelled. "You fucking whore." He noisily threw his belongings together, swearing at her the whole time. She steeled herself to take his insults—he was in pain, and she felt sorry for him even though she couldn't wait for him to leave. After a half hour he rushed out into the dark night without saying good-bye.

Rebecca sat at the kitchen table with a sick feeling in her belly. She'd been heartless and cruel, and the revelation about her affair had been unnecessary. She had just been trying to be honest, but she should have stopped herself. She should have treated him in a kind, respectful way, as she always advised her divorcing clients to do.

She noticed one of Stan's T-shirts on the floor, left behind when he so hurriedly packed, and she picked it up and buried her face in it, breathing in his damp odor. "I'm a failure," she whispered into the shirt. "Stan wasn't such a bad husband. It's my fault for wanting too much." She stayed like that for a while, and her indictment of her failures grew to include everything else that had gone wrong—the divorce from Peter, the troubles with the children, her father's death.

She imagined calling Stan and telling him she was sorry and he should come back to the cabin right away. It was dangerous for him to him to be driving on the mountain roads at night in his state of mind, the car might spin out of control and go over the edge.

Only one call was needed. But she didn't make it.

The next morning, in the cabin filled with light, Rebecca stretched out in the double bed, wiggling her fingers and toes. The scene with Stan last night had been wrenching, but it was already becoming more of a memory than a living thing. Her feeling of remorse was fading, too, and she was greatly relieved to be alone in the cabin again. The sun slanted through the window, and little dust motes floated in the light like friendly visitors. She felt as though she could float upwards with them, her body no longer bound by the gravity of Stan.

Looking out the window, she noticed the leaves yellowing on the willow tree, the first sign of autumn. She'd need to make a decision soon about what she was going to do, but that was the future and today was today. Her mind went to Daniel and the shock of seeing him last night with Colleen. How had she managed to forget that one or another Colleen could come along and disrupt their affair? That denial was over now. On this fine day she'd celebrate her freedom from Stan and her return to reality about Daniel. She'd do it by picking up her photography project once again.

She made herself a cup of tea in a chipped blue mug she'd come to love, and she ate an apple and some cheese. The next step was deciding where she wanted to go today to take photographs. She could stay on the cabin deck—but then she remembered the craggy rock she'd discovered at the top of the mountain. She hadn't been there in weeks, and it would be a pleasure to return.

Her cell rang. "It's me," Daniel said, all warmth and friendliness. "I've been thinking about you."

She took a moment to answer. "What do you want?"

"Colleen left, but the kids are staying an extra few days. How about I bring them by to meet you?"

"I saw you with Colleen," Rebecca said in a stiff tone.

"You did? Where?"

"Walking down the street, all wrapped up in each other. Obviously a couple."

Daniel was silent for a moment. "I'm not going to deny it."

"What is going on?"

"She and I once were involved, and we fell into it again. Call it old times' sake," he answered. "But Colleen is gone now."

"And you want to start all over with me?"

"I'd like that," he said.

"That's not going to happen," Rebecca said in a flat voice.

"Why not?"

"Isn't it obvious? I'm pissed about Colleen. I don't like what you did. But okay, you can bring the kids by. You've told me so much about them, I want to meet them."

After the call, Rebecca thought that she had made a mistake, that it would be awkward to see Daniel after this conversation. But when he and his boys tumbled into the little cabin, she couldn't help but embrace him, although it was a quick hug. Her attention immediately went to the children. She had set out the games and toys the cabin owners had left behind, and they clamored around the table, laughing and quarreling. Once they settled down, she looked over at Daniel: "When did Colleen leave?"

"Last night," he answered. "She took off more time from work than she planned."

"You had a good time together?"

"Yes."

He wasn't offering an apology, and she dropped the subject. "Stan came to Clear Lake," she said. "Unannounced. He was here for a week. I finally told him the marriage is over."

"Good for you," Daniel said.

"I didn't handle it very well."

"Nobody does," he said. "But it's a relief, right?"

"You can say that."

"Although it's sad, too."

"Yes." Her eyes filled with tears.

Daniel opened his arms and she went to him, allowing herself to feel his warmth. "How about you coming over to my place tomorrow night," he said. "I'm driving the kids back to San Francisco to their mother's place in the morning, but I'm not staying in the city."

"No," she answered.

"Because of Colleen?"

"That's right," she said, pulling away from him.

"But you and I never had a commitment. I didn't lead you on."

"No, but you didn't tell me that Colleen was a lover." Rebecca looked fiercely at him. "I need to take care of myself. I could get hurt by you too easily."

"Maybe you won't," he said.

"I'm not taking any chances."

Daniel shrugged. "Okay. I understand. Sort of."

"I went through that in my first marriage. I'll never do it again."

He looked disappointed. "But we'll still be friends?"

"We'll see," she answered. "If I stay in California, I'll need all the friends I can get."

Eli, the youngest child, tugged at Daniel's shirt. "Play with your brothers," he said.

Rebecca led the kids onto the deck, handing them scraps of bread to throw to the ducks in the water below. Eli began to strip off his clothes as the ducks passed by, ready to jump into the lake and swim with them. "That's enough," Daniel yelled. "You know that water is polluted and you have to stay out of it. We're leaving right away."

"No," the boys yelled.

"They like it here," he said, defeated. Children clearly were not his forte.

After Daniel left, Rebecca walked around the cabin, putting the games and toys away, relieved that she had held firm to her decision to keep her distance from him. She would have liked to get on with taking photographs, but now it was too late to hike to the top of the mountain, the light there would be all wrong. She pulled out the photographs she'd taken during the summer, flipping through them, trying to find some kind of internal order, but she couldn't settle into it. Daniel's visit had made her more aware of all the uncertainties in her life.

Miriam, it seemed, was one of these uncertainties. They'd talked only a few times that summer, and Rebecca had a great desire to hear her voice. Seeing Daniel with his boys had reminded her of those years when her kids were growing up and Miriam had been so central in their family. Rebecca had loved her, and she had counted on her love and understanding for years, but the question was: Could she still count on it?

When Miriam answered the phone, her voice was cool. "Stan told me the news. He called from the San Francisco airport."

"What did he say?" Rebecca asked. "I wanted to reach you first. To explain."

"He told me you want a divorce."

"That's right," Rebecca answered cautiously. "Although I didn't actually say divorce. I told him I didn't want to be married any longer."

"What's the difference?"

"None, I guess."

"I'm not surprised about this news," Miriam said, "but I'm very, very sorry."

"Me, too."

"No, you're not," Miriam voice was angry. "You're glad it's over. At least be truthful."

"You're right," Rebecca said, chastened. "I am glad."

"I assume you're not coming back here."

"I don't know. Maybe not." This conversation seemed so cold and impersonal, so different from the warmth she was used to being there. "Miriam, what's going on?" Rebecca asked.

"You're a therapist. I shouldn't have to tell you," Miriam said. "I've loved you like a daughter, and now you're disappearing from me. That's hard to take."

"I'm not gone," Rebecca said, her voice rising. "I'm leaving Stan, not you. I'll always be connected to you."

"Be realistic."

She was silent for a moment. "I guess it won't be the same between us."

"No, it won't."

"But I love you so much," Rebecca cried. "I can't imagine life without you. You're so important to me."

"I know I am," Miriam said, sounding more familiar. "And I'll always love you, too. But you've made a decision, and we can't go back to where we were before. Remember that."

"You'll be there for Stan," Rebecca said woefully.

"That's right."

"He'll need you."

"He'll have me." Miriam's voice became brisk again. "And now I have to go. He's coming by on his way home from the airport. I told him I'd cook up some hamburgers."

"I want to visit you soon," Rebecca said, still clutching.

"I'd like that."

"And the kids will stay in touch. You're their grandma."

"Of course," she answered. "Tell them to call me anytime."

After Rebecca hung up, she felt bereft. She imagined the stories Stan would tell his mother over dinner that night: "She treated me like shit, she'd have nothing to do with me," he'd begin. Miriam would interrupt, reminding him of her advice not to go to Clear Lake. "But she had an affair this summer," he'd say. "How could she do that to me? And she told me our marriage is over." Miriam would see the pain in his eyes, and her motherly sympathy and protectiveness would emerge full force. It would be enough to break the bond between her and Rebecca.

For the rest of the afternoon and the next day, Rebecca wandered around the cabin in a state of sadness. She remembered that last embrace with Miriam, when she had held on so tightly to her, and she thought about the days with Stan and the way he had left the cabin. "I've made such a mess," she whispered to herself. "And now I'm alone."

And finally, at the end of the second day, she watched as the sun set behind Mount Konocti and the sky filled with streaks of brilliant orange and red—an unusually beautiful sunset. In the water below, the ducks bobbed in their ongoing search for food, and when they surfaced they quacked noisily. Wiping away her tears, Rebecca stood outside on the deck, and a feeling of calmness seeped through her. Even though she had been hurtful, even though she was now alone, even though she had no idea what she would do next, she had the feeling that somehow everything would work out.

"I made a decision, and I can't go back," she said aloud. This time the words didn't sound so bad.

17

Two weeks later, Rebecca drove to the mountain summit overlooking Clear Lake and stopped to take in the view. From this altitude the lake looked sparkling and perfectly blue, as it had when she passed that way three months ago. The mountains beyond spread eastward, dried by the sun's searing heat. Her vision this summer seemed to have sharpened, and she imagined that she could see not only the surface of these mountains but their mighty, ancient bones.

She could see herself more clearly, too. Her thoughts about Charlie now flitted lightly through her mind rather than weighing her down as they had before. She'd once heard that people mourn for years when a loved one dies under suspicious circumstances, and she knew that's what she'd been doing. Clear Lake, sitting like a jewel below, had made this possible, the decaying water mirroring her emotions.

She had driven away from the locked cabin earlier that day, planning to be gone for a few days. She'd brought along her camera, her laptop, and a small suitcase of clothes, and she'd left Charlie's urn back in the cabin, at the bottom of one of the boxes that Maria had given her. Charlie the father had faded into the past, but Rebecca still wasn't finished with investigating how he had died. During the height of her breakdown, all thoughts about this had been far from her mind, but a few days ago she had decided she had to resume the search. The thought came when she was observing the ants that invaded her cabin in a long trail, leading from the window to the countertop to the sink.

The phrase "long trail of death" popped into her mind. She drew in a sharp breath, realizing that she had not yet reached the end of Charlie's long trail. She'd have to revisit Lana and Maria one more time to try to find the truth of what happened with him; it was her only hope. The idea was not appealing—she had already let go of so much of the past—but she had pledged to do this.

Returning to the car at the summit, Rebecca continued on the two-lane road that wound down the other side of the mountain. She was ready to get away from Clear Lake. She'd had several awkward phone conversations with Daniel since the visit with the boys, and they met once at the Kafe Kup—he wanted to show her a new section of the novel. But when they sat across from each other in the booth, his eyes, which before had enchanted her, seemed dull. "I'm not happy with you pulling away from me," he said, holding on to his coffee mug. His apologetic expression amused her, and she began to laugh. "Have a little pity," he said. When it became clear that he wasn't winning her over, he packed up his manuscript and quickly excused himself. Rebecca watched him as he left, feeling sad at the loss of him. But then a woman came into the café bringing her new puppy, a cute, energetic spaniel, and she got caught up in the excitement with the rest of the customers.

The afternoon sun slanted through the front window of the Audi, and Rebecca blinked in the light. Everything around her seemed to shine, almost like it had on that first Shabbat with Daniel. Trees and rocks and sky held a radiance that she hadn't been able to see when she had traveled along this same road in the other direction at the beginning of the summer. Rebecca had smoked grass and hashish in the past with Peter and she knew how drugs could expand vision, but here she was, and her vision had opened without any help.

Soon the road joined Highway 101, and she headed south toward San Francisco. She drove through the gently rolling hills and reached the area of the vineyards. The purple grapes were now heavy on the dark green vines, ready for harvest. After an hour, the traffic on the freeway began to thicken. Jolted by the noise and the growing number of cars, she felt herself tighten and her vision contract. If she stayed in California—and she was thinking she would now—she'd want to live away from such congestion. A cottage in the country or a small house in a seaside town would be just fine, and she'd work intensively on her photography and find a job to support herself. When Shabbat came, depending on how she felt, she'd close her doors for twenty-four hours or invite others over to light the candles and have a meal.

Rebecca had introduced the possibility of living in California to Paul a few days ago. He had been delighted with the idea. "I'd much rather come to California to see you than have you live here," he said. He went on to describe his new interest in windsurfing, a sport he and his current girlfriend, Sinalda, had taken up that summer on Lake Michigan. They were researching places where they could go to do more of it and the equipment they needed. He'd read that the winds were good in California, especially in the San Francisco area. "When we come to visit, we'll windsurf," he said in a pleased tone.

"How do you feel about me leaving Stan?" Rebecca had asked.

"Fine. I never liked him, but you know that."

"It's a loss, nonetheless," she said.

"He wasn't my father."

"Still," Rebecca said, but she didn't push him any further.

Annie, however, had been distressed by her mother's news about separating from Stan and moving to California. "We were a family," she said, her voice gloomy. "It meant something to me." She went on to say that she couldn't imagine how Stan would survive alone.

"He'll be just fine," Rebecca said, although she wasn't entirely certain.

"But what about the house? It's where Paul and I grew up. I like having it there. And all our stuff?"

"We'll have to figure that out. Nothing will happen for a while," Rebecca said. "But even if the house gets sold, you won't lose Stan and Grandma Miriam. They'll be there for you. You know that, don't you? "

"It won't be the same."

"I suppose you're right," Rebecca replied. "But you have Paul and me. I'll find a place where you can come and stay. And there's your wonderful lesbian community at the university."

"Everyone's been away this summer," Annie said, her voice edged with unhappiness. "And I've been stuck working at the mall. Karina and I broke up. She said I wasn't there enough for her, but I couldn't stand all her drama, she could carry on for hours. I haven't seen any of my other friends in weeks, and at nights I sit in my room alone. It's depressing."

"I'm so sorry," Rebecca said. "But classes will start soon and things will change."

"Can't you and Stan stay put?" Annie said. "Everything in my life seems so up for grabs right now."

"I wish I could make it easier for you," Rebecca said, meaning it more than her words could convey.

"If you want to move someplace," Annie continued, "why don't you come to Denver? It's a great city, with lots of things to do. You would be close to where I am. We could spend time together."

"I'll think about it," Rebecca answered, touched by Annie's desire.

"I don't like California that much," she went on. "It's too crowded and intense. I remember that horrible house Grandpa Charlie bought." She paused. "By the way, whatever happened to it?"

"Lana, Vicky's daughter, is selling it." Rebecca launched into the details, giving her a full report.

Annie said nothing for a moment then spoke in a tight way. "You should have told me all about this before, Mom. I deserve to know. I'm your daughter, aren't I?"

"You're right, I've drifted too far from you," Rebecca said. It had happened quickly, but if she didn't watch out, she and Annie would become distant the way she and Charlie had been.

"Don't do it again, Mom." Annie's voice sounded clear, as if she had finally said what was on her mind.

"I won't," Rebecca answered, chastened. "I promise."

"Good."

"I want to see you soon," Rebecca said. "I'll come to Colorado, or you can come here." She paused. "In fact, why don't you fly out here right away? Put the ticket on your credit card, and I'll pay for it."

"I can't," Annie answered quickly. "I've got my job."

"Don't you have two days off in a row? Like this weekend? It would be a really nice break for you."

"Yes, but it turns out that some of my friends are coming back to town then. Sorry, Mom. I hope you understand."

"Of course I do," Rebecca said gently. Annie wanted her but only on her terms.

Rebecca continued south on Highway 101, refreshed by an early dinner she picked up at a café along the freeway. As she got closer to San Francisco, she saw that a bank of gray fog had started to roll in, and she opened her window and breathed the moist air. Ahead were the glittering lights of the city. She would have liked to go directly there, maybe take in a film or visit a bookstore, but that would have to wait for another time.

Tonight she was going to Jim's house. She had called him from Clear Lake that morning. "Why haven't you been in touch?" he'd asked. "You should have let me know you were okay. I worried about you." She had apologized and then said she was coming to town and would like to stop by.

Rebecca turned off Highway 101 and headed over the Richmond–San Rafael Bridge, toward the Berkeley hills. It didn't take long to wind up the streets to Jim's house, and he welcomed her with more warmth than she expected after their uneasy parting three months ago. She looked around the living room, at its big stone fireplace, overflowing bookshelves, and Fran's grand piano. "It's the same here as always," she smiled. "It's the closest thing I have to home." Jim looked at her quizzically, but she didn't explain. She handed him a gift: two bottles of wine, a jar of honey, a box of salted almonds. "Something from up north," she said. "A peace offering. I should have stayed in touch with you, I know. I'm sorry."

Jim uncorked one of the bottles. "None for me," Rebecca said. They settled on the big easy couch, and she began to tell him as honestly as she could about the summer—her breakdown, the little cabin, Daniel, the separation from Stan. He listened, not saying much.

"Now what?" he asked when she finished.

"It looks like I'm going to stay in California."

"What about your clients?" He paused. "You can't walk away from them, can you? It's one thing to take time off from your practice for the summer and another not to come back."

"I'll have to figure that out," Rebecca said. In her deliberations about the future, she hadn't gotten as far as this.

"Unless, of course, you're okay with being a person who abandons others. Maybe you are. You're doing that with Stan."

"Ouch," Rebecca said. She'd always seen herself as being the abandoned one, hurt by Charlie and then Peter, but it was true that she was doing the same to others. She had crossed some kind of threshold, although she hadn't thought of it that way. "I'm just a human being, not perfect," she said slowly. "I'm on the same level as everyone else."

"Don't be defensive. Just realize what you're doing," Jim said. His words sounded harsh, but she knew he was speaking from concern, not hostility. He was right, she needed to make sure she could live with the consequences of her actions.

Rebecca excused herself and went into the bathroom to pee. If she abandoned her clients, causing them pain, she would always regret it. This was true. She owed them the time to work through their feelings; many of them were attached to her and would be deeply upset by her disappearance. It became clear to her that she'd have to return to Chicago for a few weeks or even a month or two to close her practice in an honorable way—but then she'd return to California.

By the time she got back to the living room, Jim had put out a plate of cheese and crackers. "A nighttime snack," he said. "I've gotten in the habit in my old age."

"Are you lonely in this big house?" Rebecca asked.

Jim nodded. "Too much time for tiger thoughts."

"Tiger thoughts?"

"When it's late at night, I can't stop myself from thinking about all the times I didn't come through for people I cared about. Even Fran. That's why I don't want you to have regrets about what you're doing."

The two of them were back on track and could even joke about what had happened at the beginning of the summer. "That was something, you riding off with Charlie's urn strapped in the front seat of the car," he laughed.

"And you scowling at me as I left."

Jim, ever practical, continued to press her about her plans. "You need to consider how you'll support yourself," he said. "It's a lousy economy out there."

"I won't starve," she said. "But that's enough fatherly concern from you. I'll figure it out."

"You'll stay in touch? Not like this summer."

"I will."

Rebecca stayed overnight at Jim's place and through the next day. After dinner she said good-bye, promising to return soon. Now she was on her way to San Francisco to see Lana. She had phoned her from Jim's house—she didn't tell him because he'd want to know what she was doing and then he'd object. At first Lana had been unfriendly on the phone, as she had expected, but Rebecca had taken a different approach, apologizing for how she'd acted earlier that summer, acknowledging that she'd been provocative and demanding. She hadn't begged to see Lana again, nor had she spoken in a threatening way, and when she said she was in town and would like to meet for coffee, Lana had agreed. Rebecca was surprised it had been that easy.

At nine o'clock that night, Rebecca entered a café two blocks from

Lana's townhouse in San Francisco. Lana arrived a few minutes later, bundled up against the fog in a long black coat. The two women greeted each other in a reserved way and ordered cappuccinos, carrying them to a quiet table over to the side. Rebecca felt pleased to be with Lana again despite their earlier difficulties, and she hoped that Lana shared this feeling at least a little. The café was dimly lit, the lights on the walls directed upward at an exhibit of seascapes. Rebecca tried to see Lana's face clearly; it seemed she was wearing less makeup, and there were some little lines around her eyes Rebecca had not noticed before. Her long blond hair was wrapped up with a scarf. Although she was still beautiful, she looked more like a regular person than an intimidating model.

Their conversation started off slowly, but it didn't feel as awkward as it had earlier that summer. "Did you sell the house?" Rebecca asked.

"Much more quickly than I expected in this market."

"That must be a relief," Rebecca said. She wondered how much Lana had gotten for it, but didn't ask.

"Moving out was a job," Lana said. She went on to explain that Charlie's leather chair had been carted up and shipped to Skokie.

"Thanks," Rebecca said. "But it will have to be shipped back. It looks like I'm staying here." She found these words agreeable as she said them.

"Getting divorced?"

"Probably."

"Good luck," Lana said quietly.

Rebecca heard sympathy in her voice tonight. Lana seemed so much more approachable, but she, too, felt softer and more open. "By the way, whatever happened to Maria?" she asked.

"She moved out a month ago," Lana answered. "She's okay."

"I want to give her a bonus or something," Rebecca said. "She worked so hard in that house."

"Don't worry about it," Lana said. "She's taken care of."

Although Rebecca would have liked to hear the details, she didn't press Lana. The conversation drifted to the pros and cons of living in California, and Rebecca said she might choose to settle further north, in a rural area away from the Bay Area. "At Clear Lake?" Lana asked.

"Definitely not," Rebecca smiled. "I can't believe I spent the entire summer in that place."

Lana looked curiously at her. "Why did you?"

"It was the best I could do. As soon as I got there, I crashed. I was going to have a grand vacation this summer, but instead I ended up in a ball, sobbing out my heart."

"I'm sorry," Lana said.

Rebecca shook her head. "It was the culmination of a lot of years. A darkness I had to go through. A psychic once told me that would happen, so I guess I shouldn't have been surprised, but I was."

"Things never turn out the way you think they're going to. At least not for me. That's the story of my life."

"From the beginning?"

"You could say that." Lana sipped her cappuccino. "It wasn't easy living with my mother."

"I can imagine."

"She switched between loving me and wanting to destroy me," Lana told her. "I never knew what was going to happen next. That was my first experience with unpredictability."

"That must have been hard."

Lana's eyes half-closed. "Oh, yes."

Rebecca sat silently, not moving, waiting to hear more.

"My mother was abusive. I guess that's the proper word for it." Lana gave a bitter little laugh. "She hit me. Often. And she dragged me out of bed at night, telling me for hours how stupid and ugly I was. But then she'd feel bad about hurting me, and try to get me to love her again. If I didn't go along with it, she became furious. Round and round we went."

"How horrible for you," Rebecca said.

A strand of Lana's hair had fallen from the scarf, and she tucked it back in. "You're a therapist. I figure you'll understand."

"I do."

"The only way I survived was to fight back. Even when my mother was being halfway decent."

"Good for you. That probably saved your life."

"That's what my psychiatrist says. But it was devastating for my mother. She wanted to possess me. When my friends came over, she drove them away with her insults. It happened a lot. Finally I left her myself. I refused to talk to her for a lot of years."

"You had to do that," Rebecca said.

"My mother fell apart. She could not tolerate being abandoned."

"By you?"

Lana's eyes flashed. "By anyone. It was her greatest nightmare."

Rebecca wanted to embrace this proud, beautiful woman or say something to comfort her. Instead, she sat quietly, finishing her cappuccino. "I wanted you to know," Lana finally said.

"Yes," Rebecca said, sensing the importance of her words. She wondered why Lana was telling her all this. It was such a turnaround from her defensiveness earlier that summer. "Your mother hit my dad, too," she said.

"I'm not surprised."

"He was getting ready to leave her."

"Mother would have gone crazy."

"And perhaps killed him? I'm still trying to get to the bottom of what happened," Rebecca said. "My breakdown at Clear Lake had a lot to do with his death. I've been filled these last six years with guilt that I did nothing to stop it, although I couldn't figure out how. And I was still mourning. That's all over now, but if you know something, please tell me." She said this in a simple way, without anger or pleading.

"I wasn't at the house," Lana said, "so I don't know. But last June you got me thinking. I didn't like you coming around, asking so many questions. You really irritated me. You forced me to deal with what went on between Charlie and my mother. The truth is I hardly saw them, and when I did, they seemed okay together. That was good enough for me."

"Quite the lovebirds, I remember you saying."

Lana smiled sadly. "But recently I've been talking to my psychiatrist about your father's death."

Rebecca's breath quickened. "And?"

"I have my suspicions." Lana paused. "I think my mother was involved."

"Yes," Rebecca sighed, relieved to hear her say this.

"I didn't want to admit it at first. But I couldn't avoid thinking how violent she had been with me when I was younger."

"What you just told me."

"My psychiatrist says that a violent woman like her could easily have struck her husband and killed him. She had that capacity. But the person who really knows the truth is Maria. I'm certain about that, although she's never said anything to me and I've never asked her. She was in the house that day."

"Maria won't talk to me about what happened. I tried several times."

"She will, if I ask her to."

"Will you?" Rebecca felt a rush of hope.

"I'll call her before I go to work tomorrow." Lana withdrew into silence, looking at her watch, obviously finished. Rebecca, too, had had enough. They left the café, going their separate ways.

18

Rebecca checked into a busy North Beach motel on Columbus Avenue. The conversation with Lana still hung in her mind, and after the quiet nights at Clear Lake, the noise of so much traffic would surely keep her from falling asleep right away. She'd take a walk in the neighborhood until she was really tired and her mind quieted, she decided.

Outside the fog swirled around the streetlights and she headed down Columbus Avenue toward the center of North Beach, where the nightlife was going strong. She came to a little square with a playground and benches. Several teenaged kids were sprawled on the grass, messing around, high on drugs or booze, and a woman her age, wearing a baseball cap, limped about muttering to herself. On one side of the square a grand Catholic church dominated the scene; it was lit with bright, welcoming spotlights although the entry doors appeared to be locked.

She gazed at the church with its two steeples, thinking it looked beautiful in the fog, and she walked over to it and sat on the stairs leading up to the entry doors. The woman in the cap began to forage in the garbage can in the park, tossing out papers and junk in every direction, making a mess on the trimly-cut grass. "Get the fuck out of here!" yelled one of the kids. The woman straightened up, swore back at the kids, then stuffed some of the garbage into a satchel she was carrying. "You're crazy," yelled another kid.

Rebecca was reminded of Vicky, who had been crazy although not in this same obvious way. She had been canny enough to protect herself, and she'd had the money to survive. But she had been the mother from hell, as Lana had said tonight. And there was something more: Lana had suffered terribly, but Vicky must have, too. She'd been plagued by a fear of abandonment, and she had driven away those she cared about, causing her nightmare to come true. Rebecca suddenly felt sorry for her.

The woman in the square began to limp toward the cathedral, lugging her satchel and several sacks stuffed with her possessions. It was almost midnight, and the traffic on Columbus Avenue had quieted down. Rebecca rose from the stairs, planning to walk briskly back to the motel—she was starting to feel unsafe at this late hour—but when she reached the woman, she pulled out twenty dollars and handed it to her. "Take care of yourself," she said. The woman tipped her baseball cap, grabbed the money, and tucked it into her coat pocket, muttering "God bless, god bless," as she headed in the other direction.

Rebecca slept through the night and awakened the next morning at eight o'clock with a feeling of excitement. She would soon learn the truth of her father's death after all these years. But she told herself to be realistic, that Maria might not have witnessed what happened even though she was in the house. The mystery might remain—a discouraging thought, because then she'd have to live with never knowing. She glanced at her watch and decided it was not too early to call Maria and make arrangements for a visit.

"*Ola*," Maria answered the phone in a light, friendly way. When Rebecca responded, she switched to English. "Lana just called. She said you want to talk to me."

"Can I come today?"

"Eleven thirty is good."

Rebecca stood in front of the mirror brushing her hair, thinking that it had grown long and scraggly over the summer. She twisted it up in back with a clip, and then she took out the clip and let it drop down again. She hadn't used any product on it since she left Chicago, but today she'd pick some up at a salon along the way. That would make it more manageable until she found a good stylist to trim it and give it a shape.

She had two hours to kill before going to Maria's house. She checked out of the hotel and wandered back to North Beach, passing by an Italian bakery with whipped cream pastries and cakes in the window. She stopped at a cafe and ordered some coffee and a croissant even though she wasn't hungry, and she took her time over breakfast. Afterward, with time to spare before leaving for Maria's house, she went into City Lights Bookstore, a three-level space with shelves crammed with all the best literature and poetry. This was her favorite bookstore in San Francisco and she remembered going there with friends as a teenager, but even here she was distracted, checking her watch to see if it was time to leave.

At eleven Rebecca crossed the Bay Bridge to Oakland, now optimistic that she would soon learn what had happened to her father. Following the directions Maria had given her on the phone that morning, she pulled up in front of a pretty blue bungalow, set on a block of tidy homes in Oakland. A fence ran around the house, and a black-and-white terrier in the yard greeted her with energetic yelps. "Stop, Chica," Maria yelled from the porch. "No more noise."

Rebecca climbed the steps to the porch and Maria greeted her warmly. She showed her into the small living room. "It's good to see you," Rebecca said.

"I'll bring us some coffee." Before Rebecca could say she didn't want any, Maria disappeared into the kitchen, returning with a tray of crisp lemon cookies and two full cups.

The two women sat on the couch. Rebecca looked around the room at the furnishings and the photographs of what must be Maria's family on the table, two old people, probably her parents, and an assortment of kids of all ages. A ceramic pot held a ficus plant, the hardwood floors looked new and polished, and white, gauzy curtains floated over the windows. "What a nice house your brother has," she said.

"He doesn't live here," Maria smiled.

"I thought you were moving in with him."

"This house is mine. Lana made the down payment for it. My brother lives close by."

Rebecca clapped her hands. "Oh, I'm so pleased."

"Soon my niece will come and live with me," Maria told her. "She's a nurse, and she has a job at the hospital. She will help make the payments."

"And you won't be alone. That's wonderful."

Maria became somber. "Lana asked me to talk to you about Mr. Stevens."

"She said she would."

"But first, I'll get more coffee." Maria jumped up again.

"Not for me," Rebecca said quickly.

"For me," Maria said.

When Maria returned with her coffee, Rebecca gazed intently at her. "It must be hard to talk about what happened," she said.

"Mrs. Stevens said I'd go to jail if I told anyone. She said the police would come and get me. But nothing bad can happen now that Mrs. Stevens is dead. That's what Lana said."

"That's right, I promise," Rebecca said.

Maria's black eyes narrowed. "Mr. Stevens got old fast in the Piedmont house. Mrs. Stevens treated him very badly. She yelled at him a lot when they were alone."

"You heard her?"

"She had a loud voice."

"And I know she sometimes hit my father?" Rebecca said, already angry. "He told me that."

"I saw her slap him." Maria lowered her voice. "Sometimes she hit him very hard."

"With what?"

"A book, a frying pan, other things. She hurt him a lot."

"And he wasn't strong enough to defend himself?"

"He was like this." Maria crouched down with her arms raised in defense. "And he yelled, too."

Rebecca could scarcely breathe, imagining her father with this frightening, violent wife. "That's how he got those bruises and that gash," she said.

"Very bad."

"What happened that day he went to the hospital?"

Maria stiffened next to her. "Mr. and Mrs. Stevens have a fight in the library, loud and terrible. I hear them. I'm afraid something really bad is going to happen. Mr. Stevens yells he's going to leave Mrs. Stevens and get a divorce. 'I'm not staying here any longer,' he says. 'No more. No more.' He walks out of the library and starts for the front door, but Mrs. Stevens picks up a fireplace rod and runs after him."

"Oh, no!"

"At the door he turns around. She lifts up the rod, ready to smash in his head. She's like a mad, crazy dog. He screams and tries to get away, but he slips on the marble floor."

Tears streamed down Rebecca's face as she heard this. "He tried to get free."

"I see everything. Mrs. Stevens standing over him, still yelling. She says he'll never leave her."

Rebecca stopped, confused. "But did Mrs. Stevens actually hit him with the fireplace rod?"

"No," Maria answered, straightening up. "Mr. Stevens was on the marble floor, already hurt. She didn't have to."

"Oh my god," Rebecca said, trying to absorb what Maria was telling her. "And where were you then?"

"Mrs. Stevens saw me in the hall, and she grabbed me. "'Don't you ever talk to anyone about this,'" she said. "'Otherwise, I'll tell the police you were the one who hurt Mr. Stevens. They'll put you in jail for the rest of your life or maybe even kill you.' I ran from her and hid in my room. Soon the ambulance came and took Mr. Stevens away."

"How very horrible for you," Rebecca said.

"I got so scared." Maria shook her head.

Rebecca felt like all the air had been punched out of her, and her whole body began to tremble. Maria put her arms around her. "It's my fault," Rebecca cried. "I should have saved my father."

"It's not possible," Maria said.

"I should have done something," Rebecca moaned.

"Nothing to do. *Nada, nada.*"

The two women sat like that for a long time. Finally Rebecca's tears subsided. She straightened up, wiping her eyes, trying to compose herself. "I'm so sorry you had to go through that, Maria," she said.

Maria's eyes were soft. "I'm very happy now."

Rebecca did not stay much longer. As she walked slowly toward the Audi, it seemed that everything she had imagined about Charlie's death had been taken apart and put back together in a new way. So her father wasn't murdered, after all. Yet he was not not-murdered. The truth fell somewhere in between, a terrible tragedy that could have been prevented but wasn't. If only Charlie had made it out the front door that day or fallen on a rug instead of the marble floor. If only Vicky hadn't been so angry, or threatened him with the fireplace rod. If only Maria had called the police, or Lana or Jim had dropped by at the right moment. And if only she, his daughter, his only child, had put caution aside and flown to California and insisted on taking him away from the house once she knew Vicky was hitting him. But none of these things had happened. The telephone didn't ring to interrupt their argument and the gardener or the laundry service didn't appear at the door, a package wasn't delivered by UPS and the burglar alarm didn't accidentally go off. It seemed that all of the players in this tragedy had coalesced to make certain that on that very day in December, six years ago, her father would die.

Rebecca felt a great freeing of her spirit as she understood this.

The categories of fault and blame eased, and she felt only sorrow. This tragedy was over now, part of the past. Her father's death, horrible as it was, had simply happened. It would remain in her heart and mind all the days of her life, but there was nothing more to do, no more penance to pay, no more grief or retribution.

And now she'd better get back to San Francisco before the traffic got too bad.

Lana had asked her to stop by her office to tell her what Maria said. The conversation would be difficult, but she would be comforted to learn that her mother had not given Charlie the final blow.

Then Rebecca would return to the cabin, pack up the urn and her belongings, and move out. The time had come to scatter her father's ashes, and she'd drive into the Sierra Mountains and search for a cool, clear stream.

Acknowledgments

I began writing *Clear Lake* in 2004 with only a vague idea of what the story would be. Alice Templeton and Wayne Rodin, members of my writing group, read early sections, as did Elizabeth Kaplan, Tom Jenkins, and Carol Edgarian. I appreciate their interest and helpful suggestions. When I finished a first draft, I put it aside and didn't return to it until 2010. Then I began to work with editors Michele Herman, who taught me so much about fiction writing, and Brooke Warner, who helped me further refine the book. Their guidance and encouragement were instrumental in bringing it to life.

During the years I worked on *Clear Lake*, many people supported and encouraged me. I want especially to thank Sandra Butler, Marcia Freedman, Marinell Eva, Jane Ariel, Arlene Shmaeff, and Linda Wilson, members of my women's group. Also Mia Tenenberg, Chana Bloch, Sandy Boucher, Jeri Cohen, Ellen Pulleyblank Coffey, Patrick Coffey, Charlie Halpern, Susan Halpern, and Janet Holmgren.

My family, old and young, knew not to ask too many questions about the book but to say they looked forward to reading it. I especially thank Michelle Holstein, Bill Holstein, Lisa Piediscalzi, Kirk Allen, Nick Piediscalzi, Itzik Orlans, Smadar Orlans, Anat Orlans, Rebecca Orlans, Michael Omer-Man, Sarah Holstein, Jackie Holstein, Nathan Allen, Elias Allen, Jack Piediscalzi, Bob Long, Kirk Long, and Jessica Dorrington. Most of all I am grateful to my husband, Jonathan Omer-Man, for his patience and good humor through the ups and downs of writing the book. He read several versions, listened to me talk about the smallest details, and his belief in the book sustained me.

It was a great pleasure to work with the people at She Writes Press. Thanks especially to Brooke Warner for her publishing smarts and creative leadership, and to Cait Levin for tracking so many details.

Clear Lake is dedicated to the memory of my sister, Marion Souyoultzis, who died in 2010. She and I discussed the book at length, and her insights helped me understand what the book was about and why I needed to write it.

About the Author

photo © Irene Young

Nan Fink Gefen is the author of *Stranger in the Midst: A Memoir of Spiritual Discovery* (Basic Books, 1997) and *Discovering Jewish Meditation* (Jewish Lights, 2nd edition 2011.) Her fiction and nonfiction articles have appeared in numerous publications. After fifteen years as a psychotherapist and teacher, she became the co-founder and publisher of *Tikkun* magazine. In 1996 she began teaching Jewish meditation, and she has trained hundreds of students in the Bay Area and nationally. In 2007 she founded *Persimmon Tree: An Online Magazine of the Arts by Women over Sixty*, where she remains as publisher. Nan lives in Berkeley, CA, with her husband, Jonathan Omer-Man; their blended family includes seven children and nine grandkids.

The author's website is www.nangefen.com.

Looking for your next great read?

We can help!

Visit www.shewritespress.com/next-read
or scan the QR code below for a list
of our recommended titles.

She Writes Press is an award-winning
independent publishing company founded to
serve women writers everywhere.